HELLSPIRE ACADEMY

VICIOUS INTENT

ALICE CORNELIUS

CRIMSON QUILL PUBLISHING

ISBN: 978-1-7640909-7-1

eBook ISBN: 978-1-7640909-8-8

Published in Australia by Crimson Quill Publishing. Copyright © 2026 by Alice Cornelius.

Author Website: http://alicecornelius.com.au/

ALSO BY ALICE CORNELIUS

HELLSPIRE ACADEMY

THE SOCIETY

FLICKER –
THE ARDENTIS CHRONICLES BOOK ONE

A Courtesy Warning from Hellspire Academy

Hellspire is not responsible for emotional discomfort experienced beyond this point.

Readers may encounter depictions of violence, physical injury, captivity, psychological manipulation, graphic sex scenes, trauma responses, weapons, explosions, and death.

If any of that feels overwhelming, we recommend taking a breath, closing the book, and reconsidering your enrolment.

Hellspire is demanding – but so is surviving the story you're about to read.

To the brave souls who chose to return to Hellspire – thank you for loving this unruly crew of disasters and survivors. May your snacks be plentiful, your sleep schedule forgiving, and your loyalty to Jossi, Maddy, and Gaz remain unshaken.

Chapter One

"Jossi, what the hell is that?" Matthew barked from the other side of the pool, and I knew exactly what he was talking about. I'd been waiting all day for him to notice it. I turned slowly, a smile tugging at my lips.

"It's exactly what it looks like...a tattoo." I smiled, and Maddy coughed, hiding her laugh.

"Did you have something to do with this?" Matthew turned on Alec with narrowed eyes, but Alec only shook his head.

"Don't blame me, man. She did that long before we got together." Alec smirked, winking my way with a devilish grin. "And she took it like a champ."

It was my turn to wink back, feel heat rise on my cheeks.

I could never get enough of Alexander.

It was just a shame that we barely spent any time together lately.

"You want to hope father doesn't find out." Matthew grumbled, making me chuckle nervously.

No, I didn't want him to find out. His strict rules not only applied to here at home, but also at school.

He was adamant that I finished my schooling, though I had no idea why. He would always say that the lessons I'd learn at Hellspire would be instrumental to my future. And it seemed like I wasn't going to have a say in what my future looked like.

Yet again, he'd control every aspect of my life.

I dismissed the dark thoughts, trying to focus on the now.

Who knew what my future held, so there was no point in worrying about it.

"This is the *best* way to spend break." Maddy sighed as she tipped her head back, legs dangled in the pool as I sat next to her. Gaz was mucking around at the other end, perfecting his backflip, apparently.

I swung my legs through the water, enjoying just being able to relax and being with the people I cared about. I'd had a busy break from Hellspire. Training. Running. Weapons. Father wanted me to not fall behind when I went back.

Alec appeared behind me and leaned down to kiss my neck, making me squirm.

"Babydoll, those bikinis are sinful, and I just want to take you back to your room and-"

"The powers gone out." Matthew stood, knocking the book off his lap. "The cameras, everything." His gaze snapped to Alec, and the two moved instantly.

Matthew was barking at us to get out of the water as Alec hauled me out by under my arms.

"What's wrong?" I breathed, turning to Alec, whose eyes were wide as he went to tow me away.

Before he could even open his mouth, an armoured car smashed through the fence with a screech and landed in the pool-house amid a cloud of dust.

Soldiers dressed in black suits, masks over their faces, swarmed out of the vehicle, raising their guns.

Oh, fuck.

"Move! Get Jossi *out!*" Matthew yelled at Alec, running toward us as we turned and ran.

Gaz was out of the water in seconds, grabbing onto Maddy's arm, faces pale.

"There's a panic room down the hall. Take her there." Matthew took off in one direction, and we in the other.

Maddy barked, "Oh, don't worry about us then," but I could tell she was scared.

Hell, we all were.

Our bare feet slipped on the polished tiles, still dripping wet from our swim. I heard soldiers inside the house, and I switched into autopilot.

Down the hall we ran, me in the front, followed by Maddy, Gaz, and then Alec. I'd had many emergency drills the past few weeks, so I knew where I needed to go, where every hidden weapon was.

Another requirement from father.

We reached a small table on my right, without breaking stride, I reached into the vase and pulled out a small handgun, passing it to Maddy to give to Gaz.

I grabbed another gun from behind a picture frame on my left, then another from a potted plant.

Gunshots sounded behind us, but I refused to look. I knew Matthew would be okay.

He *had* to be okay.

Shots cracked overhead, splitting the plaster on the walls, they were warning shots, too high to actually hurt us. They wanted us scared, and they were doing a bloody good job of it.

I heard Alec grunt behind me, and I skidded to a stop, Maddy and Gaz barely missing me.

"Keep going!" Alec yelled as he took on a soldier who had tackled him, "I'll meet up with you. Go!"

I knew Alec could handle himself, but I was still scared for him. I forced myself to turn back around and start running again. It didn't take long for more soldiers to halt our path.

One ran straight into Maddy, knocking her against the wall, a hand on her throat. Gaz bellowed in anger, but couldn't get to her, thanks to another soldier deciding now was a good time to pick a fight.

The soldier holding Maddy snarled in her face, then lifted her off the ground by the throat, her legs dangling.

My breath was sawing in and out of my tight throat. I needed to do *something*.

Without even thinking about it, I raised my arms and pulled the trigger. The shot was loud in the corridor, the soldier with Gaz spun to stare as his fellow soldier who stumbled back a step, dropping Maddy. She slid down the wall onto the floor, gripping her throat as she stared at me with wide eyes. The soldier I shot grabbed his throat, making a horrible choking noise as he staggered back a step.

I shot him again, this time making sure my aim was a kill shot.

Right in the middle of this throat, that vulnerable place where no clothing or helmet could protect you.

He fell with a thud, the first soldier raising his arms to retaliate, when another *crack* sounded, and he went down beside the other soldier.

Dead.

Gaz's arms were still raised, chest heaving as he stared at the man on the floor. His hands began to shake, the gun still clutched tightly in his fingers, his face paling. I slowly made my way to him and put my hands on his, slowly lowering the gun.

"You did well, Gaz." I breathed, turning him to look at me. "It's alright." His whole body started to shake as shock settled in.

"I...I just killed someone." He croaked, eyes wide with fear.

Maddy hauled herself off the floor and came to him, grabbing his face in both of her hands and kissing him soundly.

"You saved us." She whispered against his lips, "Come on, let's keep moving." She slipped her hands into his, and tugged him along. He took a wobbly step, but with more encouragement, he moved.

We shuffled along as fast as we could, but we could still hear fighting, shouts, and shots throughout the house. I refused to think about whether anything had happened to Matthew or Alec.

I jogged around the next corner, my feet slipping when I ran into someone.

I grunted from the impact, my feet went out from under me. But hands shot out and grabbed my upper arms, yanking me back up, giving me a serious case of whiplash.

The soldier pulled me up against him, his hands digging into my skin with an iron grip.

My heart flip-flopped in my chest.

His bright green eyes locked onto mine, but he didn't say anything, didn't move.

"Target one has been acquired. Move onto target two." The tiny voice coming from his earpiece confirmed my suspicions. They were here for something. But what?

The soldier took a step back, and me with him, his hands tightening on my arms until it was almost painful. It was useless for me to struggle, as my feet kept slipping out from under me.

Maddy and Gaz rounded the corner, nearly running into us in the process.

"What the hell?" Maddy barked, her voice croaky from the asshole who tried to choke her. "Get off her!" She yelled, taking a step toward me.

The soldier holding me snapped his eyes back to mine, and took another step, but I didn't miss the voice crackling again - "abort, drop everything and abort."

The soldier leaned in slightly, eyes narrowed under his mask, as if he were smiling at me.

"It's your lucky day, sweetheart." He winked, then dropped my arms, turned, and ran.

"What the hell?" Gaz snapped, coming to my side, looking me over. "Are you hurt?"

It took longer than I wanted to admit to find my voice again.

"I'm fine, they were told to abort," I said, gripping onto my shaking hands as Maddy put a hand on my shoulder.

Were they here for *me?* Was I the second target?

What the hell was the first?

Alec slammed around the corner, running into all three of us with a shout.

"What the hell are you all doing standing here?" His attention snapped to the soldier running away from us, disappearing around the corner. "Get in the panic room, and wait for me to come get you." He grabbed my chin and kissed me swiftly before taking off after the man.

"Come on, guys. The room's just around here." I breathed, feeling a little lightheaded. But I needed to be here for my friends, they needed me to keep a level head. I took Maddy's hand and towed her down the hall and to a large painting, found the small latch behind the frame and swung open the door. A quick fingerprint scan opened it, and we hurried inside, locking it behind us.

Maddy and Gaz wrapped their arms around each other and simply stood there, hugging.

I sank into a beanbag and stared at the wall.

Who the hell was it? And what do they want?

No one spoke for a few minutes, using the time to think about what just happened. I shook myself and forced my ass out of the beanbag and into the mini fridge, where I pulled out three cans of soft drink and three chocolate bars.

"Here, top up your sugar levels." I handed one to each, who just nodded at me, still not speaking. "Gaz, are you alright?" He looked dreadfully pale, and I swore that his legs had started to shake. I grabbed his arm and towed him to one of the beanbags and pushed him down into it, dragging another one over for Maddy.

"You did what you had to," I murmured, knowing full well how horrible it was to kill someone for the first time. He closed his eyes and shook his head a few times, Maddy gripping onto his hand so hard it was a wonder she didn't break any bones.

"I'll be...okay." He croaked. A few deep breaths later, he opened his eyes and nodded at me. "Thank you, Jossi, for saving her."

Maddy looked down at her hands, a red stain blooming over her cheeks.

"You know I would do anything for you guys. I love you both." I couldn't stop my tears as they fell unchecked down my cheeks.

I had come so close to losing one of them.

I dropped to my knees, and we hugged, holding each other as our tears finally dried up.

Now that I was over the shock and the fear, anger worked its way in under my skin.

How dare they come into my home, and attack those I love?

I stood, making my way to the far wall where a GPS phone sat. I dialled father's number, knowing he would want to know asap. Before I could press call, the door swung open and in came Alec and Matthew.

Both a little bloody and bruised. But alive.

"Oh, thank god." I cried as I dropped the phone and launched myself at Alec's, who wrapped his arms around me and held tight.

"Is everyone alright?" Matthew had to clear his throat a few times, but he was on his feet, with no obvious wounds. We all nodded, and breathed a sigh of relief.

It was over.

"Our team finally caught on to what was happening and took out the remaining soldiers. Although most of them had gone by the time our guards arrived."

"They were here for two things, they got the first, and aborted before getting the second." I breathed, stepping back from Alec, but he didn't let me go.

"How do you know that?" Matthew took a step toward me, eyes wide as his chest heaved, attempting to catch his breath.

"I heard someone through an earpiece telling the soldier..."

Shit, I didn't want to tell Alec that I'd come close to either being killed...or taken.

"What soldier? How were you close enough to hear his earpiece?" Alec's voice had dropped to a dangerous level, one that meant he wanted to shed blood.

I swallowed, unable to meet his gaze. But I knew he wasn't going to drop it.

"I literally ran into a soldier around the corner, and he grabbed hold of me. I heard the voice as he went to move."

"He was going to take you?" Alec turned rigid before me, back straightening. "What exactly did you hear?"

"I heard them say that they'd acquired the first target, and to move onto the second one. Then, not long after, they were told to drop everything and abort."

Matthew and Alec shared a look, nodded at each other, and the former left.

"Let's get out of here, clean up, and meet again in the dining room." Alec slipped his hand into mine and tugged me out of the panic room, Maddy and Gaz following close behind.

I had no idea what the first target was, and I didn't want to know what the second one was.

Chapter Two

We dressed, splashed some cold water over our faces and met in the dining room, Matthew was already talking to someone on the phone, pacing the room. Alec's jaw ticked as his fingers flew over the screen of his phone, he put it face down when I sat next to him.

"Hey, Babydoll." He leaned over and kissed me on the cheek, gripping my hand in his as the others sat. "How are you holding up?" His eyes roved over me as his thumb brushed the back of my hand.

"I'm alright, a little shaken, but I think Gaz is more freaked out. He just killed someone." I breathed, feeling a knot in my stomach, knowing how he felt.

Killing someone never leaves you. It haunted your dreams.

"I'll make sure to have a word with him before they leave." Alec leaned over and kissed my temple just as Matthew sat down, sighing.

"The house is secure, they'd cut the power and killed the cameras, but our team has managed to make sure we're all back online." Matthew was rubbing the bridge of his nose, eyes shut. "I'm going to have to call father, and he'll no doubt lose his mind, but right now, you guys need to keep this to yourselves." He looked up and met each of our gazes. We nodded in understanding. We knew how to keep a secret. "The syndicate will be sniffing around like wolves." Matthew grumbled, then his shoulders stiffened, as did Alec's. "I mean, our enemies." He cleared his throat, but I knew that he slipped up.

Who's the syndicate?

"What did they take, Matthew?" I spoke up, seeing as they weren't going to elaborate on the syndicate. I guessed that it was something they shouldn't have said. And knowing that my brother had his men flush out the house and do a stock take in the short while that we'd been here, I needed to know.

"They've taken a book from fathers office." He met Alec's eyes fleetingly before looking away. "But it was a decoy, so they won't get anything valuable from it."

Alec nodded subtly, a smile tugging at his lips. Like he was *smug*.

"I knew they'd fall for it. I just didn't expect them to attack us while everyone was here." Matthew sighed, leaning back into his chair as he ran his hand through his hair.

"You knew this might happen?" I raised my voice, eyes locked on my brother who flinched slightly. I turned to Alec for answers. Maddy and Gaz were watching this exchange like a tennis match.

Alec cleared his throat before turning his full attention to me.

"A month or so ago, I came up with an idea to make a decoy of your father's book. He keeps all sorts of records and personal information in it, and in the wrong hands, it would be catastrophic."

I raised my eyebrows with surprise. What on earth would be in that book to make it so important?

"And how did they know about this book?" I said between teeth, my anger slowly making an appearance again. I snapped my eyes to Matthew who looked a little guilty, so I turned back to Alexander, pulling my hand out of his.

"I might have talked a little loud on the phone one day out in the markets, knowing that I was being followed. I wanted them to hear that your father was away, and that I'd finish marking in his book, so he didn't have to worry about carrying it with him and risk losing it."

"So you've known this whole time that they would try to attack you?" I said slowly, eyes narrowing the more he spoke.

"Yes." Alec reached for my hand again, but I shook my head.

"That's why you've been drilling me almost every day about the safe rooms and weapons?" I snapped, and Alec even had the nerve to look sheepish. I wanted to fucking *hit* him.

"And you did magnificently, Babydoll." He said with a weak smile. I couldn't take it anymore.

"The fucking *audacity!*" I yelled, and Matthew gasped, no doubt about to tell me off for swearing. "How dare you not tell me. I've got my best friends here, and their lives were at risk! Hell, Maddy can barely talk from the bruises on her throat!" I stood up, the chair screeching on the floorboards.

Alec stayed where he was, which was the smartest move right now, because I wanted to punch him and Matthew for that stupid fucking stunt.

"I'm staying at Maddy's house for the rest of the week. I don't want to be here right now." I turned away, Maddy and Gaz scrabbling to their feet to follow.

"That was super smart, guys. Well done." Gaz snapped as he left the room. I didn't hear a reply.

I was so angry. At both of them. Matthew, I could understand. But Alec? I thought he knew better than to pull that sort of shit, and not tell me. Hell, I would have stayed away if I'd known.

I stomped up the stairs, making sure they heard each and every step.

"I'm so sorry, guys." I called out over my shoulder as they followed me. They'd been staying here with me for the past few nights. They needed to grab their things as well.

"It's not your fault, Joss. They're fucking idiots." Maddy croaked, clearing her throat, then wincing.

It only made me angrier.

While they went to their room, I slammed the door shut on mine, and just stood there for a moment trying to catch my breath, clear my head a little.

I had just killed someone.

Gaz had just killed someone.

And the two men downstairs had known something like this was going to happen, just not sure when.

My door opened, and the lock snicked shut behind me. I didn't turn. I knew who it was.

"Babydoll?" Alec said softly, taking a step toward me.

"Don't fucking bother, Alec." I growled, hastily shoving clothes into my bag. "I don't want to talk to you right now."

We hadn't had many fights, but I knew this one was going to take me a while to get over.

"Sweetheart, I'm sorry. I didn't know they would pull something as crazy as that. And if I thought you would be in danger, then I wouldn't have let you come over, or your friends." He took another step, and I shook my head, keeping my back to him. "Honestly, we only expected them to follow us in the car, try to get us while we were out and about."

"Cocky. That's what you both are. Always are when you're together."

Even as kids, they had behaved like they controlled the world.

"Please, look at me." It was his voice cracking that made me pause. I huffed out a long breath and slowly turned around, my arms folded across my chest. I raised a brow as I waited.

"I'm so fucking sorry. The thought of them hurting you makes me feel physically sick." He took another step until he was standing in front of me, close enough that we almost touched. "I thought that we had everything covered if they tried anything. The fact that they rammed us with a car shook everything up. They wouldn't have gotten in so easily, otherwise." He pulled my hands away where I'd tucked them and held tight. "I promise you, I would never willingly put you in danger. Please, don't go." I could see he meant it, but I didn't know if I could just move on already.

"I killed someone, Alec." I hated the tears that pricked my eyes, squeezing my throat. "Gaz killed someone. Maddy nearly got her throat crushed. Do you honestly expect me to simply forgive you because you've said sorry? You put us all in danger with no warning."

He opened his mouth to speak, but I shook my head, ploughing on. "I'm hurt, I'm scared, and you've broken my trust." I turned away from him to finish packing my bag.

"How can I make this up to you?" He breathed, staying where he was, not touching me.

"I don't know, but you better apologise to Maddy and Gaz before we leave." I lifted my bag over my shoulder and pushed past him.

He let me go, and followed without a word.

Both boys met us down in the corridor, the shattered glass had already been swept up, but I could still see the scars on the walls, the broken windows, the bullet holes.

This was my house. And I no longer felt safe here.

They apologised to my friends, and to me, but it didn't mean I was staying. With mournful looks on their part, I walked out the door as one of our guards pulled up out front in the car.

The car trip was silent, all of us too busy locked in our thoughts. Maddy and Gaz never let go of each other's hands as they stared out the window. Messages pinged on my phone, but I put it on silent and threw it into my bag.

Maddy's house had two levels; her father lived on the bottom level, and Maddy was allowed to take the top, including the spare room where I dumped my bag.

Maddy and Gaz stayed in her room, so I helped myself to a soft drink and turned on the TV. I needed something to distract me. No matter what I watched, all I could think about was the attack.

I turned it off with a sigh and got to my feet, heading onto the balcony to get some fresh air.

The city spread out before me, the ocean a distant sliver of blue on the horizon.

I didn't know exactly what my brother and Alec did for work. What I did know was that you had to be cutthroat. But what they had allowed to happen was reckless. Would Father approve? Surely not.

They knew our address, they got inside.

I didn't get to stew outside and stew for very long before a gorgeous black sports car pulled up out front. I frowned as a familiar figure stepped out. I shook my head and turned to walk away when he called out.

"Jocelyn, please, can we talk?" Alec looked up with puppy-dog eyes, a bunch of flowers gripped in his hands. "Please, come home so we can talk about this." He stood his ground, his voice getting louder with each word.

Damn it. I didn't want Maddy's neighbours coming out to see what was going on.

"Keep it down, will you?" I hissed, leaning over the rails, glaring daggers at him.

Maddy and Gaz wandered out, brows pulled down in confusion until they came to the rail and saw who stood there.

She turned to me, ignoring Alec down below. "You should go and talk." She said softly, and my stomach sank a little. I should have realised that those two would want time alone, to move past what just happened.

I just didn't think.

"You're right." I whispered, nodding.

How stupid could I be?

"It's not like I don't want you here," Maddy grabbed my arm as I went to walk past her. "You know you're always welcome." I nodded, unable to meet her eyes for long. "But I think just let him explain. Don't let this to come between you before you go back to Hellspire next week." Her eyes softened, and I felt deflated, beaten.

"Yeah, you're right." I sighed, attempting to give her a small smile. "If you need anything, just let me know." I grabbed them both into a tight hug, swallowing down my tears before letting go.

Luckily, I hadn't unpacked, so I just grabbed my bag and headed downstairs to a waiting Alexander.

As soon as I stepped outside, he took my bag and opened the car door for me, not saying a word.

I didn't know what to say, so I simply looked out the window as we drove away.

Halfway home, he cleared his throat, but didn't say anything, instead, pulled into a drive-through and ordered a large coffee frappe and dumplings with spicy dipping sauce.

Damn this man, and knowing my weaknesses.

Still, he didn't say a word as he handed them to me and continued the drive.

I almost groaned out loud at how good it tasted. I hadn't had dumplings for ages.

We arrived home, where he carried my bag and walked into the house. I followed, still sipping my coffee as I wondered what he was up to.

Upstairs we went, into my room, where he placed the flowers on my dresser, and dumped the bag on my bed before finally turning to me.

"Feel a little better with a coffee and some food?" He asked softly. I wanted to snap at him, but he was right. We were about to have lunch before the assholes attacked us.

So perhaps I was feeling a *bit* hangry.

"A little." I offered, unable to keep eye contact.

"Good." He gently took my hand and towed me out of the room and along the hall, to the roof.

Up there, Father had a garden put in after Gemma and my mother were killed.

It was in memory of them.

They had loved their flowers and plants. And in the entire estate, it was a small escape, a place that had seen no violence, and I loved it.

Alec slowly led me to the center where a large water fountain bubbled gently, surrounded by plants and greenery. He pulled me down beside him, then quietly took in the garden as I ate.

Even though I was upset, I could still admire how beautiful he was. His chocolate hair was growing out, almost in his light brown eyes, which looked tired as they stared at me.

"I truly am sorry, Jossi." He made no move to touch me, and for that, I was thankful. Whenever he touched me, I seemed to forget the world and fall into him and his stupid, beautiful body.

Even though I knew he meant it, it still stung.

"If I knew then what I do now, I would never have done it."

"I know." I breathed, looking down at my hands in my lap. "It just seems so...reckless." I shrugged, looking back up at him.

"Don't worry, your father is livid, and I'm sure we'll get what's coming to us when he returns."

I shivered at what that could mean.

Father was kind to me, but to others he disagreed with?

I'd heard some nasty rumours about him that kept me awake at night.

Chapter Three

We stayed in the garden, talking about everything and anything. It was good to get some things off my chest, and it seemed that Alec needed to as well.

A lot had happened last year at Hellspire, and it seemed that both of us still had nightmares about it. After hours immersed in the rooftop gardens, we knew that we should head down for dinner as the sun was starting to set.

Dinner was a quiet affair at first, then Matthew apologised again before we sat down to eat, then the two of them spent half their time on the phone to security, father, and father's personal assistants.

So I excused myself and headed to bed early.

I felt mentally exhausted and knew a hot shower would help me rest.

I woke just after midnight, a scream lodged in my throat at the nightmare.

It was the soldiers who attacked Gaz and Maddy, laughing while they strangled them before turning to me. They removed their masks, and there stood Sera and Darius.

It felt so damn real that I wanted to vomit.

I couldn't get back to sleep after that, so I read a book to help distract me, attempting to calm my racing heart.

By morning, I made sure to message Maddy and Gaz, asking how they were, just to ease my anxiety.

They both said they were coping and making the most of the short time we had left before school started. I was just thankful that they weren't more hurt.

I could deal with them coming at me, but as soon as they attacked my friends, it felt like they were yanking my heart out with rusty pliers.

"I have to go away for a few days, but I'll be back in time to take you to school." Alec had joined me for breakfast, and even though we'd talked about the other day, it still hung between us, making things a little awkward.

"No worries," I mumbled into my mug. Since the attack, I was constantly cold and jittery and couldn't seem to get warm. I was layered up so much that Matthew had asked if I was getting sick.

"I have to leave as soon as I've finished breakfast." Alec continued. His eyes were pinned on me, his fork hovering over his scrambled eggs.

I nodded, knowing that working with Father meant he had to travel. I still didn't know what they did, but knew it involved being able to drop whatever they were doing to go on a moment's notice.

Matthew told me I was better off not knowing.

We ate in silence, and as Alec went to leave, he kissed the top of my head on the way out. I couldn't stop the tears or burning in my throat as I hung my head into my hands and cried.

I was stupid to feel like this. But I couldn't banish the heaviness in my heart.

The next few days passed in a blur. Matthew came and went, wearing his fancy suit most days, as he apparently met with people. I spent most of my time up on the rooftop garden reading.

To break the monotony, I spent a few hours catching up with Janine and Bradley - my foster parents - which was lovely for some much-needed normality. They filled me in on everything they'd been up to for the past year and didn't mind letting me help myself to Mum's homemade chocolate bikies. I didn't tell them everything that had happened. I glossed over the end of the year, and just the past week.

They didn't need to worry about me anymore, but I knew they would.

I expected the security guard who drove me here to be waiting out front, but Alec leaned against his car, patiently waiting. He greeted my foster parents warmly. They thought he was simply wonderful.

He could butter up even the most stubborn person. Everyone loved Alexander Hyde.

We waved our goodbyes as we climbed into his sports car and settled in.

"Matthew said you've spent your time reading in the garden," he murmured as he pulled out onto the highway. I could feel his eyes on me every so often.

"Yeah, it's peaceful up there," I admitted, but I was done feeling like this. I wanted to make the most of our limited time together. "I want to move past this, Alec."

He nodded, reached over and squeezed my thigh, keeping his hand there as he continued to drive.

"Me too, Babydoll. I want to make it up to you."

"I know. So let's get something to eat and drink."

His fingers tightened on my leg a fraction, heating my body in seconds. I knew this was the only way to move on. And to be honest, I wanted him. I wanted the comfort of his body, of him sleeping next to me and this heaviness gone.

"You name it, sweetheart. I'll do anything."

We stopped for more dumplings, but instead of a coffee, we got wine.

The halls were quiet as we rushed through, eager to be alone and thankful that Matthew was away.

The rooftop garden was lit up with fairy lights, and the fountain's lights glowed green, blue, purple, pink. The only noise up here was the fountain as it bubbled.

It was beautiful, and just what I needed.

Alec didn't waste any time unpacking the food, pouring me a healthy glass of red wine, and we ate and drank in comfortable silence. But I could feel my need building under my skin, deep in my belly. I wasn't just hungry for food. I was hungry for him.

I downed my wine in one long mouthful. Alec's eyes widened as I swallowed and placed the glass down.

Without thinking, he threw the rest of his wine over his shoulder, ignoring the sound of breaking glass and moved toward me, shoving anything out of our way as we finally came together.

Our hands roved over any skin we could touch, working their way under shirts until nothing lay between us. He lay me down on the soft grass, kissing me until I was breathless. His lips moved down over my bare chest as he paid special attention to my breasts, his fingers slipping down between my legs.

I moaned at the feel of his touch, at the rightness of it all.

He quickly rolled me over onto my stomach, shocking me as a small shriek escaped.

"Relax, sweetheart, I'm going to give you a massage." He murmured against my skin, his hands gripping my hips. A thrill shot through me.

A massage sounded delightful.

He reached over into the bag and opened a jar of coconut oil, scooping some of it out before lovingly rubbing it into my back, the fragrant scent filled my nose.

I groaned low in my throat as his hands moved up my back and worked on my shoulders.

This was *perfect*.

He sat on my legs, just below my bottom, his cock resting against my cheeks with a delicious tease each time he moved. I was supple under his strong hands, my body had never felt so relaxed. His body slid down my legs as he continued to work his way down my back before massaging my glutes and legs.

I couldn't stop the moans and groans that he brought out of me. His fingers slipped up to cup my ass, giving it a squeeze before one slipped down to where I desperately wanted him. He slid one finger right in, and I sighed, ending on a moan.

God, it felt *good*.

He didn't keep his finger there long as he continued to massage me, but every so often he would slip a finger or two in for a few teasing moments, working me up before moving on.

It was glorious torture.

In one smooth move, his hands moved up my back, his body pressing against mine, as his cock slid right inside me. With his weight on me, his hands slipping around my neck and his cock buried deep inside of me. I cried out as pleasure rocked through me.

He began to move, and I was quickly coming undone.

"Oh, Babydoll." Alec sighed above me, his hands a delicious weight encircling my throat as he thrust deeper and deeper with each move.

He rolled me over, hooking one leg over his shoulder as he drove in deeper.

I moaned as his lips locked on mine, one hand digging into my hair, the other on my hip.

"Alexander!" I cried out as my release barrelled towards me. I couldn't stop it as it smashed into me with the force of a tidal wave. It didn't take long for Alec to follow me into oblivion, my name on his lips as he cried out.

We lay there a moment, catching our breath before he rolled off me, keeping a hand on my waist as I turned to meet his gaze.

"That was the best sex I've ever had." I breathed, my whole body tingling.

"That certainly was something." He grinned, winking at me before leaning in and giving me a swift kiss. "I want you to know that you'll never be put in that dangerous situation again." He leaned back slightly, but kept his hand on me.

"I know." I nodded, feeling my unease slipping away. "It just scared me, and it being in my own home..." I had to look away as I pushed away the tears. "I know you wouldn't intentionally put me in harm's way."

He moved to cup my face, kissing me soundly until we couldn't breathe. Without speaking, our bodies came together again, this time taking it slow as he worshipped my body, making me come twice more before we headed for bed. He slipped into the sheets beside me and held me close until we fell asleep.

It was the best sleep I'd had for weeks.

The sharp corners, the endless climb, the wind biting at my jacket. It was *freedom*. I grinned beneath my helmet, leaning into the curves, not ready for the ride to end. Months had passed since I'd been out with Alec on the bike. Now, his sleek black sports car followed close behind, my cases in the boot, his presence a steady shadow in my rear-view mirror.

I pulled into the nearest garage, tucking my bike neatly into a corner. Alec slid in front of the door a second later, unfolding from the driver's seat with that familiar crooked grin.

"You weren't trying to lose me, were you?" he teased.

"Not at all. Just...enjoying the corners." I tucked my helmet under my arm as he hefted my cases. Together, we pushed through the stream of students flooding the foyer, noise, chatter, luggage, and at the center of it all, poor Miss Somali waving her spray bottle like it could hold back chaos itself.

Hellspire Academy was exactly how I remembered it.

"Ah, Miss Mav-" she stumbled over the name, her frown deepening as she checked her clipboard. "I mean, Xanetto. There's been...a change to your lodgings. It seems your room is-"

"Just down the hall. First door on the left." The gruff voice cut across hers. A man pushed through the crowd with the force of a battering ram.

Must be the new Dean.

His presence soured the air instantly. Miss Somali's lips pinched tight, her knuckles white on the clipboard. Alec stilled beside me, brows shooting high. His glare was nothing short of lethal.

"You've moved her to a *fucking* broom cupboard?" His voice was quiet, but the steel in it made my skin prickle. He looked ready to tear the man in two as he placed my cases down in a calm manner that didn't reflect the look that was in his eyes.

The Dean sneered, utterly unfazed. "Someone else deserved her room more than...whatever name you're using these days." His brow arched, his disdain coiled and sharp.

My insides twisted. "Jocelyn. Jocelyn Xanetto. There's no reason now for me to be in witness protect-"

"Yes, yes," he interrupted, dismissive, waving a hand. Alec growled low in his chest. "Like I said. Your room is down the hall."

Miss Somali's lips had nearly vanished from how tightly she pressed them together.

"She's *not* sleeping in there." Alec's voice was a blade drawn slow from its sheath. Goosebumps rippled across my arms.

The Dean's gaze snapped to him. "You speak on her behalf? Is she unable to herself?" His eyebrows raised in mockery.

My jaw clenched, my hands balled into fists at my sides.

What the fuck is this man's problem?

"I'm the Dean," he continued coldly. "And *I* can do whatever the hell *I* want."

"We'll see about that." Alec glared, already digging through his pocket without breaking eye contact. He pulled out his phone, dialled, and lifted it to his ear with deadly calm. The Dean's face began to turn red. His lip curled like he'd swallowed something rotten.

"Excuse me, Mr Xanetto," Alec said smoothly into the phone. "We've got a problem here. The Dean's putting Jocelyn into a supply closet as her room for no apparent reason. Thought you might want a word with him."

My stomach plummeted. Holy shit. He'd called my *father*.

The Dean's jaw ticked as Alec held out the phone. He snatched it, muttering in low, furious tones.

My pulse hammered as I watched the Dean's eyes narrow.

Why did he hate me? He didn't even *know* me.

When the Dean finally shoved the phone back into Alec's hand, his glare landed on me, which was nothing short of venomous.

"Your room is on the first floor. Number five." Then, with a curl of his lip, "Thank God you're not attending here this year, Mr Hyde. You'd already be expelled for that stunt. Now get off my property. You're never to set foot here again while I'm Dean." He spun and stormed off through the crowd, leaving silence in his wake.

My mouth hung open, my pulse roaring in my ears as I turned back to Alec. Anxiety churned in my veins as I tried to get my head around what had just happened.

"Fucking asshole," Alec muttered, grabbing my cases and marching toward the stairs. "You're in my old room, sweetheart."

I blinked hard, shaking off the shock, catching Miss Somali's wide-eyed stare. Her hands were trembling.

"I'm so sorry, Jocelyn," she whispered before hurrying away. I swallowed hard and followed Alec.

What the hell was that? What did I do to deserve it?

Alec was already in the room, setting down my cases, he took my helmet and placed it down on the bed, then pulled me into a hug. I sagged against him, pressing my forehead to his chest.

"He's Jenna's uncle. And it looks like he has it in for you."

I stiffened. "*Your* Jenna?"

His grip tightened. "She's not *my* anything." He growled. "But listen to me, he obviously wants to make your life hell. Don't give him an excuse. Eyes open, and don't give him anything." He pulled back, holding my arms, forcing me to meet his eyes. The seriousness there stole my breath. "Be on your guard."

"I will," I whispered. But the warmth of being back at Hellspire had already drained from me, leaving me cold. Alec kissed the top of my head, exhaling slowly.

"Come on. Walk me to my car."

We'd just locked my door when my new neighbour's opened. He stepped into the hall with an easy swagger, shutting the door behind him. His smile flickered as his gaze landed on me. He dipped his head in greeting before strolling past.

"He looks too old to be a fourth year." Alec's voice was a low grumble as his eyes tracked the man down the stairs. "I swear I've seen him somewhere before."

I followed his gaze, watching the tall figure cut effortlessly through the crowd. There was a sharpness to him, a quiet command that made people step aside. My stomach twisted at another new face.

"Keep your distance from anyone you don't know," Alec muttered, his hand finding mine as we descended the stairs.

"I know. Keep to my friends, keep my head down, focus on my studies." I repeated the mantra I'd been drilled with, by Matthew, by Father, by Alec himself. The truth was, Alec hadn't wanted me to return at all. Not after last year. Not after the scars Hellspire left behind. But Sera and the one remaining Hyde twin were locked away. Dean Fendi had been stood down. And Paul... well, Paul had vanished into the wind.

But he wouldn't hurt me. Not Paul. We had too much history. Even if that history ended at gunpoint.

Father on the other hand, told me that Hellspire simply wouldn't let you walk away.

"Just keep your eyes peeled," Alec warned. "And let me know if anything happens. Promise me." He stopped by the giant front doors, taking both of my hands in his. His light brown eyes softened as he took a step closer.

"I promise." I leaned up, intending to kiss him, only to jump when a sharp squeal erupted beside us.

Miss Somali was attacking a squabbling pair with her spray bottle again. I sighed, tugging Alec toward the doors.

"I'll talk to you on the weekend," I said as he spun his keys around his finger. "I miss you already." I pouted, looking down at my shoes.

He grabbed my chin and angled my face up, lips brushing mine, teasing. I grabbed his jacket and deepened the kiss. Too soon, he pulled away.

"Stay safe, Babydoll." A cheeky wink, a charming smirk, and my heart already ached.

We hadn't said those three little words yet, but I knew. We both knew.

"Drive safe." I blew him a kiss, and he caught it with a grin before sliding into the car. The engine roared, and then he was gone, speeding down the hill. It didn't take long for the emptiness to come. It was quick and sharp.

I wish he were still here.

I turned back and slipped into the crowd, scanning for a familiar head of fiery curls or Gaz's booming laugh. Instead, I found myself surrounded by wide-eyed first-years, hands white-knuckled on their cases, staring at the towering halls with awe and fear. I remembered being them once, and pity stirred in my chest.

"You just gonna stand there and block the hallway, moron?" The sarcastic bite made me laugh before I even turned. Maddy stood arm-in-arm with Gaz, grinning at me like I'd been caught doing something ridiculous. The bruises on her throat had faded, she'd attempted to hide them with makeup. I doubted anyone else would notice, but I knew they were there.

"Come on, let's get out of this mess." She looped her other arm through mine and tugged us up the stairs. My new neighbour was just ahead, taking the steps two at a time. At the top, he paused, just as Maddy barked out a laugh at something Gaz muttered. He turned, his sharp gaze locking onto us. On me.

"Hey," he said, tilting his head, studying me. "You're my new neighbour, yeah?"

"Yeah, I think so." I shrugged, feeling uneasy at his intense stare.

"This is Jocelyn Xanetto. I'm Maddy, and this is Gaz." Maddy stuck out her hand for him to shake.

I cringed at the use of my full name. It still sat strange on my tongue, the ghost of Clementine never quite letting go.

"Lovely to meet you." His hand extended to me, but his eyes, intent, steady, never left mine. "I'm Jake Callahan. Transferred here for my last year."

"Where from?" Gaz asked, tucking Maddy closer to his side like he could shield her from the sheer presence of the man.

"Bellator Academy. Overseas." His smile was easy. Disarming. And dangerously handsome. "But I heard Hellspire was the best of the best."

"Damn straight it is." Maddy puffed out her chest. I rolled my eyes, tugging my friend's into my new room. "Cya later." She called over her shoulder. Only when the door was locked behind us did I let my shoulders sag.

"What the hell are you doing down here?" Maddy demanded, plopping onto the bed. "What happened to your old room?"

"The Dean decided someone else deserved it more. I was lucky he hadn't stuck me in a storage cupboard, actually."

"He *what?*" Maddy shot upright. Gaz's gasp was just as loud.

"It's Jenna's uncle," I said flatly. "He seems to hate me already. And he banned Alec from the premises while he's Dean."

"No fucking way." Gaz scrubbed a hand over his face. "He can't get away with that."

"Yeah, well, he's out for my blood, apparently." My voice wavered despite my best efforts. "Alec only got me this room because... he called my father."

They groaned in unison.

"Yeah," I muttered. "Exactly."

Maddy's jaw tightened. "Then we'll make sure he doesn't get to you. He'll have to go through us first."

"You're a good friend, Maddy." I squeezed her hand, warmth seeping in despite the cold coil in my stomach.

"Don't go getting mushy on me," she grumbled, pretending like she didn't care. But I could tell that she loved it.

Gaz flopped down on her other side. "Your new neighbour looks too old to be here."

"I agree, and so does Alec," I grumbled, falling onto the bed beside Maddy.

"-hot," Maddy said at the same time. I burst out laughing, and Gaz huffed out an annoyed breath. "I meant mature," Maddy back-pedalled, her cheeks turned pink.

"Liar," Gaz growled, pinning her down and attacking her with merciless tickles. Her shrieks filled the room, loud enough to make someone think murder was happening on my bed. I slipped away, unpacking my case with a quiet smile. For the first time since stepping foot back in Hellspire, I felt a flicker of comfort.

But still, under the laughter, under the warmth of my friends, a thought lingered.

Jake Callahan.

There was something about him that didn't sit right.

And now… he was right next door.

Chapter Four

"Sit down, and shut up." The dean's voice boomed over the hall, every student sat straight and snapped their mouths shut. He sure wasn't mucking around. "I'm Dean Orletta, and I will not tolerate any nonsense, pranks, stupidity, or bad behaviour. This school is in shambles, and I have a lot of work ahead of me to turn this place around."

The students didn't even mutter as he ploughed on with his speech. I think they were all too scared.

"If any one of you steps a *toe* out of line. You'll be expelled. The last dean here ruined this school, and I'm not going to stand for it. Tuck in your shirts, get your shit together and pull your damn heads in. Dismissed." He turned and stormed away from the podium at the front of the room, and I think every one of us was staring with mouths open in shock. Even the professors were stunned into silence, their eyes wide and panicked as they looked between each other.

Yay. Looks like we're in for a fun year.

My new timetable was...interesting. A few new subjects were surprising, but not at the same time.

Computer Hacking class, disguises 101, stealth and surveillance, and escape and evasion. I no longer had music, which made me a little sad. But seeing as today was Thursday, my first class was Languages, followed by M.O.D.L, then martial arts.

I shivered at the thought of having another year of Professor Verreth, and his sick and twisted class. But at least I'd kept up with my fitness over the break. I didn't want to be weak, or defenceless anymore.

Professor Long launched into a story about his summer break, pushing his glasses up his nose at least five times in the first three minutes. His voice was so high it was a wonder his glasses didn't shatter as he excitedly told us about his travels. My ears felt like they were bleeding by the time the class had finished, a headache already building as I made my way to M.O.D.L class.

I dragged my feet down the hall, but surprised when older students greeted me on their way past. I didn't know who they were, but apparently, everyone knew who I was now.

I sat in my usual seat, a little sad that Alec's chair beside me would remain empty. I kept my eyes forward as the rest of the class filtered in.

Professor Verreth stood at the head of the table, silver hair slicked back like polished steel, his gloves resting lightly on the table as though he were ready to get his hands dirty. His smile curved slowly and deliberately. The kind of smile that said *I already know everything about you. Don't bother lying.*

I reined in my shiver. I *hated* this class.

"Welcome to M.O.D.L," he purred. "Your classmates will wonder what we do here. Tell them nothing. If you do..." His eyes glittered as they swept the table, lingering on me until my skin prickled. "...I'll know."

I shifted in my seat, only for a chair leg to scrape loudly beside me.

My new neighbour.

He dropped into the seat next to mine like he owned it, flashing me the faintest smile before turning to the front of the class. Uneasiness coiled low in my stomach.

There were plenty of other empty seats he could have sat in.

"Today," Verreth continued, "we study domination through truth and lies. Power is not in your fists, children. Power is in your words. In the pause between them." He let the silence build, then clapped his hands once. "Let's play a game."

A murmur ran through the room. Verreth ignored it as he paced, surveying us with cunning eyes.

"You will each tell two truths and one lie. Your peers must uncover which is false. If they fail, you will own them."

"Own them?" One of the third-years asked nervously.

Verreth's smile sharpened. "Ownership is temporary control. If they cannot catch your lie, they will obey a single command of your choosing. Nothing lethal. Nothing permanent. But... binding." The room shifted, uncomfortable and electric all at once. He gestured lazily. "Callahan. You first."

Jake leaned back in his chair, arms crossed, eyes glinting.

"Fine. One: I once drowned a man in Raddock. Two: I've never lost a hand of poker. Three: I hate dogs." The room buzzed. Students threw out guesses. Finally, Verreth arched a brow at me.

"Xanetto. Your turn. Which is the lie?"

I swallowed, and heat crawled up my neck. Jake's gaze pinned me, and for some reason, I felt nervous.

"The poker one," I said finally, voice steady. "Nobody wins all the time."

Jake's smirk spread slow and dangerous, goosebumps breaking out over my skin.

"Wrong."

Laughter rippled around the table. My stomach flipped as Verreth inclined his head.

"Then you, Jocelyn, are his to command. Callahan?"

Jake leaned forward, his voice low, a smile playing around his lips. It was intimate enough that only I could hear, though I knew Verreth was watching every flicker of expression.

"Sit perfectly still," Jake whispered, "and don't move a muscle until the round is over."

Heat flushed my skin. Petty, humiliating, but strategic. I obeyed, jaw tight, every nerve alight with the awareness of him beside me as I had to sit there and stare at him. Verreth's smile was shark-like as he turned back to the group.

"Do you see? Manipulate. Ownership. Dominate. Leadership begins here, with control. Words are weapons. Silence is sharper still." By the time my turn came, my blood was boiling, but I was also taking notes. Because this class was about control, I'd damn well learn to master it.

"Xanetto, you're up."

I'd been trying to think of something while I sat there glaring, and I think I finally had something that might work.

"One: I can speak three different languages. Two: I hate mushrooms. Three: I've won a game of darts against a famous football player." I didn't look at anyone, just sat with my chin up, pretending to be cool while Verreth went around the room asking the other students.

At this point, I'd had three people who had guessed wrong.

"Callahan?" Verreth crossed his arms over his chest as he stopped at our table.

Jake's assessing gaze seemed to rove all over me and into my very soul.

"You can't speak different languages. You've travelled, yes, but you're terrible at pronunciation." He winked, making my stomach knot.

How the hell did he know that?

Verreth demanded that I come up with something to control the others, and I blurted out the first thing that came to mind. "You must dance in the front of the room for three minutes."

Their faces turned crimson as they shuffled their way in front of us and started to dance. But Verreth thought it was fantastic, as it fueled their embarrassment, and they were more prone to acting out in anger, revealing something about themselves.

As soon as the class finished, I was out of there before most people had risen from their seats.

This Jake Callahan guy made my skin prickle, and not in a good way.

I beat my frustrations out in martial arts, Maddy obviously kept up her training over the summer, as she continued to whoop my ass. It seemed like I didn't learn a thing last year.

"Come on, Xanetto, It's like you're not even trying!" She crowed, wiping the sweat from her brow with the back of her arm. But she leaned in and helped me up. I wobbled on my feet after she successfully knocked me down at least three times in the past five minutes.

"Sorry, last class was...intense." I wiped my face with the bottom of my shirt. Maddy quirked a brow as she sipped from her drink bottle.

"I've always wondered what M.O.D.L was. But I've heard you're not allowed to talk about it."

"Nope. Can't say a word, and honestly, it's a class I wish I didn't have to do."

"Alright, you lard asses, that was embarrassing! I expect better from you next lesson. Dismissed." Professor

Panchette shook her head as she narrowed her eyes. "Pyre, I can tell you've kept up your training. Make sure you get Xanetto in line, will you?" She strutted past and I internally groaned. Maddy just grinned widely at me like the maniac she is.

"Oh, goody." She rubbed her hands together, and I scrubbed my face with both hands, knowing she was going to continue to kick my ass until I was able to properly take her on.

Dinner was loud, voices echoing around the cafeteria at full volume as the new senior legacies took the spot on the couches in the middle of the room. Maddy and Gaz didn't want a bar of it, so we remained at our Pyro table, a few scared looking first years wondering where to sit after they'd grabbed a trayful of food.

"What a first day. I'm knackered already." Gaz yawned, stretching his arms wide before draping one over Maddy's shoulders. A tiny smile tugged at her lips, but she continued to devour her bolognese without taking a breath.

"It sure was something," I mumbled, feeling the back of my neck prickle as if someone were staring at me. I didn't turn, I shook it off and dug into my lasagna and got lost in the conversations around the table.

Maddy, Gaz and I made our way to Computer Hacking class. We barely made it three steps before a petite first-year blocked my path, arms folded, smug little smile plastered on her face.

"So, *you're* the girl I kicked out of her room. How do you like-"

"Cool story, bro." I shoved past her, flashing double thumbs-up. Her jaw hit the floor.

Gaz barked out a laugh, mimicking my thumbs-up as we passed, and Maddy flipped her the bird instead, laughing.

I smirked. I didn't have time for bitchy first years who thought they were better than me.

I didn't miss those stairs, either.

Class was in a room I'd never been in, and with a professor I'd only seen wandering the halls. But I'd heard he was a little...eccentric.

The lab looked nothing like the usual rooms. This place hummed, literally. Banks of sleek black computers lined the walls, cords tangled like vines, faint green light glowing from beneath the desks.

Someone had scratched *We Own The World* into one of the tables.

Professor Halix strode into the room, small, wiry, wearing fingerless gloves and goggles pushed up into his white hair.

He smelled faintly of coffee and burnt wires.

"Welcome to the internet's underbelly," he announced, clapping his hands once. "By the end of term, you'll know how to disappear someone's bank account, change an identity, or topple a company with three keystrokes. But for today? We're starting simple." He grinned, manic. "Steal each other's passwords."

Groans and mutters filled the room, but he wagged a finger. "Not guess. Hack. The one who gets the most by the bell wins."

Maddy groaned dramatically. "I can barely even remember my own password." She slumped forward onto her keyboard, the screen filling with many *MMMM's* and *XXXX's*.

Gaz cackled beside her, already pounding keys like he was born for this. "That's why you'll lose."

I frowned at my screen. I had no idea where to even start. A black terminal stared back at me. My fingers hovered over the keys, barely touching.

"We're... really doing this?" I look up over my shoulder to the professor wandering the room.

"Oh, yes," Halix said cheerfully. "And I'll know if you cheat. Start with the person to your left." He slapped down a book on each table, mine's dark blue cover was stained with something dark and had started fraying at the edges.

***Computer Hacking for Idiots*.** Was on the cover, making me snort. I skimmed through the pages, seeing scribbles and things crossed out, someone writing another way to do it under the text.

Cue chaos as the room buzzed to life. Screens flickering. Fingers flying loudly on the keys. Maddy was muttering curses while her system beeped angrily, smacking the side of it with her hand in frustration. Gaz let out a whoop as his screen displayed: ***ACCESS GRANTED – MADELINE PYRE***.

"*HEY!*" Maddy shrieked. "That's private!"

Gaz smirked. "Shouldn't have named your cat the same as your password."

"Shouldn't have *told you* my cat's name," she snapped, smacking him on the arm. Across the room, a loud bang echoed, someone's tower smoked and sparked.

Professor Halix beamed. "Excellent! Sabotage is allowed."

I was still fumbling, the screen yelling at me with each wrong answer, when a voice murmured at my shoulder. "Try cross-site scripting. Simple backdoor. Like this." I turned to look over my shoulder, and Jake's fingers flew across my keyboard before I could swat him away, and suddenly: ***ACCESS GRANTED – GARY DAVIES.***

I glared at him. "That's cheating."

"No," he said smoothly. "Professor Halix didn't give us any rules. It's on page eight." He grinned, throwing me a wink for good measure. Before I could snap back, alarms blared across the room. Every single screen went black. The projector flared to life at the front, displaying a single line of text:

– NICE TRY, KIDS. BUT YOU JUST GOT HACKED –

The words dissolved, replaced by a smiling skull wearing Hellspire's crest as a crown. The class fell silent. Professor Halix grinned wider than I thought humanly possible.

"Congratulations. You've just been hacked by last year's seniors. Lesson one: there's *always* someone watching. Lesson two, learn to watch back."

Maddy and Gaz were bickering the whole way down the hall to cooking class. But she sighed dramatically and shoved Gaz into the wall, making him stumble as she laughed and took off. He grumbled and ran off after her, cursing her and her red hair.

I huffed a laugh as I watched them disappear around the corner. Honestly, those two were like children the way they behaved. I smiled at being back here, even if most of my memories still gave me nightmares.

But this is where I met Alec. I didn't regret my time here last year, only some of the things that happened within its dark walls.

Chapter Five

Professor Damascus, in her stark white button-up shirt and matching little cap, looked like she'd walked straight out of a vintage infirmary. Crisp, clinical, and untouchable. Her dark eyes swept over us as we settled at the long lab benches, and the corner of her mouth twitched in what might have been a smile, if smiles could be sharp enough to cut.

"Alright, class. No mucking around." Her voice cracked like a whip. "Today we're learning to harvest, dry, and integrate ingredients in such a way that your victim doesn't realise they've been drugged. They won't taste it. They won't feel the effects immediately. And the only way to learn-" she tapped the polished wooden desk with one long finger, "-is to practice on each other."

My stomach dropped so fast it left me dizzy.

Damascus continued briskly, as if she hadn't just told us we'd be poisoning each other for fun.

"Half the class will prepare the ingredients, craft the meal or beverage, and observe. Take notes on physical and mental changes. The other half will ingest and report symptoms. Next lesson, we swap. And no need to panic-" her smile widened, almost predatory, "-these doses won't kill you. At worst, you'll be dizzy, confused, and mildly nauseous. Perhaps a few hallucinations, if someone is ambitious."

A nervous ripple of laughter spread through the room. I just gripped the edge of my desk and prayed I wouldn't be the unlucky one who started seeing dancing skeletons.

Damascus clapped her hands, sharp as a gunshot. "Pairs! Quickly!"

Maddy instantly grabbed Gaz, both of them high-fiving. My palms were slick with sweat as I waited for Damascus to assign the rest.

"Jocelyn," she said at last, "you're with Callahan."

Of course.

I shut my eyes briefly, exhaling. The scrape of a chair pulled beside me, the subtle scent of leather and something darker that always seemed to follow him.

"Hey," Jake said, voice light and warm. "We meet again."

I turned my head. He was grinning at me, a dimple cutting into his cheek like he knew exactly how dangerous it was.

"Lucky me," I said, aiming for light and failing. My voice had no warmth.

His smile lingered, eyes shining a little too brightly. "Not sure I believe you."

Before I could reply, Damascus was clapping again. "Harvesting station is open. Those of you brewing today, step forward. I expect creativity."

Jake stood smoothly, gesturing for me to stay seated like some kind of gentleman. "I'll fetch the good stuff," he murmured, then winked before striding to the front, where dried herbs, powdered roots, and vials of unlabeled tinctures were laid out like candy jars. I drummed my fingers nervously on the table.

Of all the people in this academy, why him? Why did my gut twist every time he was near, no matter how charming he pretended to be?

He returned with a tray balanced in one hand. He set it down in front of me, and I eyed the small collection of herbs and powders warily.

"Relax," he said, pulling out his chair. "I'm not going to kill you. Not in class, anyway." The wink and smile he gave me was teasing. But there was something in his eyes, something that made my stomach lurch.

Like he meant it, half-joking or not.

I forced a shaky laugh. "Comforting."

He set to work. Jake measured with precision, grinding powders with steady hands, mixing drops of liquid into a steaming cup of tea. He was focused, meticulous. I stole a glance at the other pairs - Gaz was already laughing too loudly as Maddy dumped half a jar of something suspicious into his food. Compared to them, Jake looked... professional. Like he'd done this before.

He slid the cup toward me, his eyes gleaming. "Bottoms up."

I hesitated, staring at the pale steam curling from the rim.

"You trust me, don't you?" His voice dipped lower, softer. I didn't bother with an answer. Because of course I didn't trust him. It felt like a trap.

I lifted the cup, forcing myself not to flinch, and drank. At first, nothing, it tasted like plain herbal tea. After a few minutes, slowly, the edges of the room softened, like I was underwater. My thoughts grew sluggish, as though each one had to wade through quicksand before it reached me.

Jake leaned forward, chin propped on his hand, watching me like a scientist studying a particularly interesting experiment. "What do you feel?"

"Dizzy," I admitted, blinking hard. "Foggy."

"Good. Means it's working." His tone was casual, but the way his gaze lingered on me felt heavier than it should.

Like he wasn't just studying the effects of the herbs, he was studying *me*.

Around us, chaos unfolded. Gaz had keeled over, groaning dramatically while Maddy cackled. Another first year was panicking because their partner's pupils had dilated to the size of saucers.

Damascus drifted between groups like a hawk, scribbling notes and occasionally smirking.

But I only noticed Jake. The way he tapped his pen slowly against his notebook. The way his eyes never left me.

"You're still upright," he murmured. "Stronger than you look."

"Why do I feel like that was... almost a compliment?" *Am I slurring?*

He smirked. "Maybe it was."

I tried to shake off the fog clouding my thoughts. "Why are you here, Jake? Really?"

His pen stilled. For the briefest second, something flickered across his face, gone as quick as it came. He leaned back, masking it with a lazy smile.

"Same reason you are. *Education*." But his tone was too smooth. Too easy. My gut twisted again. The dizziness was growing worse. I set my head in my hands, elbows braced against the desk.

"This is awful." I moaned, wanting the spinning to stop.

"Don't worry. It'll pass." His voice softened. Then, quieter, so only I could hear: "But one day, it won't be practice. You need to be wary of everyone."

The words chilled me more than the drug.

I lifted my head sharply, trying to read his face. But Jake was smiling again, casual and charming, like he'd said nothing at all.

Had I imagined it?

Damascus clapped for attention. "Time's up! Record your final notes. Subjects may report to the infirmary if symptoms linger." Around me, the room buzzed with chatter, laughter, and complaints. Everyone else was caught in the chaos. No one noticed the way Jake leaned close, his breath brushing my ear.

"You should listen to your instincts, Jocelyn." His whisper was silk and steel. "They're the only thing that might keep you alive."

When I turned to him, ready to demand what he meant, he was already on his feet, collecting his tray, whistling under his breath, playing the perfect classmate.

Friendly. Charming. Harmless.

But my unease lingered, heavy and undeniable, long after the dizziness faded.

Maddy cackled the whole way to science, laughing how Gaz was still stumbling, and still running into things.

But she took pity on him when he ran into the door frame, cursing.

Professor Zane was bouncing on his toes with excitement when we entered the room, fiddling with something that looked like a vial of dust as he gestured for us to take our seats.

It seemed like we were moving on from explosives, onto dissolvents instead.

But I struggled to pay attention, my mind still foggy and swimming from the damn cup of tea. Gaz seemed worse off as he lay on the floor in the fetal position under the table, groaning. Professor Zane made Maddy take him to the infirmary.

Britney, Carl, and Jordan, other second-years, were working on something in the corner of the room, heads bent as they argued about how much to use. A puff of smoke went up in a mushroom cloud, causing the smoke alarms to blare. Water sprayed next, dousing us in seconds. The room cursed the trio as we dripped our way out of the classroom. By the time the sprinklers shut off, the water on the floor lapped over our shoes, the tables were covered in puddles.

"What the hell, Carl?" Jordan shoved him as they made their way to the table. "You're so clumsy."

"Hey, I'm not the one who sneezed just as I was tipping it in." Carl grumbled, shoving him back. I rolled my eyes as we followed them into the room.

"Shut up, the both of you." Britney smoothed her hair off her face, our clothes wet and cold as we shivered. I tuned the trio out as I returned to my own table, but everything was too damp to continue using.

We packed away, most of the students muttering under their breath as we tidied up the room. Our shoes squelched as we walked out.

I had no appetite for dinner, my stomach churning as I made my way to my room. I sat heavily on my bed and sighed. At least we would get our phones back tonight, and I could ring Alec.

God, I missed him.

I changed clothes and forced myself back down to the cafeteria, grabbing a lemonade to help settle my stomach.

Maddy was there, but Gary was nowhere to be seen. She looked a little pale herself.

"Hey, is everything alright?" I sat heavily, closing my eyes a moment while my head settled.

"Not really. I think I gave him too much, they've had to purge his stomach. God, I'm such an idiot. I thought he was just being dramatic." She dropped her head into her hands, sniffling.

"Hey, he'll be fine. Professor Damascus told us it wasn't poisonous." I reached over and gripped her shoulder. "He's tougher than he looks."

"Better be, I ain't staying in this place without him." She grumbled, sniffed, wiped her eyes, and attempted to give me a smile. "You look pale. Still feeling shit too?"

"Yeah, I'm not hungry, but I want my phone, so that's why I'm here."

"Yeah, the way the new kid watched you today was a little intense. He took lots of notes, too." Maddy narrowed her eyes, drumming her fingers on the table.

"He is a little intense. And for some reason, he's always right there." I grumbled, taking a sip of my drink more for something to do.

"Well, he is *very* pretty to look at." She sighed dreamily as she looked around the room, no doubt to find Jake. "So, how's things with you and Alec?"

"Good." I paused, fiddling with the cuff of my cardigan. "He was away a few days, but we caught up before school." I stirred my drink with the straw, watching the ice cubes clink and swirl, the bubbles rising to the top.

"Uh oh. That doesn't sound good." She dropped her voice and leaned in. "Does it make it awkward that he's working for your dad?"

"No..." I didn't meet her eyes, but for some stupid reason, tears clogged my throat.

What the hell is wrong with me?

"It's nice to see Matthew and Alec repair their friendship, but it just means that I have to share him now. And apparently he's good at what he does." I cleared my throat and took a long drink, blinking back the sting in my eyes. Maddy reached out and placed a hand on my arm. "Which means he's always busy."

"I'm sure things will work out, just give it a little time to settle, get into a routine."

"Yeah." I forced a smile, but as soon as I was handed my phone, I excused myself and disappeared into my room. I stared at the screen for a while, mustering the courage to turn it on.

Why was I nervous about speaking to Alec? I'd shared everything with him. He knew me better than I knew myself. I shook myself for being ridiculous and switched it on, hearing the beeps of messages drop in.

Matthew, Alec, father, and Gabby.

I took my time in replying, making sure I didn't give away how I was really feeling.

A little lonely. A little scared. I didn't know what it was, but I still didn't feel safe here. Maybe it was just that I remembered all the bad things that happened here last year.

I called Alec, rather than replying to his text. I needed to hear his voice.

"Hey, Babydoll."

I smiled as his voice instantly soothed me.

"I've missed you." I whispered, lying back on the bed as I stared at my ceiling.

"I miss you too. How's school?" His voice was low, wholly focused on me.

"It's...fine. Same as last year. M.O.D.L is just as horrid, and I have new subjects this year."

"Second year is when things step up another notch. First year, they are a little more lenient. Are you alright?" I could imagine him frowning, his lovely honey brown eyes narrowing slightly.

"I'm fine." I shrugged, attempting to keep my voice light, but I could hear him sigh.

"No, you're not. I can hear it in your voice. What's the matter? Is it the dean?" His voice had an edge to it now, and I wish I'd tried harder to pretend.

"No, really. It's just a new student that seems a little intense, but-"

"Is it your neighbour?" He butted in and I cringed. He was always good at picking things up. "What's his name?"

"Jake Callahan, says he transferred from Bellator."

"Well that's bullshit, because there isn't an academy in Bellator. Stay the hell away from him and make sure to tell me as soon as anything happens." He'd quickly flipped from comforting boyfriend to full protector mode. "Do you have the knife I gave you?"

Dread settled in my stomach like a stone. But I looked over to my cupboard, where I'd stashed the dagger he gifted me after what happened at the house.

"Yeah, I've got it." I whispered, hoping I would never have to use it.

"Good. Keep it attached to you at all times. Jossi, you need to keep your eyes peeled."

"I will. I just wish you were here." I breathed, feeling my throat tighten with unshed tears.

"I know. Me too, sweetie. You're stronger than you think. Don't ever forget that."

Chapter Six

The training field behind Hellspire smelled faintly of damp leaves and gunpowder. It wasn't a field so much as a half-wild clearing ringed by thick forest, the kind of place where shadows stretched long and birdcalls were muted by the canopy overhead. A dozen students stood in two messy rows, all buzzing with nervous chatter.

Colonel Fex prowled in front of us like a restless wolf. His single eye glittered under the brim of his cap, his posture stiff but predatory. He wore a simple uniform, sharp creases in his trousers, gloves that looked like they'd been stitched from something that once lived and breathed.

"Listen carefully," he drawled, his voice roughened by smoke and age. "If you're captured in the field, your first thought should not be *who will come for me*. Your first thought should be *how will I get out*." He stopped abruptly, head turning toward us, that single eye sweeping like a spotlight. "Survival is not about waiting. It is about taking."

A ripple of discomfort ran down the line. Gaz muttered something under his breath that made Maddy elbow him in the ribs. I just tried to breathe steadily.

"Today," Fex continued, "some of you are prey. And the others hunters. You will take turns in both roles over the next few lessons. One will bind, one will escape, and the hunted must reach that flag-" he pointed to a tattered red scrap of material tied to a tree at the far end of the clearing "without being recaptured. Consider this your warm-up." His smile was thin and cruel, the kind of smile that said failure wasn't an option in this class.

Pairs began forming instantly. Maddy snatched Gaz before anyone else could. Britney got lumped with some poor, unsuspecting second-year who looked like he might faint if anyone touched him. Carl and Jordan high-fived. I scanned the crowd, looking for someone non-lethal, when a hand brushed my arm.

"Looks like you're stuck with me, sweetheart."

I turned, pulse tripping as I took in the person next to me. Jake Callahan.

Seriously?

He smiled down at me like it was the most natural thing in the world. Dark hair falling into his eyes, jaw set in a way that made half the girls at Hellspire stare too long. To everyone else, he looked harmless – charming, even. But there was something in his gaze that prickled the back of my neck.

I forced a shrug. "Fine. But don't think I'm making this easy for you."

"That's the point." His grin tilted into something sharper. "I wouldn't want you to."

I nervously patted my thigh where my knife now lived, tucked under my shorts.

Fex barked instructions, and the pairs separated into captor and prisoner. Jake gestured me forward with mock chivalry.

"After you."

The rope felt rough against my wrists as he looped it around, pulling tight - not painfully, but with a precision that made me shiver. His fingers brushed the inside of my pulse, deliberate, lingering just a second too long.

"You look nervous." I could hear the smile in his voice, his head still down on my hands. "You'll never get out of that in time," he murmured, leaning close enough that only I could hear. "But I'll give you a head start." It sounded like a joke. But the look in his eyes wasn't.

"Begin!" Fex's voice snapped across the clearing.

"Run," He breathed.

I bolted.

The ropes dug into my skin as I twisted and tugged, feet pounding across damp grass. I ducked behind the first tree I could find, fumbling with the knots, fingers working fast. Alec had shown me a trick once - slide the rope against the sharp edge of a branch, twist, pull, repeat. It burned my skin, the fibers beginning to fray. I snapped my head up when I saw Gaz stumble my way, breathing hard.

"Here, let's try to work together." He reached my side, puffing hard, but his eyes were shining with excitement.

I nodded as we took off. The trees were unfamiliar to me here; I'd never been this far on my morning run.

"Let's get these ropes off. Give me your hands." Gaz attempted to remove mine, but he grunted as he fiddled. "They're too tight. Who the hell tied them?"

"Callahan," I grumbled, and Gaz raised his brows.

"Impressive. Guy knows how to tie knots."

"Now's not the time to be impressed, Gaz!" I hissed, and he apologised before giving up. I set to work on his and had the ropes undone when I heard a slow clap.

"Not bad." Jake's voice was calm and unhurried. I spun, heart hammering. He wasn't rushing. He wasn't even running. He leaned lazily against a tree trunk like he had all the time in the world, arms crossed.

Watching me.

"You can run," he said softly. "But you're loud when you breathe. Easy to track."

The words sank like ice water through me.

"I'm going to find you, Davies!" Maddy crowed in the distance, getting closer. He shot me an apologetic look. "Sorry, Joss. Each for their own." Then took off running.

Damn it. I was still tied. Before Jake could approach, I ducked low and darted deeper into the woods, weaving between trees, careful to place each step quieter than the last. My lungs burned, but adrenaline pushed me forward.

Silence.

Had I lost him?

I crouched behind a fallen log, pressing my back into the damp bark. The clearing wasn't far; I could make a break for the flag if I were fast.

A shadow moved at the edge of my vision.

A hand shot out, seizing my wrist, yanking me up and slamming me against a tree. My breath left me in a gasp. Jake pinned me there, one hand braced by my head, his body a wall of heat and muscle against mine. His smile was all teeth, and too damn close for my liking.

"What the fuck?" I snapped, fear slamming through me so hard I barely had time to realise what was happening.

"Told you. *Prey*." He grinned as my heart slammed into my ribs.

I would not let this asshole continue to lord over me. So I relaxed as if in resignation, and he loosened his grip, ever so slightly. But it was enough.

I raised my knee, but he twisted at the last minute, and I got him right in the middle of the thigh instead. He grunted in pain as I ripped my hands from his grip and smacked him in the chin. It wasn't much, but it was enough for me to slip away and bolt through the trees. I made it out into the field and grazed my hand over the red flag, turning back to see a furious Jake behind me.

"Impressive, Xanetto. A little savagery will get you a long way." Fex nodded at me before sliding his steely eyes to Jake, then down at the blade on his hip.

Jake dipped his head once in acknowledgment before sliding the knife from his belt to cut my frayed ropes loose. The blade glinted as he sliced through the fibers, his fingers brushing mine again.

He obviously didn't like how I'd gotten away from him.

Around us, the class erupted in groans and laughter. Gaz claimed he'd escaped in record time until Maddy smacked him with a stick. Britney was berating her partner for being too slow. Jordan had fallen and broken his glasses, and Carl had fallen chasing him and rolled his ankle.

Everyone else bought Jake's act. Only I noticed that when he leaned close to murmur, his voice was barely audible.

"Careful, Jocelyn. The hunt for people like you doesn't stop when class ends."

I whipped my head to him, heart hammering in my chest as he winked, then wandered away.

What the hell is he playing at?

I changed quickly, Maddy laughing at how awesome it was to play hunter - claiming how fun it would be to run away from Gaz. I was just glad that next time, I would be the one to find someone. I didn't like the feeling of someone after me, especially when it was someone powerful, dangerous, and intimidating.

Gaz and Maddy fell heavily onto the table at lunch, still bickering about our last class. But she shoved him away before turning to me.

She paused as she watched the Dean stalk through the cafeteria. She narrowed her eyes as she tracked him, making sure he was out of earshot.

Every time I passed him in the halls, it was like his glare was filled with fire, burning into my back until I'd turned the corner.

"You know that nasty first-year who took your room?" She picked at her nails with a pocketknife, not even looking at what she was doing.

"Yeah. She's been sneering at me since." I smiled. I'd heard her bitching about me, but honestly? I didn't care. I had bigger things to worry about than some snooty first-year.

"She thinks she's king shit, right. Strutting around because she kicked you out of your room. But I have a plan to knock her down a peg or two."

I turned to see her grinning like a madwoman, and I returned the smile.

"Count me in."

"Perfect. Swing by my room after lights out."

By the time Maddy let me in, Gaz was already there, shoving something into a duffel bag.

"So, what's the plan?" I flopped down onto her bed, watching the two as they stood at the foot of the bed, like they were ready to give a presentation.

"Right. So, we either have to draw her out and sneak in, or do it during the day when she's not there." Maddy began pacing, her hands behind her back. "I'm thinking another fart bomb; that shit stinks for *weeks*." She turned and grinned, and I knew all too well how much one of those things reeked. "And if we do it just after she leaves for the day, it has time to stink her stuff out for hours before she realises."

"Perfect. I'll get the bombs, you, Mads; make sure you keep her downstairs." Gaz grinned, rubbing his hands together. "Oh, and I'll make sure to leave a note telling her if she tells, then everyone will know her dirty little secret." He was pacing like Maddy was, and I frowned, cocking my head to the side.

"Which is?" I turned to Maddy, and she just shrugged. Gaz tipped his head back and laughed evilly.

"Oh, that her parents are frauds. They're broke and have been caught stealing from charities and are now being sent to jail."

"Oh, that's perfect!" Maddy cackled, jumping up and down. I felt a twist in my stomach at how she must be feeling. But that gave her no right to treat the rest of us like garbage.

We decided on a day and time and got to work.

Maddy made sure to create a distraction that blocked the hall after the snooty first-year and her friends passed through. Gaz snuck into her room and planted the note and the bombs, rigging them so they would set off in a matter of minutes.

About half an hour later, he sat down at the Pyro table, breathing hard but grinning. He nodded once, then dug into his breakfast. That was all the confirmation we needed to know that he succeeded.

I could hear her from here, boasting about how good the view was and how she had her own bathroom.

I smirked into my coffee.

She wouldn't be bragging soon.

I made my way to my next class, M.O.D.L. I now had the class twice a week, and that was two too many times in my opinion.

The room was darker than usual. A single golden lamp glowed above the round table, casting shadows that made every face look sharper. Professor Verreth stalked behind us with the ease of a predator pacing its cage, the soft click of his shoes against the polished floor the only sound.

"This exercise is simple," he purred, fingers steepled. "You will take turns dragging secrets out of your partner. You don't have to be correct - you only have to convince the rest of us that you've made them reveal something.

That's where the skill lies: making them bleed truth, or at least making the audience believe they have." He paused by my chair. His eyes were like polished steel, impossible to read. "And remember, an unguarded tongue is more dangerous than any blade. If you slip... well." His slow smile sent a ripple of unease through the room. "You may regret it."

No pressure, then.

The pairings had already been decided. The class was a carefully curated group of ten, all top of their classes. My stomach tightened when I saw Jake slide into his seat across from a quiet boy named Elijah, who looked like he'd rather melt into the floor than go toe-to-toe with him. Of course, Jake caught me looking, and smirked, like he'd already won a game I didn't know we were playing.

I was paired with a sharp-eyed girl named Cleo, whose expression suggested she wanted to peel me open like an orange. Fantastic.

Verreth clapped once, silencing the room. "Jocelyn and Cleo. You're first. To the front."

The others watched with that mix of anticipation and bloodlust that seemed to thrive in this school. I took my seat opposite Cleo at the smaller table in the center, heart hammering.

"So," she began, leaning forward, voice sweet as poison, "I hear you run every morning. Alone."

I swallowed. "So?"

"So maybe it isn't just for fitness. Maybe you're meeting someone. Or maybe you're running from something. Interesting habit for someone who was hunted all year. To be alone out there." Her smile widened, waiting for me to flinch.

"That's cute," I said lightly, matching her smile with one of my own. "But if you want to talk about habits, maybe you should explain why you always sit facing the door. Afraid someone might come looking for you?"

Her pupils flared, just slightly and her finger twitched on the tabletop. The watching students murmured. Verreth's voice slithered across the room: "Point to Jocelyn."

Cleo narrowed her eyes, but I was already tuning her out. Because across the room, Jake and Elijah were making their way over.

Jake leaned back in the chair, legs stretched, smile lazy and amused. "You always volunteer for clean-up duty after dinner, don't you?"

Elijah frowned. "So?"

"So... funny thing. That's usually when the professors leave their papers unattended while they go out for a smoke. You like reading things that aren't yours, don't you?"

"I don't-" Elijah's protest died in his throat. His gaze flickered just once toward Verreth, like he were afraid of being caught. And there it was: a slip.

Jake's smile sharpened. "See? You've already admitted it." The students murmured again, some impressed, some annoyed. I, meanwhile, couldn't look away.

Jake didn't push. He never needed to. He set traps in silk and waited for you to stumble. He didn't press Elijah, didn't gloat, he just let the silence work, let the boy's own panic do the bleeding for him.

And I noticed things, like the way Jake always smiled before he struck, as if softening the blow. The way his hand flexed under the table every time he was about to lie. The way he mirrored Elijah's posture, subtly, just enough to make the other boy lean closer, relax, lower his guard.

It was a performance, but also a mask. I couldn't tell how much was practised habit and how much was just... him. My stomach knotted. Professor Verreth had told us on the first day that predators spotted openings. And Jake Callahan was nothing if not a predator.

When it was over, Jake caught me watching again. His smirk widened, like he knew exactly what I'd been doing, studying him the way Verreth wanted us to study each other.

And for one, tiny flicker of a moment, the mask slipped. His smile faltered, his eyes sharpened, and the weight of his stare pinned me like a butterfly to a board. Then he winked, leaned back, and laughed at something Elijah said, the picture of easy charm.

But the unease lingered in my chest like smoke.

Chapter Seven

Professor Damascus tapped her clipboard with one immaculate, gloved finger, the sound sharp as a knife point.

"Today, we switch. Those who prepared last class will test. Those who were tested on will prepare."

My palms were already sweaty. I knew this moment was coming, but knowing it and living it were two very different beasts.

"Remember," Damascus continued, sweeping her gaze over us like she was cataloging our future failures, "your concoctions must be undetectable. Taste, smell, texture. If your partner suspects, you've failed. Their only job is to consume, and you record the symptoms. That will be graded just as harshly." She smiled, and it was wrong - bright as a chef on a cooking show, but underneath it pulsed a dark glee.

"Begin."

Maddy and Gaz already had their heads bent together, whispering like they were plotting a heist instead of mixing ground roots and berries. I envied them. At least they got to fail or succeed together.

Me? I glanced at Jake. He was leaning back in his chair, arms folded, looking like he'd been waiting all morning for this.

"Your move, partner." He smiled, looking at ease in this class. Hell, he looked at ease in every single class we had together.

I forced myself to exhale through my nose and made my way over, trying to focus on the array of ingredients spread across the table: dried fungi that looked suspiciously like shrivelled ears, powders that clung to my fingertips like dust, vials of thick liquid the colour of spoiled honey.

The assignment: induce mild disorientation without altering flavour.

I crushed one of the dried mushrooms, careful to scrape the pieces fine enough to vanish when stirred into broth. My stomach churned at the smell, but I layered it with a squeeze of the honey-thick extract, stirred. Perfect.

I slid the bowl across to him. "Bon appétit."

Jake raised his brows, grin sharp. "If I didn't know better, I'd think you were trying to kill me."

"Not today," I muttered, attempting for one of his usual barbs.

He held my gaze as he lifted the spoon, then swallowed the mixture in one go. The smug smile never left his lips, even as I set up my notebook, pen poised. For the first two minutes, nothing. He leaned back, completely unbothered, like he was going to coast through this untouched. I started to think I'd messed it up.

Then his smile wavered. Just slightly. But enough that I caught it.

"Symptoms?" I prompted, writing the header in my notebook.

"Fine," he said easily, but the word slurred on the edges. His hand tapped against the desk, too quick, too restless.

"Fine," I echoed, jotting it down. "Loss of fine motor control, slight speech slur."

His eyes narrowed. "I didn't slur."

"You did."

"Didn't."

I bit my lip to hide a grin. The concoction was working, disorientation creeping in around the edges, loosening his polished composure. He tried to lean casually on his elbow and nearly knocked the bowl off the desk. I caught it before it spilled and wrote, *clumsy*.

Jake scowled, trying to straighten, but his balance was off.

"You're enjoying this too much." He growled, glaring at me but it lacked its usual bite.

"Only a little." It was nice to see him becoming undone for once.

The others were starting to notice. Gaz snorted as Jake swayed in his seat, muttering something to Maddy that earned a laugh. Even Professor Damascus's lips twitched, though her eyes stayed cold.

"How are you feeling?" I asked, trying to sound professional.

He blinked at me. Slowly. "Like... the room doesn't know which way is up."

I scribbled it down. *Spatial disorientation.*

He leaned closer suddenly, so close I could see the faint stubble on his jaw, smell the clean bite of whatever cologne he wore. "If you ever poison me outside this classroom," he murmured, "I won't be this forgiving."

A shiver raced down my spine. I told myself it was just the intensity in his voice, not the threat behind it.

I cleared my throat and pulled back. "Noted. Symptom: paranoia."

That got a laugh from Gaz so loud Damascus snapped at him to focus on his own work. Jake, meanwhile, grinned again, but it was crooked now, teeth flashing.

I should've felt victorious. He was unravelling in front of me, and I was the one cataloguing every slip, every stumble. Instead, I just felt... unsettled. Because even disoriented, even drugged, Jake Callahan looked like he was still calculating ten steps ahead.

And worse - like he was letting me win.

God, what a horrible day. And a Monday to boot.

I still had the rest of the week ahead of me.

I couldn't wait to climb into my comfortable bed and sleep the rest of it away. But what I wouldn't give to have Alec snuggled up beside me.

Maddy and Gaz were bickering about something, completely ignorant of the rest of our table. Britney gave me a small wave on her way past.

I didn't know much about her. Last year she was as quiet as a door mouse, but this year she seemed to be finding her feet. I hadn't talked to her much, but she seemed nice. She also admitted that she was scared witless of Maddy, which made me snort.

I wrote Alec a letter, seeing as I wouldn't talk to him until the weekend, and I needed to get some things off my chest. He's taught me how to write in a code he invented, so that I could say what I needed to, and anyone else who read it would think I was being a little vapid and spoiled.

But I told him that Jake Callahan was more than he seemed, and that I thought he had it in for me.

A little far fetched? Probably. Paranoid? Probably.

But there was something about him that put me on edge.

And the fact that he was normal with everyone else, but with just me, he was terrifying.

The classroom wasn't a classroom.

It was the entire north wing. But the class Stealth and Surveillance, obviously needed a large space.

Professor Morayne, thin as a dagger, with a voice that carried through the room, stood before us in the darkened corridor.

"The world is not conquered by those who shout," she said, adjusting the black gloves on her hands. "It's conquered by those who are not seen. Not heard. Not remembered. You will learn to stalk shadows, to read movement, to watch without being watched." She smiled then, sharp and humourless. "And you'll do it today."

The rules were simple, or so she claimed. We were split into two groups: Trackers and Ghosts. The Ghosts had to make it from one end of the wing to the other without being caught. The Trackers had to catch them, by spotting them, tagging them, or, if they were bold enough, outsmarting them.

The prize? Survival points toward our overall rankings.

The penalty? Hours cleaning the kitchens under Damascus's watchful eye.

My luck, I was picked for the role of Ghost.

Gaz fist-pumped at being a Tracker, while Maddy groaned. "I can't be invisible, I sparkle too much," she crossed her arms, earning a few laughs. Jake, of course, was a Tracker too. His eyes flicked to mine across the hall as if he already knew he'd be the one hunting me.

Morayne snapped her fingers. "Ghosts. You have two minutes. Go."

I darted into the shadows with half a dozen others, heart hammering. The wing had been transformed into a maze of obstacles: overturned desks, draped curtains, vents cracked open like dark maws, even sound-triggered alarms on some doors. It was like a high-stakes game of hide-and-seek, except if you lost, you'd never live it down.

I pressed myself flat against a wall, counting my breaths. Already, I could hear the Trackers being released, their footsteps deliberate, echoing down the corridor.

"Come out, come out, little Ghosts..." Gaz's voice sing-songed. He was having way too much fun.

I edged toward a vent, hoping it wasn't booby-trapped, when I caught a flicker of movement ahead – Jake. He was silent, scanning the dark like a predator. His strides were slow, deliberate, as though he had all the time in the world. My pulse spiked, my palms becoming sweaty.

He stopped suddenly, head cocking. For a terrifying second, I thought he'd heard me. But then he murmured to another Tracker, "*Check the curtains.*"

I used the distraction to slip through the vent opening. It was narrow, dust coated my hands, but at least it muffled the sound of me sneaking through on my hands and knees.

"Two Ghosts tagged!" Morayne's voice rang out somewhere behind. "Trackers, sharpen up!"

I inched forward until I reached another grate, peeking out, only to freeze. Jake was standing directly in front of me, scanning the hall like he knew I was there.

How the hell did he get there so quickly?

"You're breathing too loud."

I bit down a curse, heart racing. He hadn't seen me, not really. He was bluffing. Right?

The sudden *clang* of metal told me otherwise. Jake bent down, gripping the edge of the vent, eyes locking with mine in the dark. My entire body jolted.

Before he could reach in and haul me out, I scrambled forward, kicking him in the chest and ran across the room into another vent, leading to the next room. I scrabbled through on my hands and knees as fast as I could, my landing was messy, but as soon as I got to my feet, I sprinted before anyone could tag me.

"Ghost spotted! Hall three!" Jake's shout echoed, and suddenly, Trackers were converging.

I ducked through a cluster of desks, weaving fast. A hand brushed my sleeve. I twisted away, slamming into a door and bursting through. The alarm shrieked.

"Penalty! Ten points lost!" Morayne's disembodied voice announced gleefully in the distance.

"Damn it," I hissed, stumbling forward, only to slam into a chest.

I looked up and internally cursed.

Jake caught me by the wrist, not unkindly, but with a grip that was firm enough to make my breath catch. His chest was heaving, so he'd obviously taken the quickest route to beat me there.

His eyes glittered in the dim light. "You're quick," he murmured. "But you panic. That's when you make noise.

That's when you get caught." For a moment, it wasn't a game anymore.

Then he tapped my shoulder. "Tagged."

My scowl only made his grin widen.

I was actually glad for metalwork next. It meant that I could hammer away, imagining it was Jake's infuriating face.

The steam quickly enveloped us, masking the room in a thick haze.

The more I did this class, the more I enjoyed it.

Gaz stood next to me, finishing up his work with a curved sword. It was truly amazing.

"You're actually really good at this, aren't you?" I leaned on the table and wiped the sweat from my brow. It was always so damn hot in there.

"I enjoy it. I used to make stuff with my dad in our garage all the time. Not weapons, but other things." He smiled fondly as he finished his final touches. Professor Wood beamed at his finished product, showing it off around the room. Gaz blushed so hard his cheeks looked like tomatoes.

Geography passed quickly, another lesson without Jake, thank goodness. I didn't like how he stuck in my brain, that he consumed so many of my thoughts, and not in a good way either.

Was he trying to intimidate me?

Check.

Was he trying to always be one step ahead?

Check.

I really needed to see Alec this weekend and to share my worries.

He would know what to do.

It was my first class in Disguises 101. I wasn't sure how this class would work, but I knew it was going to be all sorts of weird.

The classroom looked like a costume department had thrown up in it.

Racks of clothes crammed the walls: uniforms from every branch of the military, business suits, maid outfits, lab coats, even what looked suspiciously like priest robes. Wigs hung on mannequin heads, sunglasses piled in baskets, and drawers overflowed with makeup and latex putty.

Professor Quinn, our instructor, stood in the middle of it all. She was tall, severe, with crimson lipstick painted in a sharp cupid's bow. Her eyes gleamed with mischief, though her tone was ice.

"Rule number one of disguise," she said, heels clicking as she paced. "It's not about hiding who you are. It's about convincing the world you're someone else. If you can't sell it, you die." Her gaze skimmed the room until it landed on Maddy, who'd already picked up a wig.

"You. Put that down. You don't choose your disguise. I do."

Maddy groaned, dramatically returning the wig. "What, no self-expression allowed?"

Quinn smirked. "Express yourself in your obituary."

The class laughed nervously.

The Assignment was that each student would be given a random disguise, five minutes to put it together, and then had to fool the rest of the class into believing their cover story. Quinn promised brutal honesty in judging, and apparently had no issue humiliating us in the process.

"Confidence, detail, and improvisation," she snapped her fingers. "That's how you pass."

Maddy ended up in a janitor's jumpsuit, armed with a mop. She leaned on it like a sword, dramatically declaring, "I am Boris. I clean... everything."

Gaz, immediately suspicious, started interrogating her: "Boris, what kind of bleach do you use?"

Maddy blinked. "The... one in the blue bottle?"

"Wrong," Quinn barked. "You're dead."

Gaz himself was shoved into a postal worker's outfit. He went overboard, flinging junk mail at people as he strolled past. "Sign here, ma'am. Don't mind the suspicious ticking package!" Half the class was in stitches, but Quinn narrowed her eyes. "Too much performance. Not enough believability. Dead."

My turn.

Quinn shoved a blazer into my hands and a slim pair of glasses.

"You're a corporate executive. Five minutes."

I did my best, straightened my posture, slicked my hair back, and tried to look important. When it was my turn, I adjusted my glasses and introduced myself as *Vanessa Clarke, VP of Operations at Orion Technologies.*

Quinn's smile turned razor sharp. "And what exactly does Orion Technologies do, Miss Clarke?"

My brain scrambled. "Uh, cybersecurity. Government contracts. Defence systems."

Her eyebrow arched. "Impressive. And who's your largest competitor?

I didn't have the faintest clue, but knew that I was decent at lying when I had to.

"Murdoch Enterprises." I held my head up high, channelling some arrogance to help. "We are neck and neck at the conventions each year."

Quinn turned her head as she thought for a moment, nodding with a smile on her lips. "Alright, you live."

I wanted to fist-pump the air, but kept my cool.

Now, it was Jake's turn.

He got the role of a paramedic. He slipped into the uniform like he'd been born in it. When Quinn grilled him, he rattled off medical jargon with frightening ease.

"Blood pressure is dropping, patient's tachycardiac, epi's not working, prepping for intubation," he said, tone clipped and confident.

Even Quinn looked impressed. "Convincing. You live."

By the end of the lesson, half the class had been "killed" and the survivors were riding the high of impressing Quinn. Maddy swore revenge on Gaz for tripping her up, and Gaz promised his fake mailman routine would go down in history. But it made sense. If we were going to put on a persona, pretend to be someone else, then we needed all the information, the receipts to back it up.

Chapter Eight

Even though I kept up with my running and weights over the summer break, Professor Kiyoko still kicked my ass.

I was wheezing, hands on knees, within the first ten minutes, but at least I made it over the obstacle course. More than most of the first years could say. Gaz, of course, was bouncing on his toes like usual. Annoyingly chipper.

The thought hit me like a blast of cold air. Déjà vu. I remember feeling like this after our first class, but Sera was here. I immediately shut the thought down. I refused to think of Sera and what she did to me last year. She was locked away and never to be let out again.

Alec and Gabby never spoke about her either, and for that, I was glad.

"Hey, you alright?" Gaz placed a hand on my shoulder, making me flinch. "You're a little pale. Did you push yourself too hard?"

"No, I'm alright. Just had a flash of Déjà vu." I tried for a smile, but it came out a grimace. His face fell, as if he knew exactly what I was thinking.

It must have been worse for them. They spent three years as friends and never suspected a thing.

"Yeah. I don't like to think about that either. Come on, let's head over to the weights."

We continued our class in silence, my thoughts too busy trying to shove Serephine Vale back into the locked, metal box I kept her in.

Professor Omara greeted me with a thin smile as I entered weaponry class. He was one of the few who knew almost everything that happened last year. Especially the horrible incident that ended up with seven deaths, and me with a bullet wound to the leg. I still had the scar, shining silver on my thigh.

I tried not to look at it.

This year, we would be working on how to make our own bows and arrows, how to dismantle and rebuild a machine gun, and how to make our own grenades.

Honestly, this school was completely mental.

Professor Omara clapped his hands once, the class snapping to attention. "Today," he announced, "we build something silent. Something patient. Something far more intimate than a firearm."

A few students exchanged looks. Silent and intimate at Hellspire usually meant one thing: deadly.

He rolled out a long wooden crate onto the table and pried it open with a crowbar. Inside was a neatly arranged row of raw materials – wooden staves, carbon limbs, coils of bowstring, small vials of resin, and a selection of arrowheads that absolutely shouldn't be legal. Serrated, barbed, needle-thin, some dyed matte black and other gleaming like surgical steel.

Professor Omara gestured me forward. "Xanetto, you're demonstrating."

I swallowed. *Great.*

He placed a stave in my hands. The wood was smooth and deceptively warm.

"This," he said, "looks like a stick. It isn't. With the right shaping, it becomes an extension of your intent. A bow does not kill quickly. It kills deliberately."

I forced a smile. "Comforting."

A few students chuckled, but Omara ignored them. He guided my hands.

"Step one: find the natural curve. Every stave has a spine – push against it, and it pushes back. Respect the tension. You force it too soon, and you weaken it. Much like people."

He made me bend the stave slowly, feeling for the point where it resisted. We marked the inside curve with chalk.

"Step two: carve the belly."

He handed me a drawknife. "This is where precision matters. Remove too little and the bow is stiff. Remove too much, and it will snap the first time you draw it. And it *will* snap toward your face."

Gaz in the back quietly muttered, "Awesome."

Omara shot him a glare. "If you lose an eye, you fail the unit."

He moved on to stringing demonstrations.

"The string must be waxed, reinforced, and looped correctly. Incorrect knots mean misfires. Misfires mean broken noses, broken fingers, or broken pride – depending on which you value more."

Then he brought out the arrows.

"Your shaft must be straight as truth." His gaze flicked to me for a heartbeat too long, as if he knew how many lies I was currently juggling.

"Fletching's control stability. Arrowheads control intent. Choose your intent wisely."

He laid out the choices – broad-heads for maximum internal damage, barbed heads for tear-out injuries, bodkin points for piercing armour, and needle points for stealth kills.

Most kids our age were worried about how many followers they had on their socials. We were choosing what kind of wounds we preferred to inflict.

"Today," Omara concluded, "each of you will craft one arrow. By the end of the week, you will craft a bow to match it. By the end of the month..." A slow smile stretched across his face. "...you will demonstrate accuracy under pressure."

At Hellspire, 'pressure' could mean anything from moving targets to simulated hostage scenarios. If we were lucky.

I glanced down at the silver scar on my thigh as if I could see through my stockings.

Lucky wasn't usually in my vocabulary.

I wasn't used to seeing the Dean stalking the halls. He was always there, always watching with his black, beady eyes. I felt like he was waiting for me to stuff up, to have a reason to expel me. So I made sure to keep my head down, trying my best in my classes, and not to bring any unwanted attention on myself.

I had enough enemies as it was.

After failing our stealth and surveillance class, I had kitchen duty before breakfast. So now I had to get up earlier to make time for my morning run. I made sure to change up my running routine since Cleo had called me out on it in class. I usually liked to run the same tracks, but I had paranoia chasing after me now.

It was still dark as my lungs burned in my throat, the sky beginning to lighten on the horizon. Hellspire was stunning, and the trees surrounding it were peaceful. It was just too bad about the atrocities that happened within its thick stone walls.

At least in the short time when I ran, it was just me, and the peaceful trees surrounding me. It was too early for the birds just yet, I missed their calls, their cheerful chirps as they greeted each other.

Thursday passed in a blur, and Friday too. I was looking forward to the weekend. Where I would meet Alec down in Greensville. I'd managed to ignore Jake as much as possible, but he still kept one eye on me.

I thanked Miss Somali when she handed me my phone, eager to spend my evening catching up. But there were was only one message that pinged in, and it was from Matthew.

Hey Joss. Sorry to be the bearer of bad news, but Alec is away for work and is unreachable until Tuesday next week. He said to say he's really sorry, and that his letter should be on its way to you. Have a good weekend, stay safe - Your doting big brother.

My stomach plummeted, and I hated how I felt tears pricking my eyes. Catching up with Alec was all that had been keeping me going the past two days, hell, the whole week. And now, I wouldn't speak to him for over a week.

"You alright there?" Maddy's concerned voice shattered my spiralling thoughts.

"Yeah, fine." I plastered a smile on my face, shoving my phone away, but her frown only deepened.

"You're lying. What's the matter? Don't tell me Alec isn't coming?"

I couldn't answer, my throat was clogged and I didn't want to cry in the middle of the cafeteria. So I just shook my head, shoved out of my seat and got the hell out of there. Footsteps followed, and I knew Maddy was coming after me. She caught my door before it could shut behind me, and she surprised me by wrapping me in a tight hug.

"He's a dick for leaving you hanging." Her voice was muffled, but I heard its steel.

"It's work. He can't say no." I sniffled, her lion's mane an easy place to bury my face into.

"Still, he's a dick. Let's spend the weekend together. Gaz is catching up with his dad to watch the football." She pulled away and threw me a cheeky wink. "Girls day."

"That sounds great. Thanks." I wiped my tears and cleared my throat, taking a deep breath in and blowing it out slowly, my tears drying up.

"Alright, we're leaving about eight." She gently punched me in the arm before hightailing it out of my room. She wasn't one for emotions.

Greensville was in full swing.

The bus had been full of students, all ready to get some shopping in, tattoos, and all sorts of mischief I didn't want to know about. I had no idea what Maddy had planned, but I was happy to tag along.

I braided Maddy's hair into two plaits on the bus, seeing as it had grown so long in the twelve months that I'd known her. But the year felt much longer than that. I felt like I'd known Maddy my whole life.

The bus parked, the students scrambling to get off, spreading every which way.

I felt a prickle at the back of my neck, making the hair on my arms raise as I turned, but saw no one. I rolled my shoulders with unease as I followed Maddy through town. She wanted to do some shopping for clothes, and I was fine with that. I wouldn't mind getting a few things as well.

The prickling feeling followed me through town, down every street, even into the mall. I tried to ignore it, but as soon as I was in the building, it only grew.

"Any word on loser Manfred?" Maddy asked as she picked out a black top, checking herself out in the mirror before wrinkling her nose and putting it back.

"No. No one has seen him since last year. Which I'm not complaining about." I checked out a pair of runners.

I do need a new pair.

Mine were getting rather worn from the gravel tracks.

"Good. Hopefully, he never shows his stupid face again." Maddy wandered over to the jumpers, flicking through them hanging on the rack.

We wandered through the store, Maddy finding bargains left, right, and center.

"But we're off to Imperial Heights this year for our tournament. We haven't found out what we'll be doing yet." Maddy smirked, and I knew she was thinking of the same thing as me.

I softly laughed as I remembered our prank last year. Yeah, they hated us, and for good reason. We made our way to the checkout, Maddy's arms full of goodies.

"Are they the type to try to prank us back?" I placed my new runners down at the counter, thanking the cashier after I paid him. Maddy threw her armful onto the conveyor belt, ignoring the young kid behind the counter as he began scanning painfully slowly.

"Oh, absolutely. And after that embarrassment last year, they're going to be out for our blood." She drummed her nails on the counter, impatient as the kid began to sweat. "But we're going to be ready. You just have to watch out, you left a rather big impression on Jenna and Paul last year."

"Yeah, but they both graduated, so I should be in the clear, surely?" I swung my bag a little nervously, hands becoming sweaty as I thought about them both.

If Jenna's uncle hated me this much, she must hate me so much more.

"They were the popular ones. I'm sure some of them are still in contact. And don't forget how the dean hates you. She's obviously told him all about it." She turned and huffed a loud breath as the kid's face turned red, eyes darting anywhere that wasn't Maddy.

The poor kid finally finished and bundled it all into one bag, practically shoving it into her arms after she paid, before bolting. Maddy only laughed.

"Come on, let's get something for lunch."

We parked ourselves in a cosy booth at the back of a café when the door pinged. Four men looked around, and their gazes snapped right to us. A slow smile spread across their face, and my stomach dropped as they came our way. They spread around, blocking any way out, and crossed their arms, smirking evilly down at us.

"Can we help you?" Maddy turned and glared at them, crossing her arms over her chest, but I didn't miss how she grabbed the knife off the table first.

"As a matter of fact, you can." One of them grinned. They all had the air of superiority, their hair perfect, their clothes expensive.

I would bet that they're Imperial assholes.

"You're just the girl we're looking for." One of them leaned in, but Maddy flashed her knife, and they leaned back slightly, but kept their eyes on me. "You're Clementine Mavis, aren't you?"

My old name shocked me, and I blinked. I'd thought that my name had been exposed everywhere by now.

"What's it to you?" Maddy barked, but they wholly ignored her.

"Calm down, spitfire. We're just here to pass on a message." He reached into his pocket and drew out an envelope, placing it on the table and sliding it toward me. "We look forward to seeing you at our school for the challenge. If you make it, that is." The ringleader winked, and my stomach turned to ice. "And no boyfriend here to protect you this year, what a shame." He smirked, and they peeled away, disappearing like they were never there.

I was almost shaking. I didn't want to know what was in that letter.

"What the fuck was that all about?" Maddy breathed, looking over her shoulder before leaning on the table, "Are you going to open it?"

"I don't want to." I breathed, eyeing it like I was about to explode or something.

"Let's not open it here. But when we get back, make sure we have gloves on or something. If it has anything to do with Imperial Heights, then it can't be good."

We were halfway back to the next bus out of there when a woman stepped out in front of us on the footpath, and I heard Maddy gasp, stopping dead in her tracks.

"Madeline." The woman purred, and my brows shot so high they must of been hiding in my hairline. This immaculate woman before me looked the spitting image of Maddy, but twenty years older.

"M-Mother." Maddy had to clear her throat, but her hands were balled into fists by her sides.

"Look how you've grown. You're a woman now." She smiled, but it looked forced.

I instantly didn't like her.

"Of course I'm grown. The last time you saw me, I was twelve." Maddy hissed, and I took a tiny step next to her, letting my arm brush hers. "What the hell are you doing here?"

"Don't you speak to me like that, young lady. I'm your *mother*." The fake smile disappeared, and her face transformed into a cold mask.

"You stopped being my mother the day you walked out on us. So *you* don't have the right to speak to me like that. Now get the hell out of my way." Maddy growled and pushed past this woman, and I made sure I was right there beside her.

"I'm disappointed in your choice of friends, Madeline. *She* and her family are not nice people." She called after us, her voice cutting and sharp. The blood in my veins turned to ice as we continued walking, and Maddy only shoved her middle finger in the air, storming away. Her chest was heaving, her eyes so dark as she ground her jaw. She stormed onto the bus and planted herself at the back, not meeting my worried gaze. The bus was mostly empty, as people still wanted to spend the rest of the day in town.

"How...how *dare* she," Maddy ground out between clenched teeth. "I fucking hate her." She turned to me and took my hands in hers, squeezing tight. "And fuck her for telling me who I can be friends with. You're my ride or die, you know that, right?" The vulnerability in her eyes made my heart clench.

"And you're mine, Maddy. She doesn't deserve to be in your life."

"And she won't be. I won't let her."

Maddy let go and stared out the window of the bus the whole trip back to Hellspire. As soon as we arrived back, she took off into her room, not even glancing back at me as she almost ran.

Poor Maddy.

But I turned and made my way to the empty science classroom, grabbed a pair of gloves and goggles to be extra safe, to open the letter.

Chapter Nine

I broke the seal with shaking fingers, the knife sliced the paper too easily. Inside was a folded sheet, but as I pulled it free, something fine and white sifted down like snow.

Not snow. Powder.

It coated the letter, dusting the table in a pale film.

My stomach dropped.

What if it's toxic? I wasn't wearing a mask. *Shit.*

The letter slipped from my hand as I ran to the storeroom, and ripped off the gloves and scrambled for a mask, lungs aching from the breath I'd already taken. With fresh gloves on and a mask, I unfolded the letter with trembling fingers.

Clementine Mavis. Or should I call you Jocelyn Xanetto?

You're a fake, and you don't deserve him. I'm coming for you. I asked Eliza Marshall, and she decided this one would be suitable.

I hope you like my little gift.

Jenna Orletta

Ice flooded my veins.

Jenna.

Of course.

And who the hell is Eliza Marshall?

I shoved the letter away and stumbled to my feet, hands shaking so badly as I staggered my way to the shelves. I nearly dropped the evidence container I was shaking that much. The powder got swept in with clumsy strokes, the letter sealed into a ziplock bag, my anxiety flaring as hot as the sun in my chest.

Think, Jossi. Think.

The academy had testing kits somewhere - Damascus made us learn how to use them last year - but my thoughts were scattered, heart hammering. I turned and fumbled through the storage cupboard, muttering under my breath, when a hand clamped down on my shoulder.

I nearly screamed. Spinning around, I collided with Jake Callahan's eyes.

He looked me up and down, slow and assessing. Then his gaze cut to the table behind me, the evidence bags, the container, the powder.

"What the hell is this?" His voice was a low growl. His grip on my shoulder tightened when I tried to shrug him off.

"None of your damn business, Callahan." My voice was sharp, but it came out thinner than I'd like. I move to push past him, but he stepped sideways, blocking the door completely. A wall of muscle and menace.

"Move your giant body and get out of my way." I snapped, yanking down my mask, completely over him barging into my life every second. For some reason, that made him smile. Not kindly.

"What was in that letter?" His eyes narrowed. "Why the protective gear?"

Before I could stop him, he crossed the room and snatched up the ziplock bag. His eyes flicked across the words, brows knitting, jaw tightening until he hissed, "Who the hell is Jenna?" He shook the packet at me.

"None of your damn business," I snapped again, ripping off the goggles and gloves, tossing them down into the bin. I made a grab for the letter, but he just held it above his head, out of reach.

Asshole.

His smirk was infuriating. "When someone mails you poison, yeah, I'd say it's my business."

Before I could argue, he snatched the test-kit right out of my fumbling hands. I lunged for it, but he was already snapping gloves and a mask on like he owned the place.

"Jake-"

"Sit." He didn't even look at me as he spooned a careful sample into the vial, sealing it again once he got enough. The liquid swirled. His movements were efficient, practised. He tossed his gear into the contamination bin, waiting, jaw tight.

"I was handling it fine," I muttered, glaring from the stool where he'd shoved me.

"I'm aware," he said, tone clipped.

The vial shifted to a deep, unnatural blue.

His face changed.

"Shit." He spun toward me, urgency sparking for the first time in those dark eyes. "Did you inhale it? Touch it bare-skinned?"

"What?" My pulse spiked. "I didn't-well, I didn't have a mask when I opened it. I... I might have-"

"Fuck sake, Jocelyn." Before I could finish, he grabbed my wrist and dragged me toward the window. His grip was iron, unyielding. In the next breath, his hand was under my chin, tilting my face up to the light.

"What are you-"

"Hold still." His thumb pressed under my chin, his other fingers prying open my eyelid. His breath was too close, his voice a low snarl. "You've been poisoned. The whites of your eyes - they're already clouding."

Poisoned.

The word slammed into me, knocking the air out of my chest.

I stumbled, and he shoved me down into the chair, his movements sharp. My pulse raced so hard I could hear it in my ears. The room tilted, the floor sliding sideways, nausea crawled through my veins.

"Stay awake." His voice cut through the haze. Then he was gone, darting across the room, rummaging for something - antidotes, neutralisers, I don't know. My vision was swimming, hands clammy, skin too hot. My heart flopped heavily in my chest, stuttering.

"Jake-" My voice came out strangled and a little weak.

He was suddenly back, kneeling in front of me, one gloved hand gripping my face, the other holding a vial of something sharp-smelling under my nose. His eyes locked onto mine, furious and desperate.

"Don't you dare shut your eyes, Jocelyn," he snarled.

The edges of my vision blurred to black. And the last thing I heard before darkness tried to swallow me was Jake swearing violently, my name a growl in his throat.

My pulse stuttered, then lurched. My fingers were ice, my vision started tunnelling.

"Jocelyn - stay with me." Jake's voice was harsh, sharp, like he could command me into survival. He fumbled in his pocket, ripped open a small injector pen with his teeth, and plunged it into my thigh.

I jolted. A burn ripped through my muscles, heat flooding into my bloodstream like liquid fire. My cry was ragged, as air rushed back into my lungs. My heart was a hammer again, too fast, too hard.

Jake's face was right there, his eyes blazing with something I couldn't read. Fury, fear - both? His fingers gripped my jaw, steadying me when the room lurched sideways. I shut my eyes to stop the room from spinning.

"Eyes open. *Now.*" His tone was lethal, and commanding. And for some reason, my body listened to him more than to myself. My lashes dragged upward, barely.

"That's it," he muttered, softer now. "Don't you dare check out on me, Xanetto. Not yet."

I tried to speak, but my tongue was thick, and too heavy. His hand dropped from my jaw only to find my wrist, finger pressed hard against my pulse point. His frown deepened.

"Too fast. Dammit." He yanked a second vial out of his pocket, this one tiny and filled with clear liquid. He broke the seal, tipped it against my lips. I tried to turn away, but his grip was iron.

"Drink it."

When I resisted, his eyes flashed - and for a fraction of a second, the mask of control slipped. His voice cracked raw and urgent.

"*Please.*"

It stunned me enough that I let the liquid touch my tongue. It was bitter, a sharp chemical taste on my tongue, but I swallowed.

Heat spread through me again, this time steadier, dulling the panic clawing at my chest. The nausea eased, though my hands still trembled. I sagged forward, into the solid wall of his chest before I could stop myself.

He went rigid. Then his arm slid around me, holding me up, steady but not gentle. His breath brushed the top of my hair.

"You're going to be fine," he muttered, low. "But for fuck's sake, Jocelyn - don't touch things like that again. Not when I'm not there."

The words barely registered over the pounding in my ears, the way my whole body felt foreign, not mine. My voice came out as a rasp.

"Why do you care?"

For the first time since I'd met him, Jake didn't have an answer ready. His silence was deafening.

When he finally spoke, it wasn't the explanation I expected.

"Because if you die..." He trailed off, jaw flexing. Then softer, "Bad things would happen if you die."

He eased me back just enough to look into my face. His eyes flicked across my features like he were memorising them. Then the mask slid back into place, his voice a cold blade.

"Don't tell anyone about this. Not your friends. Not Alec. No one. Understand?"

I managed a shaky nod, though a thousand questions burned on my tongue, especially how he knew who Alec was.

Jake exhaled, finally loosened his hold, though his hand lingered at my elbow until he was certain I wouldn't collapse again. He gathered the letter and powder into a second sealed bag, his jaw ticking.

When he finally spoke again, it was in that same low, sharp tone that made my skin crawl with unease.

"She's not your biggest problem, Jossi. Not by a long shot." He turned and stormed out of the room, taking the evidence with him. I remained in my seat, my legs feeling too weak to hold my weight just yet.

God, what the hell does he mean by that?

And not for the first time, I wondered who the hell he was, and what he wanted with me.

I eventually dragged my ass back to my room, slowly, my hand dragging along the wall to keep me steady as I locked my door behind me. I fell onto my bed and just stared at the ceiling. My eyes felt so incredibly heavy. I was completely exhausted, and I wanted nothing more than for the day to be over.

I was roughly shaken awake, and instinct took over, I opened my mouth to scream, my fist flying. A large hand clamped over it, cutting the sound.

"Shh. It's just me." The voice was low, and urgent. My eyes flew open to pure blackness, the shape of a man on my bed. His breath was ragged, harsher than I'd ever heard from him.

Jake?

My arms pushed weakly against him, but they felt like wet noodles, drained of strength. He finally pulled his hand away, leaning back but not leaving my side.

"Get off," I rasped, blinking through the haze of half-sleep.

"I thought you were dead," he hissed, his face too close. "I had to make sure." His fingers dragged through his messy black hair before he stood.

"I'm *fine*," I muttered, curling back toward my pillow. "I feel like shit, though."

"Your body needs time to heal." His voice was gravelly, and he didn't move from my side.

"Then leave so I can." My eyes shut before he answered. Sleep dragged me under again, but a single thought clawed its way through the fog.

The door had been locked.

How the hell did he get inside?

By morning, hunger gnawed at me. I showered, tugged on leggings, an oversized Hellspire hoodie, boots, and padded down to the cafeteria. It was blessedly quiet, barely past dawn. The steam of my coffee fogged my face as I cradled the mug, eyes fluttering shut.

"Miss Xanetto."

I nearly spilled it all over myself in my surprise, snapping my eyes open. Dean Orletta's bulk loomed across the table, his glare sharper than any blade.

"Good morning, Dean Orletta," I croaked, throat feeling raw after yesterday.

"Why are you down here so early on a Sunday?" His bark echoed in the cavernous cafeteria, arms folding like a wall of disapproval.

"I woke early and got hungry. Am I not allowed to eat yet?" I sat straighter, but his brows only sank lower.

"Don't be smart with me. You're lucky you're still here."

What the hell is this guy's problem?

My mouth snapped shut. Any answer would only be ammunition.

"I've got my eye on you. One misstep, and you're out." He growled, then turned on his heel and stormed off.

I rolled my eyes, stabbing at my omelette. His anger burned in my head long after he was gone.

Jenna's little letter hadn't taken me out.

Was he angry about that? Was he the one who told her where to find me in the first place?

Unease curdled my stomach. Appetite gone.

I left the half-eaten omelette behind and slipped outside, and into the woods. Running always cleared my mind. The sun was peeking over the horizon, the coldness in the air snapping in my lungs as I pushed myself. I probably should of been taking it easy. But I didn't want to be alone in my room.

The path was worn, the grass beaten down by my shoes over the past few weeks since we'd been back. The whisper of trees, the trill of birds. It was constant, grounding, resetting.

Just as I was feeling calm, a gasp ripped from me as I was yanked sideways, swallowed into the press of a hard chest. My head tucked beneath a chin, cocooned by strong arms.

"What the-"

"Can you use a gun?" Jake's urgent voice burned hot against my ear. The crack of gunfire exploded through the woods. He grunted, the sound raw. I froze, eyes wide.

"I'm fine. Kevlar." His hand smothered my mouth before I could cry out again. "Can you shoot?" He repeated, and I nodded frantically, my heart in my mouth. He shoved a cold weight into my shaking fingers - a handgun. My heart lurched.

"The people chasing you are out to kill," he hissed, still shielding me with his body as more shots sounded closer now, the words sinking like stones in my stomach. "So don't miss."

My breath caught. Out to *kill?*

"On your right!"

He shoved me free. Instinct took over. I spun, saw a man barreling straight for me. My hands rose, both fists gripping the gun. The shot cracked through the dawn.

The man crumpled.

Dead.

My body shook, bile clawing up my throat, but there was no time to think. Another cry split the air.

Jake spun, his own gun pressed to a man's temple. The crunch of bone and bullet echoed as he fired.

I flinched, hands trembling around my weapon. Another man shoved the corpse aside, gun raised. He was too close, but Jake moved like a phantom. A flash of steel, and his knife slit across the man's throat. A spray of blood painted the trees and me. I staggered, staring at the carnage, the weight of the gun slick in my hands.

"Run, Jocelyn!" Jake barked, shoving the dying body away before wrenching the gun from my stiff fingers. "My team have just arrived, and if they catch you, you'll never see your family again." His eyes were wild and desperate as they met mine. "*Run*, for fuck's sake!"

I bolted.

Branches tore at my arms, lungs burning, the blood on my clothes cooling sticky against my skin. My heart thundered as if it might burst.

Behind me, Jake's voice crackled over a radio: "Target escaped while disposing of assassins. Regroup."

The looming silhouette of the academy rose ahead, its walls suddenly the only safe place in the world.

My legs nearly gave out as the question slammed through me:

What the hell is going on?

Who the fuck is Jake Callahan?

Chapter Ten

I slammed my bedroom door shut and made sure to lock it behind me. The chain slid into place with a decisive click. My chest heaved. Every breath burned as if I'd sprinted for miles. My skin was clammy, my heartbeat too fast, too loud.

Assassins.

And what the hell did he mean that if his team got me, I'd never see my family again? Were they going to *kidnap* me?

I needed answers. But first, I needed to get these stiff, bloody clothes off me. I started stripping down to my bra and undies, when my window slid open, the sound slicing through the silence like a knife. I whirled, half-dressed, clutching the bloody shirt to my chest for cover.

Jake landed soundlessly inside my room, his movements predatory, practised. His eyes caught mine in the dim light, and the look on his face was terrifying. Cold, hungry, relentless.

"Get out," I snapped, but he ignored me, moving forward, steady and unhurried, backing me up until my shoulders slammed into the wall. His hands slapped against the plaster beside my head, caging me in.

The impact reverberated down my spine.

I was trapped. Panic clawed at me, but I fought to keep my breathing even. He leaned in, close enough that our breaths mingled, his shadow swallowing me whole.

"Who the hell are you?" My voice was a whisper, but it was laced with steel. His gaze roved over my face, unreadable. Then, slowly, he lifted a hand. His thumb brushed along my jaw, smearing away blood I hadn't realised was there. He studied it on his fingertip, and when he looked back at me, his expression was unreadable.

"I'm your worst enemy." His breath ghosted across my lips, his words low and lethal. "Those people out there want you dead. I won't let that happen." He paused, his voice dipping darker. "I need you alive."

I shoved him, but he didn't move. He pressed closer instead, pinning me with his sheer presence. My pulse was frantic.

"You know what's funny?" His mouth twisted in a cruel smile. "Your father's file called you a pawn. Said you'd break if pushed. But here you are, shooting a man like it's nothing."

My jaw clenched. "It's not the first time I've shot someone," I admitted, not daring to let him see how he affected me.

"Oh, I know, sweetheart." His eyes glinted with something dark, and admiration twisted into mockery. And before I could demand answers, his hand clamped my chin, angling my face upward. Then, his mouth crashed into mine.

Shock rooted me to the spot. His grip tightened around my throat, forcing the kiss deeper, stealing air and thought.

I shoved him away, hard. He only staggered a step, laughter curling around me like smoke.

"If you want your friends alive, you'll keep this to yourself, Doll." He winked, mocking. "Not Alec. Not anyone. Because you won't like me when I get mad."

Rage boiled up, burning away the fear. My hands balled into fists. "How dare you-"

"Oh, come on, sweetheart." He chuckled, infuriatingly smug. "I know you enjoyed it."

My fist flew. He caught it easily, yanking me closer until I was flush against him again. His breath was hot against my ear.

"You call it fear," he murmured, "but underneath, I know you love it. You crave it. You love the danger. Same as me."

"*Fuck you.*" I snapped, fear coursing through me at a million miles an hour.

His laugh was low and lethal as he let me go. He slipped back to the window, offering a mock salute before vanishing into the morning as if he'd never been there at all. My hands trembled as I stared at the empty frame, fury crackling in my veins. I grabbed the bloodied clothes, shoved them in the bin, and drenched them in lighter fluid before setting it alight. The flames ate them alive, smoke curling out the window as my fan whirred.

My chest heaved as my thoughts spiralled.

And for the first time in a long time, I didn't know what to do.

And that scared me the most.

I was not ready for Monday.

Not for the weight of Jake's threat. Not for the feel of his mouth on mine, seared into memory like a brand I never wanted. I tried to comfort a grumpy Maddy, but Gaz seemed to be handling that better than expected. But the first lesson of the day, escape and evasion, had me breaking out in a nervous sweat.

No wonder Jake was so good at everything. The perfect student. The perfect predator. And now, knowing what I know, the thought of being locked in a room with him made my pulse spike.

On my way to class, I heard some professors grumbling to each other behind the door, but it was ajar just enough for me to hear.

"This year's recruits are soft. The syndicate won't accept them like this."

I almost stumbled, catching my bag before it hit the floor as it slipped off my shoulder. Recruits?

Doesn't he mean students? The voice sounded like Professor Morayne's.

I stumbled my way to class, my mind spinning. What the hell was going on here? What is Hellspire under all its false facades? I shook my head and pushed open the door, only to be led to what looked like bunkers out the back, nestled amongst the trees.

Colonel Fex ushered us into the training area. "Today's exercise is simple," he said, his tone razor-sharp. "You're prisoners. Captured. Restrained. Locked in. Your goal:

escape before the time runs out. Fail, and you're dead. Or worse." My stomach twisted.

We were herded into groups of four, wrists bound tight with zip-ties. Maddy, Gaz, Britney, and I.

Across the room, Jake leaned against the wall, arms folded, watching with that damn smirk like he already knew how this ended. We were ushered into a small, interrogation-looking room, the smiles of Fex and Jake were enough to set my nerves on edge.

The former slammed the door shut, locks engaged, and darkness swallowed us whole. Maddy swore under her breath. Gaz tugged at his bindings, muttering profanaties. Britney was trying to kick the door to no avail.

My mind whirled. I couldn't let the panic in. I needed to focus. I looked around the room and tried to think about what Gabby and Alec had taught me over the break.

"Stop moving," I hissed. "Give me your hands."

"What?" Gaz whispered.

"Hands. Now."

I could only see the whites of his eyes as he shuffled his way toward me. I felt along the floor until my fingers closed around a jagged nail sticking out of the baseboard.

Perfect.

"Get over here." I pulled his hands toward the wall. I wedged the nail up, sharp enough to bite into the plastic.

My wrists ached as I dragged Gaz's tie against it, sawing, sawing, until with a sudden snap, he was free.

"Holy shit," Maddy breathed.

As soon as I cut my own, I worked them loose one by one, adrenaline pushing me faster.

My wrists were still raw from the zip-ties as I stood up, flexing my hands. The bunker smelled like damp stone and old metal – the kind of place that felt like it had seen a lot of terrified people over the years.

"Okay," I whispered, scanning the room as my eyes finally adjusted. "We've got...stone walls, one very unfriendly-looking steel door, and absolutely nothing else useful."

"Great," Britney murmured. "I'm so glad we're at a school for geniuses."

Gaz snorted as he shuffled toward a stack of abandoned supply crates. "There's gotta be something in here. Something sharp? I'll take that rusty nail at this point."

Maddy kicked the door again, just because. It still didn't budge. "That's it. We're dead."

"No," I said. "We're Hellspire students. We're annoyingly hard to kill." My eyes landed on the metal shelving bolted to the back wall. Bolted...loosely. Really loosely. "Gaz, help me with this."

He got the idea immediately. Together, we rocked the shelving back and forth until the bolts groaned and one popped out, ricocheting across the concrete.

“Don't stop.” I hissed. We kept at it until the whole shelf tore free from the wall. It crashed onto the floor, sending up an explosion of dust.

Maddy blinked. “We're building a fort? Fantastic. That’ll stop the bullets.”

I ignored her dramatics. The shelf frame was an old steel pipe. Bendable. Breakable. Brutally effective if you knew what you were doing. I wedged my foot against it, pulled upward with everything I had, and felt the metal scream before it finally snapped into a long, jagged-edged bar.

Britney let out a low whistle. “That's the hottest thing you’ve ever done.”

I huffed a laugh, grinning. “Give me a minute.” I stomped with my heel on the end of the pipe, attempting to squash it enough so I could wedge the metal bar into the gap between the door and its frame, right at the lock. After a few curse words later, it was thin enough to wedge in there. The leverage was good. The angle was perfect. This was exactly like the breach exercise Professor Fex ran last week. Only this time, we didn't have him yelling in our ears.

“Back up,” I warned. Gaz braced beside me. Together, we heaved, the metal groaned, and the stone cracked. Then – nothing.

“Again,” I said, sweat already dripping down my spine. We drove our combined weight into the lever. The lock plate screamed. Dust showered from the doorframe. A hairline crack snaked through the stone.

“We’re close,” I gasped. But that's when I heard it – boots crunching through the dried leaves outside.

The captors were coming back.

“Okay,” Britney whispered, panic rising. “New plan?”

“Nope,” I panted, “same plan. Just faster.” I looked around the room, desperate for anything, when Maddy wandered over and grabbed the old emergency light from the wall – still wired, still functional. She tore the casing open, yanked out the battery pack, and twisted the exposed wires together until sparks spat onto the floor. She looked up with an evil grin as smoke curled up instantly.

Britney coughed. “Oh, brilliant! Gas ourselves before they can shoot us!”

“It's a *distraction*,” Gaz snapped, rolling his eyes.

“Just get by the wall – when they open the hatch to check, we finish the breach.” I breathed, hoping they couldn't hear us. Heavy footsteps thudded right outside.

“Maddy – now!” I hissed.

We threw our weight onto the metal bar one last time.

CRACK.

The lock plate ripped out of the stone with a violent metallic screech just as the hatch opened and a masked man shouted, "What the -?"

Gaz grabbed the door, yanking it inward with a grunt. I lunged forward, ramming the broken end of the bar into the doorframe to wedge it open.

The man stumbled back, choking on smoke, and we bolted past him and spilled into the training yard, gasping and laughing. Free.

Applause cut through the air.

Jake, stood there with Colonel Fex. Arms folded, lips curved in that smug smile that made me want to both punch him and scream.

"Well, well, that was efficient...and unpredictable," Fex said as he glanced at the destroyed lock, the cracked stone, the smoking light fixture. "I'll admit – I didn't think you'd get out."

"Neither did I." Jake's voice sent shivers over my skin. "Beginner's luck," he drawled. But his eyes, oh, his eyes, were sharp and unreadable. He hated it. He hated that I beat him at his own game.

I squared my shoulders, chin high, and met his gaze with a spark of defiance I couldn't smother.

"Guess I'm full of surprises."

And for once, he was the one who looked away first.

The rest of the day, I was doing my best to ignore Jake, but his presence was demanding and always there. M.O.D.L made it impossible to get away from him, from his hard gaze and smirking face. Whenever he leaned over, letting his arm brush mine, I'd quickly pull away. He chuckled low in his throat, and I bristled each time. If we were in a different class, I'd hiss at him. But not in Professor Verreth's class. I was almost too scared to *blink* in this class. But Jake slid something over my desk. It was a letter, but this one looked a little damaged. I met his gaze, frowning in confusion.

"A letter came in for you, sweetheart." He winked, and I snatched it away from him. He still stayed close, as if he intended to read over my shoulder.

"Why the hell do you have *my* letter?" I demanded, keeping my voice so low it was a wonder he could hear.

"I screen all your mail, Jocelyn. Nothing gets by me." I whipped my head to glare at him, outraged that he reads my letters.

"*How dare-*" I began, but he snatched it off the desk and shoved it into my lap, right as Verreth prowled by. The professor raised a brow, but continued, berating another student for their messy handwriting.

"It seems like you're not the only one hiding things." He whispered into my ear, goosebumps breaking out over my skin. The bell rang, signalling the end of class. I shoved the letter into my pocket and tried to get as far away from him as possible. But I didn't mistake his quiet laugh.

In cooking, we got to pair up with different partners, and I made sure to grab Maddy. But what annoyed me the most? Jake was laughing with Gaz. *Laughing*. Like he hadn't shoved me against him two nights ago while bullets snapped past my ears. Like I hadn't watched him slit a man's throat without blinking.

In the harsh light of the classroom, he was just another transfer. Handsome, friendly, dark hair falling into his eyes like some kind of tragic book boyfriend. The girls already whispered about him in the back rows.

Pretty sure I was grinding my teeth for the rest of the class.

"Jake seems to have chilled a little, almost cool," Maddy whispered as we packed our things away, but I had to bite my tongue. I wanted to yell at her that he was the bad guy, the enemy. But I couldn't. His warning was ringing in my head like a bell. I didn't answer, just nodded absently as I pretended to focus on putting the vials away in their proper spots.

"Joss?" Maddy nudged me, eyes flicking to where Jake was grinning, casual and easy. "You look like you want to stab him."

"Maybe I do," I muttered. Jake must have felt my glare because he glanced back, catching my eye. That smile didn't falter. If anything, it widened. And for everyone else, it looked charming.

But I saw it for what it was.

Toward the end of the class, I ducked into one of the empty supply rooms to pack away my gear when a hand shot out, dragging me between the shelves. We stopped when my back hit the wall, a yelp stuck in my throat.

Jake stood too close, the playful grin gone, his eyes dark as obsidian. The air between us felt heavy with danger.

My mouth was dry. "What do you want?" I snapped, but it sounded forced, fear choking my throat.

His hand braced beside my head, boxing me in. "What do I want? *Need*, sweetheart. My team-" his mouth twisted, "-they're circling. Hungry. They'd love to snatch you up, tie a nice little bow around you, and deliver you to the highest bidder."

I swallowed hard. "And why haven't they? Who the hell are you?" I balled my hands into fists, ready to strike. I was sick of this man cornering me.

"Because I told them no." He ignored my other demand as he leaned closer, so close his breath ghosted over my cheek. "Because I said you're mine." Fear knifed through me, but I forced steel into my voice.

"I don't belong to you." I snapped, and for a beat, his eyes softened, something almost regretful, but it vanished just as quickly. I shoved him in the chest, but he didn't budge a centimetre.

"No. But right now, I'm the only thing standing between you and a black van with no windows. Don't forget it." He pulled back slightly, scanning me with a predator's calm. "Your father has something my people want. And if we don't get it..." He let the silence hang, dangerous and heavy. "...you'll learn just how creative my team can be."

"Then why save me at all?" The question broke out before I could stop it.

Jake's mouth curved, not quite a smile. More like a secret. "Because I haven't decided what to do with you yet."

Before I could respond, voices echoed outside the door. Jake stepped back, the mask sliding neatly back into place. By the time Gaz shoved the door open, Jake was leaning casually against the shelves, his grin boyish and harmless.

"Just helping Joss with... reaching the high shelves," he said smoothly as Gaz's eyes swept over us.

He snorted. "Right. And I'm the Queen of Hearts." But Jake only winked at him, slipping out the door like nothing had happened. Leaving me fuming, my heart hammering against my ribs. The echo of his words rang in my head.

I'm the only thing standing between you and them.

And I hated - *hated* - that I believed him.

"Are you alright?" Gaz blocked my way, arms folded across his chest. "You're very pale." He was staring at me with narrowed eyes, but I needed to plaster a smile on my face and act like nothing was wrong.

"Fine. I just felt a little dizzy, and Jake helped put the extra stock up for me." It was a pathetic excuse, but I needed to get out of there. I needed some fresh air. "I'll see you at dinner." I smiled and gently pushed past him. But I knew he didn't believe my lie. I grabbed my bag and got out like the room was on fire, leaving a confused Maddy and a suspicious Gary behind.

The letter was burning a hole in my pocket since M.O.D.L, and I was desperate to read it and to be alone. But it was going to have to wait until I was back in my room. And while I was at it, I needed a lock for my window.

Maddy was distracted with homework due tomorrow to notice my distraction at dinner, but Gaz shot me worried looks all night. But I excused myself early, my appetite no longer there. I wasn't eating much lately, and my clothes had begun to feel a little loose. But I would worry about that later. I had more pressing things to think about.

Making sure my door was locked, I sat down on my bed and unfolded the letter. It looked like someone had kept it in their pocket for a while before delivering it, the creases evident and slightly wrinkled.

Clementine, Clem, Jocelyn, Jossi - I have no idea what to call you anymore. How I love that you're back at school, doing normal things, oblivious to the absolute hell I've been through. But I won't fail, my dearest. I'll make sure to send you gifts, maybe starting with Gabrielle's pretty hair. She does love her long locks.

I so look forward to seeing you, as I've now gained my freedom. Make sure you tell your little Alexander I say hello, seeing as he's been hunting me since I got out three months ago. Anyway, I digress! See you soon, my darling. I can't wait to catch up.

Love Sera xoxo

Oh, fuck.

Chapter Eleven

Sera had escaped, and no one thought to tell me?

Had Gabby and Alec been hunting her all this time and didn't think I should know?

I was livid, terrified, and I wanted someone to tell me the fucking truth for once.

I slammed the bathroom door behind me, chest heaving, knuckles white as I gripped the porcelain sink. Cold water splashed against my face, but it did nothing to wash away the feeling still clinging to my skin. Every time I shut my eyes, I saw blood, the image of bodies hitting the forest floor, and my loved ones dying around me, especially what Sera did to me last year.

The lock on the door clicked. My head snapped up to see him leaning against the tiles, arms crossed, like he hadn't just left a trail of corpses behind the other day.

"You-" My voice cracked, coming out more desperate than I wanted. I forced steel into it. "Leave me alone."

Jake's gaze dragged over me, sharp and unreadable. He didn't answer right away. He just stepped closer until the mirror reflected us both, me, trembling, wild-eyed, and him, calm and seemingly carved from shadows.

"I'm afraid I can't do that," he said finally, voice low and dangerous. "I don't want to remind you to keep this to yourself. I don't want to hurt your friends."

My stomach hollowed out. "Leave them out of this."

"Then learn how to hide your emotions better!" He snapped, his eyes met mine in the mirror, and I flinched at the weight behind them. "Every move you make. Every word. Every step. And the wrong person knowing too much about you?" He leaned in just enough for his breath to ghost against my ear. "That gets people killed."

Gabby's face flashed in my mind. Her notebooks. Her wall of questions. Her stubborn, infuriating determination to dig until she hit bone. Jake's jaw tightened like he'd read my thoughts.

"Tell your little detective friend to back off. If she knows what's good for her."

I spun on him, fire burning through my veins despite the fear. "Who the hell sent you here? What do you want from me?"

His smirk was gone, replaced with something harder, something almost regretful.

"Want?" he echoed, then shook his head. "Doesn't matter what I want. What matters is that you stop pretending this place is safe." His hand shot out, catching my wrist, not rough, but firm enough that I couldn't pull away. His voice dropped, urgent now. "Don't trust anyone, Jocelyn. Not your professors. Not your classmates. Not even your friends."

My chest squeezed. "Not even Alec?"

Something flickered across his face then, jealousy? Pain? But it vanished so fast I couldn't be sure. He released me, stepping back into the shadows.

"Especially not Alec."

The door unlocked with a soft click, and by the time I blinked, he was gone. I stood there shaking. I turned to the mirror, my reflection so pale. The warning echoed in my skull, sinking like poison into my bloodstream.

Don't trust anyone.

I ran back to my room, my pulse skittering all over the damn place. I fumbled with my burner phone, pacing my room like a caged animal. Jake's warning was still rattling around in my skull like a loose bullet, but I wouldn't let my friends get hurt because of me.

She picked up on the third ring.

"Hey, sugar, make it quick, I'm knee deep in cross-referencing handwriting samples."

"Gabby, listen, you need to- " My voice cracked. I pressed my palm to my forehead. "You need to drop this case on Jake. Now. Whoever we're poking at, it's bigger than we think. And-"

The line cut out with a thunderous *boom.*

"Gabby?" My blood iced. "*Gabby!*"

Static filled the phone, then nothing.

I didn't think. I just moved. Snatching my helmet, I tore out of my room, sprinting down the hall like the devil herself was on my heels. My bike was my only thought - then get to Gabby. But when I burst through the courtyard, he was there. Standing in the middle of the path like he'd been waiting for me, dark eyes unreadable, his hands up like he could stop me with a look.

"*Move.*" My voice shook with rage.

"You don't want to go there, Jocelyn." His voice was sharp. He must have somehow hacked into my phone, too.

"I don't care!" I shoved past him, my heart hammering. "She could be...she could be *dead!*" I didn't give him a chance to argue. I ran to the garage, threw off the sheet, and kicked my bike to life. I shoved my helmet on, zipped up my jacket, my tyres screeched against the stone as I shot past.

In the mirror, I caught him running into the garage. I didn't have time to think about why he was following me. I needed to get to Gabby.

Thank god she had an office in Greensville, so it took me no time at all to get down the mountain.

By the time I reached Gabby's office, smoke was curling into the night sky, flames licking out of shattered windows. My stomach plummeted.

"Gabby!" I kicked the stand down, not caring if the bike fell as I stumbled forward, choking on the acrid smoke as I yanked my helmet off. A figure staggered out of the haze, coughing, soot covering her face.

Gabby.

Relief punched through me so hard I almost dropped to my knees. But then Alec was there, rushing to her side from the shadows, sliding an arm around her, his face twisted in fury and panic.

"What the hell happened?" I croaked, stumbling toward them - and then gunfire.

The air cracked with bullets, so close the sound tore at my eardrums.

Something slammed into me hard, driving me to the pavement. My scream lodged in my throat. I looked over my shoulder, and my stomach dropped. Jake's body covered mine, shielding me from the hail of bullets. His vest absorbed the impact with sickening *thuds*.

"Are you *insane?*" I gasped, shoving at him as he rolled off.

"Still breathing, aren't you?" he barked, shoving a fresh clip into his gun. "That's three times now, princess. You gonna start keeping score, or do I have to?" He fired shots into the dark. Someone grunted.

Alec's voice thundered, rough and furious. "Who the *fuck* are you?" He stalked toward us, still holding Gabby steady with one arm, rage burning in his eyes.

Jake's laugh was sharp and humourless as he raised his weapon toward the shadows and fired. Another grunt sounded from the darkness. The look he levelled on Alec would make me wither.

"She's alive because of me. Three times. That's all you need to know."

Alec's face settled into a terrifying cold mask. "What the fuck do you mean three times now? Let her go." He snarled, and I could barely get enough breath into my lungs.

"I've been the one who kept her safe this year. Where the hell have you been?"

Alec's face twisted, his free hand curling into a fist. "Don't you *dare-*"

"Don't I dare what?" Jake snarled, baiting Alec and stepping closer, his voice low and lethal. "Point out the truth? While you were off playing errand boy for Daddy Xanetto, I was here. Taking bullets for her. Keeping her alive."

The air between them crackled, electric, seconds from detonating into a fight neither of them would walk away from clean.

"Enough!" I shouted, my voice breaking. "Both of you!" The sharp wail of sirens split the night, distant but racing closer. Jake's jaw clenched. He grabbed my wrist, tugging me away. "Let me go." I snapped.

He ignored me, as usual. "We need to go. Now."

Alec's eyes burned into mine, torn between fury and worry.

"Take your fucking hands off her." He snarled, taking a step toward me.

"We don't have time for this shit." Jake snapped, tugging me along. "They're almost here, and I'd run and hide if I were you, making sure your secrets go with you."

"What the fuck is that supposed to mean?" Alec snapped, his nostrils flaring as he looked at Jake's fingers wrapped around my wrist, taking a step towards us.

"I know Sera's escaped." The breath was lodged in my throat as Alec's face fell slightly, his mouth pinched into a thin line as he finally met my gaze.

"I was going to tell you, Jossi." He tried to take a step, but Gabby groaned.

I cleared the lump in my throat. "We'll talk about it later. Go, get her taken care of." My breath caught in my throat, and the hurt on his face nearly brought me to my knees. But Jake's grip on me was as hard as iron.

"I'll get Gabby out. Don't you trust him, Joss." He pleaded, and Jake scoffed behind me. Gabby, still coughing, tried to wave me off, her voice rasping.

"I'll be fine. Go." Her words hit like a punch to the gut. But Jake was already pulling me toward my bike, the sirens shrieking louder, the world burning around us.

And I realised - It wasn't just the building that had blown apart tonight.

It was everything.

The ride back passed in a blur, but all I could see was Alec's hurt expression.

Jake took off as soon as we hit the road.

It was too close back there.

The halls were quiet, the quiet that pressed on your ears until you swore you could hear your own heartbeat. Everyone else was asleep, or sneaking down to the kitchens for midnight cake, but I couldn't calm my racing heart.

Not after tonight.

I closed my door softly, the ash still burning my nose as I suck in a long breath. A shadow peeled itself off my wall, and I sighed.

"Don't you have someone else to stalk?" I grumbled, placing my helmet down. He pushed out of the shadows, closing the distance with an easy swagger. My back hit the wall before I realised I'd been retreating.

Jake tilted his head, studying me. He leaned in, not touching, but close enough. I caught the faint scent of leather, smoke, and gun oil.

"You know, most people would thank me. I kept you from getting caught and killed tonight. Could've let them take you out, but I didn't." The asshole had the nerve to sound smug.

"Why?" I bit out, annoyed he thought he could keep cornering me like this.

His smirk deepened. "Maybe I like watching you squirm. Or maybe..." His gaze flicked to my mouth for one unbearable second. "...maybe I'm curious. What makes the Xanetto princess tick? Everyone here whispers about you, but none of them really know."

"I don't owe you anything," I snapped, forcing steel into my tone. "You don't get to play hero and interrogator in the same breath."

Jake chuckled low in his throat, straightening just enough to let me breathe again.

"See that fire? That's what I wanted to see. You'll need it soon."

"Fuck off, Callahan," I growled, shoving him in the chest, but he didn't budge.

"Cracks between you and Hyde?" He leaned in, and I was scared he was going to kiss me again. I fumbled for the knife on my thigh, but he caught my wrist, halting me. "Naughty, naughty. You were really going to stab me, were you? Not after I saved your life, *again*."

"I don't need you to save me. I need you to get the *fuck* out of my face." I hissed, shoving him with my spare hand, but something in him snapped. His hand gripped my throat, squeezing so tight I could barely get a breath.

"Watch how you speak to me, sweetheart." He snarled, "Because I might be the only one who can keep you alive. You have *no* idea what they want to do to you." He snapped, getting so close that I could see each of his eyelashes. "Don't push me. You won't like me when I'm angry." He dropped his hand, and I gasped in a breath, my heart flip-flopping in my chest.

Rage boiled over, and I was sick of him bullying me.

My fist cracked out and hit his jaw. I hadn't used my right hook for a while now, and it felt damn good. He stumbled back a step, a hand going to his face. I didn't back down, I swung again, but this time, he was ready.

He grabbed my wrist, and held it so damn tight it burned.

But what he did next surprised the hell out of me.

"Good, I need you to fight. Stop cowering and fight back!" He snapped, shoving me. But I used the wall as leverage and pushed myself back towards him. He ducked my next punch, but didn't anticipate my foot kicking him in the stomach. My room was so small that he tumbled onto the bed with a chuckle.

"Now get the fuck out of my room." I breathed, fists clenched by my sides as he got to his feet.

"I want to see more of that fire, Jocelyn." He winked, and softly closed the door behind him.

Chapter Twelve

The rest of the week, letters kept coming.

Every night, I returned from class to find them waiting on my bed. Jake would have been the one to put them there, seeing as he read my mail now, too.

And every single one was from Sera.

They were photographs. Of me, of Gabby, of Alec, Maddy, Gaz. Some from years ago, some from last month. Pictures I didn't even know existed. Her notes were short. Taunting, promises and threats.

Next time, I'll send something more personal.

I didn't let myself imagine what that meant. I shoved the envelopes into a drawer I barely opened, but the sickness stayed in my gut, a constant rot under my ribs. I didn't know what to do about it.

Dean Orletta's eyes burned every time I crossed him in the hall. As though he knew. As though he wanted me to know he knew. I kept my head down, took my notes, pretended to eat, but food soon lost its taste. By Friday, I was pushing salad around my plate when a senior Legacy burst into the cafeteria at a run. He was pale, drenched in sweat, his hands shaking as he stumbled towards the teachers' table. He bent low, whispering. He had the whole room's attention. But the reaction was instant.

The teacher's chairs scraped back with a squeal. They rose as one, their faces blanching. One clutched his mouth. Another muttered a curse under her breath. Then they swept out, moving quickly, tightly together.

The cafeteria hushed. Every head turned as we watched them leave.

"What's happened?"

"What's happened?"

It was as if a single invisible thread tugged the students to their feet. One by one, row by row, they moved toward the doors. Maddy and Gaz shared a wide-eyed look.

"Come on," Maddy whispered, her fingers locked on my sleeve, and dragged me into the tide of bodies. I didn't know if I wanted to go or not.

The southern wing courtyard laid ahead, its vines and flowers wilting under the weight of so many footsteps.

Silence blanketed the air, thick, and unnatural. The closer I got, I could hear gasps, choked sobs. A scream that broke into gagging. I froze, dread pooling cold in my stomach. More than one student turned and retched over the stone wall. Someone ran. Another cried.

I almost didn't want to see. I would bet that it was going to be a body.

A presence settled beside me. I didn't need to look.

"You don't want to see it, Jocelyn," Jake murmured. His voice, soft for once, slid down my spine. His brows knit, his mouth tight as he shook his head slightly.

But I couldn't stop myself.

I pushed forward and the crowd parted. Maddy gasped behind me, Gaz cursed as voices became desperate.

"Jossi, don't-" Gaz tried to grab my arm, but I broke free of their hands and stepped through.

The body lay sprawled across the cracked courtyard. Limbs severed, deliberately, carefully, and placed back in their rightful positions, as though someone had tried to *reassemble* her - a grotesque puzzle.

Blood pooled dark beneath the joints. And scrawled across the stone in thick, dripping letters:

JOCELYN
COME PLAY WITH ME

My breath caught, my body locking in place as I looked over the poor girl lying broken before me.

Elspeth Grady.

Her name surfaced through the fog. A second year. She'd sat beside me in music class last year, pencil tapping to the rhythm as she thought. Long, wavy brown hair. Blue eyes.

People said we looked alike.

My throat closed. Bile clawed upward, hot and sour.

I gritted my teeth, forcing it down and turned my gaze away. My legs carried me backward through the parting crowd. It felt like walking through water. Mutters surged around me, shock turning to hysteria. Professors barked orders, herding students back inside, their voices swallowed by chaos.

Maddy and Gaz appeared at my sides, their hands clamping onto my arms, dragging me with them. I let them, too stunned to fight. By the time we reached my room, my skin crawled as if ants marched beneath it.

"Who the fuck would do that?" Maddy paced my room, her voice sharp.

"It's Sera," I croaked. The sound of my own voice startled me. I couldn't look up, couldn't stop staring at my hands twisting in my lap.

"No." Gaz froze. His gaze locked on mine, horror widening his eyes.

"She's been sending me letters," I whispered, throat tight. "Telling me she's escaped. That she's coming for me."

Maddy's curse cut through the air. "How the fuck did she get out? Why hasn't anyone told us?" Her hands tore through her hair, leaving strands sticking up like she'd stuck her finger in a power point. "Is she here? Is she inside the academy?"

"I don't know." My voice cracked, but I forced a breath, slow and steady. "But I'm not going to sit around and let her get me. Not again." I stood, feeling restless as I paced.

"Why the fuck didn't you tell us?" Maddy snapped, and I shook my head.

"I don't want to involve you guys. You've already been through enough because of me."

"Yeah, well, too late for that."

I fell heavily onto my bed, mind spinning. I needed a plan, anything.

Because I knew Sera.

And I knew she wouldn't stop until she had me.

That night, Maddy crawled under my blanket beside me, neither of us willing to face the dark alone.

Sleep didn't come easy. Not with the smell of blood still clinging to my memory. Not with Sera's taunts rattling through my skull.

I received another letter the next day, and it was the worst one yet.

My dearest Clementine,
I hope you liked my gift. I spent a lot of time preparing it for you.
I write to you with happiness today. I've been joined by a good friend of mine, someone I haven't seen since the accident last year.
But no matter, we're together again. But he's not the same. Not since you killed his other half.

Oh, gods.

We are both looking forward to seeing you, hopefully sooner rather than later.
Love Sera, and Darius xoxo

No. No, no, no.

I dropped the letter and sank onto my bed, my head in my hands. She'd gotten Alec's older brother out of prison. And they were both coming for me, let alone the assassin's Fendi had sent after me. I collapsed into bed and cried myself to sleep.

"Babydoll." A whisper pried me from my sleep, and I groaned, thinking I was dreaming. "It's me." I sat bolt upright, rubbing the sleep from my eyes as Alexander sat on my bed.

My Alec, he was *here*.

"Is it really you?" I whispered, and he reached out and linked his fingers with mine.

"I had to see you. After what happened, I needed to see that you were alright." I could barely see him, but I could see worry framing his mouth as his eyes darted over me. A loud sob burst between my lips, and he pulled me in for a hug, holding me tight. He leaned down and kissed the top of my head, gently rocking me side to side. "I'm so sorry, about everything." He breathed, rubbing a soothing hand up and down my back.

"Why didn't you tell me?" I croaked, sniffling into his chest. He pulled me back and looked me in the eye.

"I didn't want to worry you. I know how stressful second year is."

"I'm stronger than you think," I grumbled, and he smiled sadly at me.

"I know you are, sugar. But I worry for you, especially since I'm not here." He ran a thumb over my cheek, but his expression changed in an instant, eyes narrowing. "I need you to tell me who the hell that Jake Callahan guy is, and what the fuck did he mean he's saved you three times now? What aren't you telling me?"

Here we go.

I scoffed, leaning back further so I could give him my best glare.

"You're one to talk. You didn't tell me that Sera and Darius had gotten out. Now she's sending me letters every few days. Photos of you, me and the others. She's stalking us, and she says she's coming for me, and soon. Not to mention the dead body in the courtyard today."

He sucked in a surprised breath, his jaw ticking. "I'm handling it." He growled.

"Are you? Because what about when Fendi sent assassins after me, and they would have killed me if it wasn't for Jake."

Shit. I shouldn't have said that.

"What the *fuck?* Assassins? When the hell did this happen?" He yelled, and I shushed him, pulling him back down beside me, more than aware of Jake in the room next to mine.

"Keep your damn voice down, will you?" I hissed, and he narrowed his eyes. "It was a few weeks ago. I was out for a run, and they came at me. He was already out there and took down two of them."

"And you didn't tell me because...?"

"You weren't *here*. We were meant to catch up on the weekend, but Matthew told me you'd be away the whole week. Not even a message from you."

"I couldn't say no. I had to go without warning." Regret laced his tone, and I softened a little. I knew how persuasive my father could be.

"I know. But you've been hiding things from me too."

He sighed, rubbing a hand over his face. "I didn't come here to argue. God, I've missed you so much that I dream of you every night."

Those words alone made me melt, and I grabbed his face, and brought his lips to mine. His hands instantly cradled my face as he kissed me back.

"We don't have to-" Alec murmured against my lips, but I ignored him as I stripped my top off. I needed him more than anything right now.

We wasted no time in shedding our clothes, our hands always in contact with each other in some way.

Tonight wouldn't be slow and gentle. We were too fired up for that. We needed to feel that we were okay, both alive.

He palmed one of my breasts, and I moaned quietly, missing the feeling of his touch. I reached between us and grabbed a fistful of him, slowing working him up and down. He groaned low, his hand slipping into my hair. Our tongues danced as he laid me down, he was a welcome weight above me. He paid special attention to all my sensitive spots, making me gasp and quietly moan.

"Stop mucking around, I need you, Alexander." I breathed, and he wasted no time in lining me up and sliding all the way in.

Oh, god, yes.

The feeling was exquisite. I tipped my head back as he slowly slid out, then eased back in. I could spend all night right here, but for now, I needed *more.*

I bucked my hips up and he chuckled darkly, making my nipples harden. He pulled out again and slammed into me so hard I cried out.

"Oh, god." I gasped, which made him sigh. I felt his smile against my neck.

"If I'm your god, then you're about to become my religion." He grunted, and I moaned as I threw my head back, feeling that fire burn within me.

I didn't care that we were being noisy, I didn't care that Jake could probably hear us as Alec continued his punishing rhythm. He leaned back, flipped me over, pulled my ass into the air and slid right back in.

"Oh, you feel so good." He breathed, his fingers digging into my hips as my back arched. I couldn't fight the wave building in me, and there was no way I was going to be able to keep quiet.

My mind was blissfully empty as we lost ourselves in each other. It had been so long since we'd been together. I'd missed us. Missed this. He hit that sweet spot, and I cried out, my release hitting me so hard I went weak at the knees. But he held me there as he found his own, groaning quietly as he came. I was breathing heavy, it was like I'd just ran a damn marathon, but my mind felt a little quieter.

We flopped onto the bed beside each other, catching our breath, smiling like Cheshire cats.

He gently trailed his fingers down my cheek, before resting it on my neck. He froze, his eyes darkened slightly, and his face changed in an instant.

"What are those bruises on your neck?" He sat, eyes roving over the rest of me for any other hurts. "Who the fuck wrapped their hand around your throat?" He growled, and I could see that inner fire, that beast that wanted out and to destroy. I needed to think quick, because if I told him it was Jake, he'd be right over there smashing his door down in seconds.

"It was one of the assassins the other day, but I killed him. I'm okay." I sat up and placed my hands on his chest, willing him to calm. "I'm really okay." I breathed and pulled his face back down to mine. He was still breathing too heavily, and I needed to distract him. I climbed over onto his lap and kissed him hard. His arms wrapped around me and held me close as he slowly relaxed against me.

His hand rubbed my back in soothing motions, and I could feel him stirring beneath me as we got lost in our kiss.

"That was weeks ago." He started, but I silenced him with another kiss.

"I'm okay. I'm not hurt." I whispered, trying to convince him, as much as myself, as I slowly lowered myself onto his shaft, and he tipped his head back with a low moan. "Oh, Alexander," I murmured as I sat fully on him to the hilt.

I dug my hands into his hair, gripping tightly enough that it almost hurt. But we needed this pain to make ourselves feel alive. I wasted no time and began to move, the fire quickly ramping to maximum heat in seconds. His hands moved around to grip me on the ass, and I came undone. I tipped my head back as I clenched around him, my release hitting me in wave after wave. He cried out, wrapping his arms around tight as he joined me.

By the time we peeled ourselves off each other, we were sweaty and sated.

"I don't want to leave you, but I have to." He sighed, keeping me tucked in close, his body cocooning me. "I wish you could come with me."

"I know." I tried to savour being held by him. "I wish you could stay," I admitted. Having him there with me would make the world of difference. I wouldn't be so scared every day. But he couldn't know that. No one could.

"I'll try and get a weekend off to see you, alright?" He kissed my shoulder, then climbed out of bed, dressing as I rolled over to admire the view. I nodded, giving him a small smile. I wasn't going to hold my breath though. I didn't want to be disappointed like last time.

He leaned down and kissed me, lingering. I wanted to tug him back to bed, but he pulled away, giving me that damn crooked smile I loved.

"Stay safe, Babydoll." He winked, blew me a kiss and snuck back out the window, shutting it quietly.

I walked over to the window and bolted it. Sighing as I climbed into the still warm bed, I rolled onto my back and blew out a long breath.

God, I felt so alone already.

I ran a hand over my face and forced myself out of bed, and ducked to the bathroom across the hall to get ready for sleep.

My bed was cold when I returned, but it still smelt like him, and I smiled. Sleep found me soon after, and for once, no nightmares.

Chapter Thirteen

Another week dragged by, more letters, more photographs, each one a fresh weight on my chest.

Jake barely spoke to me now, choosing silence over taunts. I much preferred it that way. Whatever crawled under his skin, at least it meant I could breathe, focus, and pretend for a moment that my world wasn't collapsing.

I swore that I saw Sera in the halls, in her pristine school uniform. I always did a double-take, thinking I saw her in the back of the classroom. But every time I turned back, she was gone.

I was starting to think that I was losing my mind.

I even saw Darius a handful of times in the cafeteria, out in the yard, and walking the halls.

I didn't dare share these thoughts. It would be a one-way ticket to a hospital where they'd dress me in a white jacket.

Group work became my refuge: Maddy, Gaz, and now Britney. She was calm and steady. Her soft laugh and wide eyes were nothing like the sharks circling in the rest of our year. Maddy insisted Britney was too gentle for a place like this. I disagreed. The fact that Britney was still kind after surviving there for a year? That was strength. If I didn't have my friends, this place would have devoured me long ago.

"Where did you spend your summer break?" Britney asked during science, her gloved hands flipping through ratios of powder-to-liquid.

Today's project? A compound that ate through steel like water through sugar.

"With family and friends." I jotted down numbers, pretending my chest didn't ache at the thought. "But they're always busy."

Her lips curved downward, her fringe slipping into her eyes. "Mine too. My sister just moved overseas." She forced a laugh. "She was my best friend. Now she's gone."

"I'm sorry. That must be hard," I murmured, marking the page that listed how much corrosive was needed to strip different alloys.

"Thank you." She tucked her black hair back, slapping a braver smile in place. "We write letters. She likes the old ways."

"Same." I couldn't help a small smile. "Alexander and I do, too."

"That's sweet." She grinned, cheeks flushed as she gathered supplies. "Ready to melt some stuff?"

"Hell yeah." Britney cracked a wide grin.

We set up, while across the room Gaz and Jake laughed together, the sound grated like nails. Maddy got stuck with a third-year more concerned about her manicure than the compound eating her gloves.

But Professor Morayne's words from last week gnawed at me:

This year's recruits are soft. The Syndicate won't accept them like this.

What did he mean? Where do Hellspire's students really go after graduation?

I shoved the thought aside as Professor Zane prowled like a jackal, snapping out half-hints and praises. I was pretty sure he even jump-scared the table in the front, making Jordan and Carl scream and drop their vials. I sighed and shook my head, glad he had already passed my table.

The intercom sputtered overhead, Dean Orletta's voice slicing through the air:

"ASSEMBLY. STRAIGHT AFTER CLASS. MANDATORY."

A ripple ran through the room, full of chatter and unease. Maddy shrugged from across the room as our eyes met, but her knuckles whitened around her pipette.

"That man terrifies me," Britney whispered, lowering her goggles.

"Same," I muttered, adjusting my mask before the acid hissed onto steel, smoke curling upward.

"He does seem to particularly hate you though," she grumbled, watching the hole bloom through the metal. "Why can't they hire someone who doesn't prey on students, doesn't hate them, and actually wants us to thrive?"

"Apparently that's too much to ask." I snorted, but her laugh softened the tension until her gaze drifted across the room. To Jake. To the way he leaned toward Gaz, his shoulders shaking in laughter. Her cheeks flushed, green eyes catching the light.

"I'll admit," she sighed, "Jake Callahan is ridiculously gorgeous. But... he seems a little obsessed with you." She wrinkled her nose, and I snorted despite myself.

"He's a pain in my ass," I muttered.

Britney's gaze sharpened, unexpectedly serious. "Is he... hitting on you? Doesn't he know you're with Alec?"

"No." The lie slipped too easily. "He knows. He's just... protective. Like an older brother."

Her laugh was dry, disbelieving. "He doesn't look at you like a brother, Jocelyn. Especially when you're not looking." The words lodged in my gut like a shard of glass. I shrugged, forcing a smile. "He's a little intense sometimes, though, don't you think?"

I need to change the subject, and fast.

"I can introduce you to him, if you want."

Her cheeks pinked, eyes sparkling. "Would you? Really?"

Across the room, Jake said something low to Gaz, and both men laughed again, oblivious. Britney tucked her hair back, smiling at the sight.

"Absolutely," I murmured, already plotting. "I'll make sure you meet him after class." And if she was willing, I'd set Jake Callahan on a thousand dates, anything to drag his dark eyes, his too-close attention, away from me.

We filed into the hall, the scrape of shoes and the murmur of voices swallowed by the sheer weight of silence pressing down on the room. At the front, the dean and professors stood like statues, hands clasped, eyes fixed forward. They weren't talking to each other. They weren't talking at all.

They looked... nervous.

"Hurry up," Orletta snapped, the words cracking like a whip. Instantly, the students stilled, spines straightening, voices dying away.

"We have a guest assessor joining us for the next two months. She will be overseeing your classes, ensuring you're... where you need to be." A chill skittered over my skin as the woman strode onto the dais.

Her heels struck the floor like gunshots, each sharp step echoing off the vaulted ceiling. Long, silken hair fell like molten gold down her back, a slash of blood-red lips curved into something that wasn't quite a smile.

Her gaze swept over us, a predator measuring prey. She nodded once at Orletta, then folded her hands in front of her as though she owned the place.

"Miss Hemlock," Orletta barked, "may pull you aside for a word at any time. Nothing to worry about. Just... do your best." His eyes roved over us, lingering on a few students. "Don't disappoint me. Dismissed." The professors ushered us out with brisk, pale-faced efficiency. Their tight lips and darting eyes told me more than words ever could.

If *they* were rattled, then what the hell were we about to face?

"Jocelyn."

I turned to find Oliver Upton falling into step beside me on the way to the cafeteria. Another legacy, but one of the rare ones people actually liked. Tousled blond hair, easy grin, shirt sleeves rolled carelessly up, his uniform half-untucked in open defiance of Orletta's standards.

"Hey," he said lightly, "got a sec?" He flicked a glance around before jerking his chin toward an empty classroom. I hesitated, then slipped inside with him. The lights stayed off, shadows stretching long and thin across the desks. "Wood and Omara want the works up and running again. They need all hands."

My stomach sank. Illegal weapons. Again.

"Of course they do." My voice was flat, but the memory of last time made bile rise in my throat.

"Tuesdays and Thursdays night," he said, rubbing a hand through his hair. "We're doing twice a week now.

Demand's doubled, Anton Karrev requires more than last year, apparently."

"Who?" I frowned, crossing my arms. Was this the man who was buying them off us?

"Oh, forget I said anything." He winced, scrubbing at his neck. I caught it then, a faint smear of pink lipstick on his neck. I hid my smile. Oliver Upton was Hellspire's worst-kept secret: a legendary lay with half the school, and the swagger to match. He reminded me too much of Paul. Too charming. Too easy. Too dangerous in his own way.

"Alright. Around ten?" I asked, already stepping back toward the door. But his hand curled lightly around my wrist, halting me.

"Yeah. Ten." His grin sharpened, teeth white in the dark. "Hey, while I've got you. You still with Hyde?" The megawatt smile would've made most girls melt.

"Yeah. I am." My gaze locked on his, frowning slightly.

He only smiled wider. "No worries." With a wink, he slipped back into the hall, leaving the faint scent of his cologne in the empty room.

I rolled my eyes, waited a beat, then followed. The shadows pressed in on either side of the corridor, every creak and whisper prickling the back of my neck.

I hated walking these halls alone.

I tugged my hood low, boots heavy on the stone floor as I met Oliver in the hall. He winked, as casual as ever, before pulling up his own hood and leading the way. The corridors were mercifully empty, our footsteps muffled as we slipped into the supply closet and down beneath Hellspire's skin.

The heat hit me first, steam rising from the belly of the operation, machinery clanging in rhythm with whispered orders.

"Ah, Miss Xanetto. Lovely to have you back." Wood greeted me with a warm smile, I returned it hesitantly.

"This way."

Oliver vanished into the haze while Wood guided me to a battered workbench. Omara was already there, leaning over maps and papers, scratching his chin. He glanced up, gave me a curt nod, then gestured to the spread of documents.

"We need a drop in Mangalore. You're familiar with the terrain?"

My eyes skimmed the maps, old names and landmarks stirring unwelcome memories.

"Yes. I know the routes. What do you need?"

"The best meeting point for a new client. Travel time. Risks." He straightened, pinning me with a look that said this wasn't a request. "You'll take a truck, run the route with GPS, stay ten minutes in the zone, then return."

My breath caught, but I forced myself to nod. Weakness was blood in the water here.

"Good," Omara says smoothly. "We've recruited a new helper. Callahan. He claimed he knows Mangalore too. He'll be your muscle."

The floor dropped out from under me. A shadow moved, and Jake stepped into view with that faint, infuriating smile. Of all people, it *had* to be him. I'd take Oliver Upton's smug flirtation a thousand times over.

"Settled," Wood said brightly, pressing the keys into my palm. "We'll be watching."

The truck loomed ahead, patched up from last year's bullet holes like nothing ever happened. I wrenched the door open harder than I meant to, climbed into the cab, and slammed it shut. Jake followed, effortless as ever, grinning like a cat with cream.

The warehouse door rolled up, and we lurched out into the night, the road unspooling beneath us as the stars glittered above.

I gripped the wheel, knuckles white. The truck was massive, the mountain roads narrow, and worse, I could feel his gaze burning into me.

"You look a little... uneasy." His chuckle rumbled low, amused. I didn't answer. Silence was better than giving him what he wanted.

"Thought you weren't speaking to me," I muttered finally, eyes fixed on the winding road.

"I've been... preoccupied." There was a smile in his tone, smug and unhurried. "Still. Just the two of us, hmm? Shame the truck's rigged with live-stream GPS."

My head whipped toward him, fury sparking, but his smirk only deepened.

"Eyes on the road, sweetheart."

My pulse spiked, heat crawling beneath my skin. He leaned back, hands laced behind his head like he was lounging on a beach instead of plotting my ruin. "My people are getting impatient. They want to know why I haven't delivered you yet."

The words were casual. But their meaning deadly.

"And why haven't you?" My voice shook. The cab was too hot, the air too thin. Sweat slid down my spine.

"I told them it's not that simple." His eyes glinted in the dark, fixed on me. "Told them they can't... play with you yet. Not until I wring more information from you. About your father."

Play with me. My stomach lurched. I flicked on the aircon, needing some air.

The lights of Greensville flickered on the horizon. We would bypass it for the city. At least an hour more with him in this cab. An hour too long. Not to mention the hour or so return.

"What information do you need?" My whisper trembled, but the question slipped out anyway, fuelled by panic.

Jake's smile was slow, merciless. "That's for me to know, sweetheart. Not you."

"But I might know what you need, then you could leave me alone." I almost pleaded, hating how desperate I sounded.

"No, this information is top secret, only those in your fathers inner circle will know."

Chapter Fourteen

He let the conversation die, but the silence was worse. I didn't want to imagine what his 'people' would do if he ever delivered me to them.

Torture? Death? Something worse? The only question that festered is why he was holding back. Why he hadn't already handed me over.

Not that I was complaining, I quite liked my head where it was, thank you very much.

"Sera is becoming a problem." The words sliced through the dark cab like a knife. My head jerked toward him before I could stop myself. He was already staring at me, gaze locked, sharp enough to cut skin.

"Watch the road." His tone snapped like a whip. I wrenched my eyes forward, though my chest felt too tight to breathe.

"She's gathering more helpers. I've already taken out three trying to crawl their way into the academy. What happened the other day-" his voice hardened "-won't happen again."

Bile rose in my throat. I swallowed it down, steadying my breath, counting to ten in my head like it would stop me from throwing up.

"But then there's Fendi." He exhaled sharply, rubbing his face as if even saying the name was exhausting. "That man doesn't know when to quit. I've got my team chasing him down now. I told them he's a distraction from my real mission."

Real mission.

The words lodged like glass in my chest. I didn't know why he was telling me any of this, Jake never shared, never opened up. This was the most I'd ever heard him talk about his world, his plans. It should have felt like progress. It only felt like horror.

"And what is your real mission?" My voice was quieter than I wanted, but it still managed to break the tension. "Other than to kidnap me?"

His smirk was immediate, a little cruel. "Oh, sweetheart. Wouldn't you like to know?"

"You're infuriating," I snapped, heat spiking in my cheeks. "You threaten me, then you tease me, then you drop classified secrets like breadcrumbs. I can never get a read on you."

"And that's exactly how I like it." His grin turned sharp and predatory. "I want you looking over your shoulder. Always. Never let your guard down, especially with that new assessor." His voice dropped to a growl. "*Miss Hemlock*."

The name alone made my spine stiffen. "Who is she? What does she really want?"

"You don't want to know." He didn't soften his tone, didn't even pretend to. "The students who fail to meet her standards… disappear. Quietly. No one sees them again."

A chill sliced through me. Another weight on the endless pile of things to fear.

"But you don't need to worry." His voice shifted, smooth as silk, and somehow that was worse. "Your grades are immaculate. You're smart. Smarter than most here."

I scoffed, rolling my eyes, refusing to let him manipulate me with flattery. He was a liar. Verreth's golden boy. I didn't buy it for a second.

"Excuse me if I don't believe you." I muttered under my breath.

His laugh was low, almost fond, which made my stomach twist. He reclined his seat, tossing one boot over his knee, casual as if we weren't hurtling down a mountain road with death shadowing both our steps.

"I always tell you the truth, sweetheart." The words chilled me more than lies ever could. "I'll admit, though, introducing me to Britney was clever." His grin returned, sly and knowing. "She tries to talk to me constantly. Especially when I'm tracking you."

My blood turned molten. "You *what?*"

"I've got trackers on you." He said it like he was commenting on the weather. "Sewed them into your clothes."

"*You-*" Rage roared up my throat, hot and choking. "How *dare* you-"

I whipped toward him, glare blazing, but the truck jerked violently. Jake's hand was already on the wheel, yanking it straight.

"For fuck's sake, Jocelyn. You'll kill us both." His voice lashed at me. "Pull over. I'm driving."

Before I could argue, he reached over and killed the engine, swerved the truck to the side, and in one fluid motion, slammed on the hand brake. He unclipped my belt and hauled me out of the driver's seat.

"Get your fucking hands off me!" I thrashed against him, fury spitting from every nerve. He ignored me, muscling me into the passenger side, buckling the belt himself with infuriating calm. Then he slid into the driver's seat, clicked his own belt, and restarted the engine like nothing happened. Within seconds, we were back on the road, moving smoothly into light traffic.

"Relax." His tone was maddeningly even. "I've been driving a lot longer than you. Now you can scream at me without killing us both."

I slammed my arms across my chest and turned to the window, seething, jaw clenched tight enough to ache. My pulse was still wild, rage boiling beneath my skin. He didn't speak again, which was both a mercy and a curse. Silence gave me too much space to think. Too much space to process everything he just told me.

Sera's soldiers clawing at Hellspire's walls.

Fendi still hunting me like prey.

Miss Hemlock's shadow looming over us all.

Just another normal year at Hellspire.

We found a spot for the drop point down by the bay, waited the ten minutes, then turned back toward Hellspire. Two hours just to get here, and now the silence in the cab pressed in, thick and unbearable.

I was about to break it, to ask about Sera and her people, when headlights flared in my side mirror, blinding, fast, and not slowing down.

"Uh... Jake." My voice cracked. "I think someone's coming right for us."

He checks the mirrors, shaking his head. "Fuck." He snarled. The truck lurched as he swerved, tires screaming, the world tilting as we took a corner far too fast. Metal shrieked as the pursuing car slammed into us, the impact spinning us like a toy. For one heart-stopping second, we balanced on two wheels, then gravity won. The truck tipped, the world turned sideways, and we slammed onto our side with a shuddering crash.

Pain detonated up my arm, blinding white, ripping the breath from my lungs. Jake was already out of his belt, leaning over me, hands cupping my face.

"Tell me you're alright." His voice was low, rough, and desperate.

"My arm-" My words choked out, fractured by agony. "Oh, gods."

Shots hammered against the truck's belly, echoing like thunder. Jake cursed, sliced my belt free with his knife, and dragged me against him before I could collapse. Glass bit into my legs as he kicked through the fractured windscreen, hauling me out into the night.

"Run. Hide until I come for you." His command was clipped and urgent. He shoved me behind him as two figures appeared at the truck's flank.

And then I froze.

"Clementine," Paul breathed, smiling like he was greeting me for coffee, not stepping out of the shadows with a gun at his hip.

"Jocelyn," I snapped, teeth bared as I clutched my ruined arm. But my throat went dry when I saw who was beside him. "Jenna." I curled my lip over my teeth in a snarl.

She smiled, sharp and cruel. Jake went statue-still beside me. He slid one arm around my waist, the other levelling his gun.

"Why aren't you dead?" Jenna hissed, her voice dripping venom.

"I'm...hard to kill." The lie came out hoarse, ragged with pain. My vision spotted white at the edges, but I didn't dare falter.

Paul turned on Jenna with horror. "What did you do?" He balled his hands into fists, shaking at his sides.

"I sent her a little gift." Jenna shoved him, and to my shock, he growled at her.

"She's *mine*. You don't touch her This was only meant to make them pull over." His gaze cut back to me, softening. "Look at you, darling. They've hurt you. I'll take you away from this."

My stomach lurched. What the hell was happening?

He stepped closer. Jake raised the gun higher. "Take another step, and you're dead."

"Oh, come now," Jenna crooned, fluttering her lashes at him. "We just want her. Then we'll be on our way." She stepped forward half a step. "I don't believe we've met. I'm Jenna Orletta." She extended her arm out for him to shake, and my mouth dropped open in shock.

"I don't give a fuck who you are. You're both dead if you take another step." Jake barked, keeping his gun pointed at her.

"Oh, come now. No need to be so...violent." She simpered, fluttering her lashes at him.

"Clem," Paul pleaded, ignoring Jake entirely. "Sweetheart. I'll help you remember who you are. Who *we* are." Delusion and madness danced in his eyes, they shone too bright, as if he were fevered.

"Who the fuck are *you?*" Jake barked.

"I'm her *boyfriend*." Paul's face twisted with hate. "So take your filthy hands off her."

Jake laughed, short and cruel. "You're insane."

"She's *mine!*" Paul roared, and then he was charging. I hastily threw my knife, but didn't get a chance to see if it landed, as Jake shoved me hard. I hit the ground, landing on my broken arm, and agony tore through me like fire. My scream dissolved into a whimper as the world tilted.

Gunfire cracked. Someone cried out. Fists met flesh with sickening thuds, and snarls filled the night.

Then silence.

I blinked through the haze. Paul was sprawled in the dirt, unconscious, blood streaking his temple.

Jenna lay in a heap beside him, limp as a rag doll.

Jake breathed hard, gun steady in his hand, chest heaving. He looked back at me, eyes flashing.

"Stay awake." His voice was gravelly, command threaded with panic. I tried to answer, but only managed a groan. My arm throbbed, my vision swimming. He crouched, pulling a phone from his pocket. A few clipped words, low and lethal: "We've got a mess. Pick up, now. Bring the van."

"The crash was detected. We're nearly there." I heard Omara on the other end, but my head was swimming so much I might have imagined it. Jake pocketed the phone, then gathered me against his chest like I weighed nothing. His gun dangled loosely from his other hand, but I knew he'd fire without hesitation if anything moved in the shadows.

The last thing I heard before the darkness swallowed me was his heartbeat hammering under my ear, and the crunch of tyres approaching fast.

I woke with a gasp, sterile bright lights burned my eyes as I blinked awake. I felt like I'd got cotton wool in my head, all fuzzy and numb.

"Easy." A deep voice rumbled to my right, and I blinked, trying to get the person into focus. "They've fixed your arm, but you're on some serious painkillers." A face finally swam into view, and I shut my eyes again, lying back on my pillow.

"Do I know you? And what the hell happened?" I groaned, trying to move my arms, but my body didn't want to obey.

"Very funny." He sighed. I opened my eyes, frowning as I looked at him.

"I've never seen you before in my life." I met his lovely green eyes. He *was* rather beautiful. A muscle ticked in his jaw. He closed his eyes, took a deep breath and opened them again.

"Paul and Jenna are currently in our holding cells underground. The dean doesn't know yet."

"What?" I forced my eyes back to him, feeling completely confused. "Why the hell are you holding Paul? And who's Jenna?" He sat forward, eyes narrowed on me as he looked me over.

"What do you remember?" He breathed, knuckles white as he gripped them tightly on the edge of my bed.

"I...I remember having dinner with my mum and dad, then...nothing. It's blank. What is wrong with my arm? Where am I?" I frowned, and his eyes widened, his face paling a little. He stood and grabbed my chin, moving my head side to side. He lightly brushed my skull with his fingers, and I hissed in pain, swatting his hand.

"Ouch. That hurts." I grunted, moving my head out of his grip. "What the hell?"

"What the hell?" He hissed, suddenly in my face, and I sucked in a breath. Should I be afraid of him?

"Who are *you?*" He probed, and I raised one brow, rolling my eyes.

"Clementine Mavis."

Chapter Fifteen

I didn't understand why he was so upset. I hadn't lost my memory. I remembered everything perfectly well, thank you very much.

The man - still nameless to me - snatched a phone from his pocket and dialled with clipped precision. His voice was low and urgent, like he was afraid I'd hear the words. Within moments, the curtain whisked open and a man in a white coat stepped in. He smiled but it was too bright, too rehearsed, and my stomach twisted a little.

Why do I feel so uneasy?

"Ah, good evening, Miss Xanetto. I heard you've had a little trouble with memory loss."

I froze. The name slammed into me like a punch. My name. My *real* name.

Oh God. They know.

My breath quickened, throat closing around it. I flung the sheet back, ready to bolt, but the stranger blocked me with a firm, careful hand on my wrist.

"You're safe here," the doctor said softly, but the way his eyes skimmed over me felt clinical, detached.

Not safe at all.

"Where am I?" My voice cracked, air tearing through my chest like fire. "Where are my parents?" I couldn't breathe. I couldn't-

"Look at me." The man with black hair and green eyes barked, and something in his tone made me obey, like a command I'd heard before. His gaze pinned me, relentless. "Your name is Jocelyn Xanetto. For the past year and six months, you've been living at Hellspire Academy. You killed one of the Hyde twins in your first year. The other is rotting in prison because of you."

The words landed heavy, impossible. I shook my head, recoiled, but he caught my hands in his, iron bands that refused to let go. "I'm Jake Callahan," he pushed on, each word ragged with desperation. "You're best friends with Madeline Pyre and Gary Davies."

I wrenched at his grip, panic clawing at my throat. "This is madness! I've never heard of those people before, or Hellspire!" I needed to get out of here.

His jaw tightened. His voice lowered to a growl. "You're in love with Alexander Hyde."

The name punched the air from my lungs. My gasp felt too loud in the sterile room. I ripped my hands free and clutched at the sheets, shaking my head so hard my vision blurred.

"*No*. No, I'm with Paul. Paul loves me. He's...he's my boyfriend." My voice cracked as I searched the room, eyes darting for my parents, for escape, for *anything* that made sense. "I want to go home. Where are my parents?"

Jake leaned closer, voice rough, urgent. "Jocelyn. Look at me. You were in an accident. Your brain's protecting itself. That's all this is."

"No!" My plea turned into a sob. I snapped my gaze to the doctor, desperate, silently begging him to see the truth, that I *do* remember. That I wasn't crazy. But he just exchanged a look with Jake, unreadable, before a sting bit into my arm. I thrashed, tried to pull away, but Jake held me still.

"Don't-" My voice slurred. My limbs turned heavy. My eyes closed against my will.

Darkness swallowed me whole.

Images flickered past. Too fast. Too blurred. Faces I didn't recognise, yet my heart ached as though it knew them. A boy laughing in the sun. A girl's scream. A violin's string snapping tight. My fingers reach for them, but they slipped away like smoke.

"...reset her brain?" a voice muttered near me, sharp with frustration.

"Rest. Her mind's protecting her," the doctor answered. "If you force it, you'll lose her completely." Footsteps faded. Another pair approached. The curtain whipped back with a shriek. I snapped my eyes open.

"Jocelyn." The way he said my name made me flinch. Like it belonged to me. Like I belonged to him.

"I need you to remember." He sat, leaning forward, elbows digging into his knees as he fixed me with those burning green eyes. "You're at Hellspire Academy. You've bled for it. You've *killed* for it. Do you understand? Paul tried to have your friends executed. You survived a shootout when you showed up to save them. You were shot and nearly died."

I clapped my hands over my ears. "No. Stop." My voice was hoarse, trembling. "I don't believe you."

But he didn't stop. His voice sharpened like a blade.

"You found Cooper's body strung up with your own violin strings. Sera carved messages into the corpses of your fellow students and left them for you. Jenna poisoned you. Three assassins hunted you through the woods. And you-" his voice broke, just for a heartbeat, "-you killed one of them before they could put a bullet in your skull."

"*No.*" I sobbed. My stomach heaved, bile burning my throat. "That...that doesn't happen to me. I've been safe. I've been travelling with my parents. I've been-"

His hands seized my face, forcing my eyes to his. His lips crashed against mine before I could breathe.

And suddenly, it all unraveled.

Heat flooded my chest, spreading through my veins. Images detonated in my head - Alexander's piercing gaze, Maddy's lion's mane, Gary's laughter. Paul's hand reaching for me. Jenna's smile as she saw us standing before the wrecked truck. Blood on my hands. Screams in the dark.

I ripped back, gasping, shaking, as it slammed into me all at once.

"Oh, God."

Jake's hands fell away. I collapsed into my palms, shoulders shaking, sobs tearing free. The pain, the loss, the weight of every memory came crashing back, suffocating me.

Too much. Too real.

"You remember." Jake breathed, sitting back.

I couldn't speak. My throat felt tight, the words strangled before they could escape. I just nodded, eyes fixed on the blanket in my lap, anywhere but him. Raised voices echoed down the hall, footsteps pounding closer. I scrubbed my eyes with the back of my hand, plastering a bright, brittle smile on my face just as the door banged open. Maddy and Gaz rushed in, out of breath and wide-eyed.

"What the fuck happened? Did you break your arm?" Maddy dropped to my side, clutching my hand like she was afraid I'd vanish. There was fear in her eyes, and it sliced through me like a blade.

"I'm alright, Mads." My voice cracked. I almost preferred the numbness of forgetting. Almost.

"No, you're not." Gaz's tone was sharp with a twinge of suspicion. "What the hell is going on?"

"She fell down some stairs." Jake said smoothly, arms folding across his chest. A smile ghosted his lips, infuriatingly calm. "Sounded like a herd of elephants."

"I did not!" I snapped, but it only made his smirk widen.

"I'll leave you with your friends." He strode out without another word, and suddenly the air felt lighter, easier to breathe. But the reminder burned in my chest - I couldn't forget who he really was.

My enemy.

"Seriously? Stairs?" Gaz narrowed his eyes at me. "Were they made of glass?"

I reached for my head instinctively and winced when my fingers brushed the shallow cuts.

"I don't know. I can't remember. They say I've got short-term memory loss." The words tasted like ash.

"Seriously?" Gaz muttered.

"Did Jake push you?" Maddy leaned in, whispering urgently.

A nervous laugh burst from me. "No. He's the one who found me."

"He wouldn't do that," Gaz scoffed, running a hand through his hair. "Jake's a solid guy."

If only he knew. My guilt twisted tighter.

"I'm fine now. Really." I forced a smile. "Can you walk me to my room?"

"Of course," Maddy shook her head, but helped me out of the bed.

We slipped out together, silence pressing heavily. Eyes followed me down the corridor, most of them curious.

"I called Alec. He's on his way." Gaz said as I unlocked my door.

Warmth flared through me, fierce and sudden. "Thank you."

I hugged him with my good arm, clinging tighter than I meant to. Maddy joined in, and soon I was buried in them both, fighting back tears.

"I don't know what I'd do without you." My voice broke. "What am I going to do when you both leave?"

"That's ages away. Don't bother thinking about that yet." Maddy sniffled, wiping her own eyes. "And I'm not crying! I got something in my eye." She grumbled, and I smiled at her as she sat beside me. "I don't trust Britney." Maddy blurted, and I frowned and leaned back a little.

"Why?"

"She's...too nice."

"Mads, we've been over this." Gaz rolled his eyes and pulled out the chair at my desk and sat on it backwards. "She won't replace you. Trust me, there is no one else out in the world like you." He winked, and Maddy huffed, but her cheeks turned pink.

"Still. Don't tell her anything she could use against you."

"Alright. I won't." I nodded, attempting to keep my face straight.

They smiled, reassured, and fussed over me. I smiled back, but my heart ached.

"Want us to wait until Alec arrives?" Maddy asked.

"I'll be fine." I waved them off. "Just need a nap."

When the door shut, I finally let out the breath I'd been holding. My head was spinning. My body ached *everywhere.*

And deep down, I knew this mess was only getting worse.

Gentle fingers grazed my face, stirring me awake. My lashes fluttered open.

"Alexander," I sighed, wrapping my arm awkwardly around him as he pulled me into his lap. His chest was a wall against my cheek, steady and safe.

"What the hell happened, Babydoll?" His voice was raw, threaded with fear.

"I don't remember. The story is that I fell down the stairs..."

"She was in a car accident." The voice slid through the quiet like a knife. I jolted, Alec's body going rigid beneath me. In a blur, he had his gun out, aimed into the shadows.

Jake stepped forward, calm and seemingly unfazed that a gun was pointed at his chest.

"What the fuck?" Alec growled, easing me off his lap. "How long have you been standing there? Why the *fuck* are you in her room?"

He sauntered closer until the barrel pressed against his chest, his expression unreadable.

"You want the truth? Put the gun down." Jake glared at Alec, jaw clenching.

"Tell me now, or I pull the fucking trigger." Alec's voice was all steel, his knuckles were white on the gun.

I clutched the blanket tight, heart hammering, useless in my sling. Jake tilted his head, mocking.

"Your ex, Jenna, and Paul Manfred ran us off the road, flipping the truck. I dragged her, bleeding, out through a shattered windscreen. She had a broken arm, and a concussion. She woke up thinking she was *Clementine*." His voice dripped venom on the name. My stomach flipped, heat prickling my skin.

Alec cursed, lowering his gun. "That doesn't explain why you're here." He snapped, but turned and grabbed my hand instead, holding too tight, panic in his eyes.

"Fuck. Jossi."

"They were put in holding cells," Jake continued, cold and precise. "By the time I got back to interrogate them, they were gone. The guards had their throats slit."

"Someone inside," Alec muttered, letting go of my hand and pacing hard.

"Orletta," Jake snapped. "Who else? He's fed them her location before. Her lackeys gave her an envelope filled with poisonous powder. She's lucky to be alive."

Alec's head jerked toward me, horror blazing across his face.

"You didn't tell me she tried to kill you!" His shout rattled the walls. He stormed back, gripping my hand like it was a lifeline.

"What could you have done?" My voice shook, breaking under his fury. "You're not here anymore Alec. Every weekend you're gone. I barely even hear from you anymore."

His face drained of colour, devastation etched into him.

"Jossi..." he whispered, voice cracking. He whirled on Jake, his hand slipping from mine. "Why are you always here? Always around her? What the hell are you doing - are you sleeping with her?" His voice cracked on the last word, like it burned his throat to even say it.

The words hit me like a whip. My gasp was stuck in my throat.

Jake's eyes flashed, deadly calm. "No. But I've saved her life more times than you can count." His voice sharpened into a snarl. "And she would never betray you like that. Don't you dare insult her."

"You speak like you know her better than I do." Alec shoved Jake hard in the chest.

Jake only took a single step back, shoulders loose, eyes burning. The tension between them crackled, thick and violent, and I knew if I didn't stop them now, blood would spill.

Chapter Sixteen

"All you need to know is that right now, I'm the only one keeping her safe." Jake shoved back, but Alec held his ground.

"Why the fuck are you following her?" Alec growled again, fists trembling at his sides.

"You want the truth, Hyde?" Jake sneered, pushing him again. Alec relented one step, fury simmering under his skin. "I've been sent to gather intel on her and her father. By whatever means necessary, I have to get that information. And we need her alive. So I've been following her, taking out all the assassins Fendi keeps sending. Keeping Sera and your brothers' minions out of the academy. It's a fucking full-time job!"

Oh, my God. He's told him everything.

I glanced to Alec, whose chest was heaving, his jaw locked so tight I was afraid his teeth would crack. His eyes were shards of onyx as he continued to glare at Jake.

"And what happens if you can't get your information?" His voice was quiet. Too quiet. A lethal calm that stole the breath from my lungs.

"Then Jocelyn will be taken and used as leverage."

Oh, fuck. He really said it.

"The fuck you will." Alec's growl was animalistic as he stalked toward Jake, but Jake whipped out a gun, the barrel glinting as it swung, not at Alec. At *me*. My heart lodged in my throat as I flinched back, breath stuttering. Alec froze mid-step, every muscle pulled taut.

"I don't want to hurt either of you. Especially Jossi." Jake's eyes flashed my way before locking on Alec again, and the sound of my nickname on his tongue made my skin crawl. It was too familiar. Too personal. "That's where you can help."

"What do you want?" Alec spat, his voice shaking with barely restrained fury.

"I want information." Jake leaned closer, forcing Alec back step by step, like a predator circling prey. "I want you to give me what information you have on Gordon Xanetto, and his whereabouts, where he goes, who he talks to."

Alec's face drained of colour. His knuckles whitened as they clenched into fists.

"He'll kill me if he catches me giving the enemy information like that."

"Is it worth her *life?*" Jake snarled, pointing at me again. My stomach dropped as his words sliced through the air. "Because I don't want to know what they'll do to her once they get their hands on her. We all know what a brute Gordon Xanetto is. He'll take a lot of persuading. Who better than his last remaining, darling daughter?"

I wanted to vomit. They were speaking about me as though I were already gone. As though I wasn't even in the room.

"You're not taking her *anywhere!*" Alec roared, ready to launch, but Jake's tone was deadly calm.

"I will if I have to. Unless you give me something in the next two weeks. Then I can't stop them. I've delayed them as long as I can. They want that information *now.*"

"I can't." Alec's voice cracked as he dragged both hands through his hair, gripping the back of his neck like he was about to tear himself apart.

"You can't stop me, Hyde. Unless you give me information every few weeks. Otherwise, this might be the last time you see her."

"And if I kill you right now? What happens then?" Alec snapped, his hand darting toward his gun again, but Jake only scoffed, unflinching.

"Then they'll move in straight away and take her. And kill anyone who gets in her way. You. Her friends. Everyone."

"No." My voice splintered as I forced myself to wobble to my feet, heart hammering so loud it almost hurt. I wedged myself between them, my broken arm trembling in its sling. They towered over me, eyes like blades, both too dangerous, too unyielding.

Alec looked down at me, his pain carved into every line of his face.

"And tell your little detective friend to back the hell off." Jake growled, and I whipped my head toward him.

Shit, Gabby is still digging?

"She's next on my list if she doesn't stop. And I won't make the same mistake as the others last time. She won't survive this."

"You know that telling someone like her to back off, means she's getting close," Alec growled, tucking an arm around my waist.

"And if it comes to that, Jocelyn will be leaving the school in the boot of my car." Jake snapped, baring his teeth like he could barely contain his anger. "Does she mean so little to you?" Jake whispered, a cruel taunt, and I swore my stomach plummeted to the floor. "That you'd rather save your own skin than hers?"

"Don't you *dare-*" I snapped, but Alec swung before I could stop him, his fist cracking against Jake's face. Jake staggered, wiped the blood from his lip with his thumb, then grinned, a bloody, wild grin that chilled me to the core.

"Here's my number. Use a burner phone each time you send me new information." He tossed a folded scrap of paper onto my bed, turned, and slipped out the door, his shadow leaving chaos in its wake.

"Jossi. Please, know that I would never-" Alec turned to me, his eyes begging, but I pressed a shaking finger to his lips.

"I know. Don't let him into your head."

"Why are you so calm about this?" His voice trembled.

"Because I've known since he saved me in the woods from Fendi's assassins. Obviously, I wasn't allowed to tell anyone. He's tracking my every move. Bugging my phone. Reading my letters. There's no hiding from him."

"I'm *not* going to let that happen." Alec's vow cut sharp, but I shook my head, feeling a little hollow.

"How? You're across the world half the time. I can't even reach you. What's stopping him from breaking in and dragging me out of bed one night? It could be at least three days before anyone could get in contact with you." Alec opened his mouth, then snapped it shut again.

"Then I'll quit. I'll-"

"You and I both know no one walks away from my father." My voice fractured. And then, because I knew it was the only way to keep Alec safe, the words I'd been dreading slipped free, acid on my tongue. "I think... we shouldn't do this anymore."

The way his face collapsed made my heart split clean in two.

"What are you saying?" His whisper was so soft it shredded my heart, my soul.

"This isn't working, Alexander. I can't see you, and I can barely speak to you. It won't work while I'm still at Hellspire, and all the extra stress..."

"Don't do this, Joss." His voice cracked, his shoulders caving as he took a stumbling step forward. I stepped back, tears burning trails down my cheeks.

"You and I both know this isn't what we want, but it's not *working*. You can't afford to have me distracting you. You need to focus on your work. I'm just a nuisance to you."

"Don't push me away when things get hard. Fuck work. I want *you*. You're the best thing to ever happen to me." His growl was guttural and raw, and I couldn't look at him anymore. My chest was torn apart. He reached me in two strides and grabbed my face between his trembling hands, forcing me to meet his eyes.

"I love you, Jossi." his voice broke over the words, and my heart stuttered. "I should have told you before, but I was terrified. I didn't want to scare you off. But I fucking love you so much." Tears streaked down his face as he begged me to believe him.

God. I can't do this.

"Alec." My sob wrenched free. "I love you too. But this isn't working. When I graduate, we can talk."

"By the sounds of it, you might not even be here to graduate. I can't let anything happen to you. Please. Come with me, leave right now." His thumb brushed my tears, smearing them into my skin as his face crumpled.

"You know that's not an option. I would never be allowed to leave. You need to focus on your job. Forget about me."

"You know that's never going to fucking happen!" His forehead pressed to mine, breath ragged, desperate. "I don't care that your father wants you to finish your schooling. It's not worth it, trust me." We said nothing for a moment, as his words sank into my mind. "Let's run away together. Just the two of us."

The idea was incredibly tempting. But I wouldn't do that to him. He deserved better than being hunted down by not only my father, but Jake and his team as well.

"I won't be the reason to ruin your life."

"My life isn't worth living without you in it." He seemed to crumple into himself.

That stopped me in my tracks.

"If you want space... then I'll give you space." His voice shattered, and my heart went with it. "But know that I'll do everything in my power to keep you safe. I'll wait for you, because I'm never letting you go." His kiss was fierce, searing, but over too soon. And then he was gone, climbing out the window, disappearing into the night like a ghost.

The silence after was deafening.

I fell to the floor, curling in on myself as great, heaving sobs ripped through me. It felt like someone drove a blade straight through my chest and left me bleeding and hollow. I cried until my throat was raw, until the night swallowed my grief whole, and I felt nothing but the ache of him.

I woke in my bed, tucked in tight, and went to roll over, only to wince, my arm screaming in protest. For a second, I didn't even remember getting up off the floor last night, but I couldn't bring myself to care. Alec was gone. I had pushed him away. Pushed away the best thing to ever happen to me.

It's for the best. I repeated the words in my head like a prayer, like a mantra. If I said them enough, maybe they'd feel true.

He'll be better off without me.

I sat heavily at the table, a bowl of cornflakes in front of me. The spoon dragged in lazy circles, milk sloshing, but I couldn't seem to bring myself to eat. I felt hollow. Gutted. Alec had filled my world with light and heat, and now I'd torn it out by the roots. My chest ached with every breath.

I'd woken with my mind fuzzy, confused and not sure where I was. It took me at least five minutes to figure it out after I looked outside and at my uniform.

A freezing cold shower had helped.

I shook my head and forced myself upright, jabbing the spoon into the cereal like it might ground me.

I did this. I need to live with it.

"Hey, is everything alright?" Maddy slid in beside me, coffee clutched tight in her hands. Her sharp eyes raked over me, too perceptive for my liking.

"I broke up with Alec." My voice cracked on his name, and I kept my gaze locked on the swirling milk. If I looked at her, if I saw pity in her eyes, I'd shatter.

"No fucking way. Why?" she hissed, leaning close, grabbing my hand like she was afraid I might disappear if she let go. "What the hell happened last night?"

"He's already got too much going on with work stuff." I shrugged, trying to summon indifference, but it came out hollow. "He doesn't need my drama distracting him." But the truth sat like a stone in my stomach: I'd pushed away the best thing in my life.

"Oh, Joss." Maddy's arms wrapped around me, pulling me in. I held myself rigid, clinging to my composure with white-knuckled stubbornness, because if I cried now, I wouldn't stop. "If you ever need to talk, I'm here," she murmured against my hair.

"Thanks, Mads." I pulled back with a weak smile, but she didn't return it. Her eyes were heavy with sadness. Gaz wandered over, took one look at me, then the two of us, and I swore he considered bolting. But Maddy shot a hand out and clamped onto his wrist.

"Can you get Jossi a cup of coffee, please?" Her tone left no room for argument.

"Uh, yeah. Sure." He scurried off, lingering too long by the machine.

"Thank you, Gaz." I cradled the steaming mug when it was finally set in front of me, pressing it close. The warmth seeped into my palms, but inside, I felt nothing but cold.

Avoiding Jake all week was a miracle in itself. Every time I caught sight of him across a hall, his shadowed eyes tracking me, I ducked away. He looked frayed, with dark circles beneath his eyes, tension carved into his jaw, but I refused to ask why. I couldn't afford to.

That nasty first year had started to smirk at me again if we passed in the halls. Like she had a secret I didn't know. I'd simply smile back, like I didn't give a shit about her. Her smile would falter, just a little, but her eyes were narrowed in hate.

I pushed her aside in my brain, just like everything else that didn't require my immediate attention.

The assessor's presence was like a knife to the throat. Her heels clicked against the stone floors, a sharp warning as she stalked the rows in class. She watched everything. Everyone. Professors snapped at us, their own nerves fraying under her scrutiny. Even Omara looked stressed, and that alone was enough to make me sweat.

Four second years vanished with her, and never came back. Then two third years. Another fourth year next. My skin prickled every time she passed me in the halls, though she always smiled, dipping her chin in greeting.

Somehow, that smile was worse than her scowl.

By the last class of the week, I was unravelling. My nerves shredded. I wanted to crawl into bed and vanish. Instead, I sat at my desk, staring down at ingredients for small smoke-and-flash bombs.

"Van Muntz!" Zane's shout cut through the room. We all turned to see him beaming at Jordan as if he'd just invented fire. "That was... amazing!"

Jordan shoved his glasses up his nose, trying, and failing, to hide his grin. "I accidentally tipped too much gunpowder in, and... *boom*," he said with a shrug, smug as hell. Zane laughed, clapping him on the back like a proud father.

"Boom indeed."

I sighed, glaring down at my tray. If I didn't make something explode soon, I'd fail. I reached for a vial, mind whirring with calculations, when a strangled curse ripped across the room.

Jordan's face was ghost-white, his glasses slipping down his nose. "Oops."

The entire room seemed to hold its breath.

Then the world punched me in the chest.

A concussive blast thundered through the air, hurling us off our seats. My scream tangled with others as I hit the floor, the world ringing, my body rattling like a rag doll.

"Take cover!" Zane bellowed, diving behind an overturned table as fire tore across the room. Alarms shrieked. Crimson warning lights strobed. Heat licked at my skin as I rolled for cover, glass shattering overhead in deadly shards. Screams filled the air, pain, panic, raw terror.

"Fucking Jordan always has to take it too far," Gaz snarled, crawling over broken glass toward Maddy. She yanked shards from her hair, wincing as they snagged her scalp.

"Do you think he survived?"

"No way." Gaz peeked over the table, then went rigid. His face drained of colour. "Shit."

I forced myself to look.

Blood painted the ceiling in a spray of red. Chunks spattered across the floor, the walls, and our desks. My stomach lurched. My hands shook.

"Oh, God."

"It's like he was vaporised." Maddy's voice was low, almost reverent. Then she added, "At least he went out with a bang."

"*Maddy*," Gaz snapped, but there was a tremor in his voice, his mouth twitching as though he couldn't decide if he was horrified or fighting a laugh.

"What? Everyone's thinking it."

I pressed my hands harder against the floor, my chest rising and falling too fast.

This school was *terrifying*.

Chapter Seventeen

I was curled on my bed with a book when someone pounded on my door hard enough to rattle the hinges.

With a groan, I peeled myself up, cold floorboards biting at my bare feet. Britney smiled when I cracked the door, and I blinked in surprise. She'd never come looking for me before.

"Maddy asked me to fetch you. A bunch of us are heading into town, and not to leave until you agreed to come."

"Oh." I hesitated, then forced a smile. "Alright. I'll just change and meet you there." She waved brightly, promising to wait by the bus. I tugged a jumper over my head, still smoothing it down when my door swung open without warning. Jake leaned against the frame, arms crossed, smirk carved across his face.

"Going somewhere?" His brow arched, like he already knew the answer. Of course he did, he always knew.

I rolled my eyes. "I'm guessing you're coming?"

"Yup." He fell into step beside me as I locked my door, not that it mattered. Locks apparently meant nothing here.

He was in a hoodie, black jeans, a cap shoved backward on his head. He looked like the average jock who should more worried about catching the game.

"Your friends are up to something," Jake muttered.

I glanced up, frowning. "Are you snooping on them too?"

"Because they're being targeted as well," he said flatly. "And Madeline is about to rope you in."

I shut my eyes, fighting a smile.

They're going to prank Imperial again. Our trip to their academy wasn't far off.

"Excellent," I murmured. "I look forward to it."

Jake scoffed but didn't tell me I shouldn't do it. That was something. But his words made me uneasy. Who was targeting them?

The bus rattled down into Greensville, full of singing, shouting, and someone throwing balled-up paper. Gaz volunteered to drive down, as long as someone else drove back.

Jake slouched at the back with the other fourth-years, laughing at something one of them said. He looked massive compared to them, his shoulders twice the size, his jumper straining at his arms.

Maddy was grinning at her phone, typing furiously. She wouldn't tell me what was going on, it was a surprise.

We tumbled out of the bus, scattering into groups. Maddy hooked her arm through mine, tugging me close as Gaz caught up, pushing between us and slinging his arm over both of our shoulders like he was claiming us.

They'd barely left my side since Alec and I broke up. When Maddy told him, Gaz had wrapped me in the biggest hug, and they hadn't let me be alone since. I was terrified of what I'd do when they left.

At the craft store, Maddy prowled the aisles, eyes sparkling far too brightly. She loaded our basket with glitter. Buckets of it. And spools of thread. And sewing needles. The cashier stared, utterly baffled. I couldn't help but laugh. Gaz lugged the bags toward the café where we always regrouped. My chest twinged as I sat down.

Last time we were here, Cooper was still alive. I shoved the thought away. Our group was smaller now, but still together. The bell above the door chimed, and a familiar voice sang out.

"Hey, y'all, room for one more?" Gabby strode in, heels clicking, golden hair swinging as she tossed it over her shoulder. My smile was instant. I rose and wrapped her in a hug, and she clung longer than usual.

"I'm sorry, sugar. It can't be easy."

"Thank you." I blinked hard, swallowing the ache in my throat. She settled beside me, espresso martini in hand within seconds, turning her sharp gaze on Maddy.

"Fill me in. All the gossip."

"Don't look at me," Maddy chirped, grinning. "Joss is the magnet for trouble."

Gabby's eyes glittered as they locked on me. "Oh, I'm well aware." She softened, tilting her head.

"How are you, after..." I stiffened. I never told Maddy or Gaz the full truth of Gabby nearly being blown up.

"I'm fabulous," she purred before I could finish my sentence, smoothing her skirt. "New office, better view. Much better." The waiter nearly dropped his tray when she winked at him.

Gaz leaned back, sipping his beer. "What was wrong with the old one?"

"I outgrew it," she said simply, smiling like she knew something none of us did.

Right. They definitely don't know then.

Her gaze sharpened, cutting straight through me. "Now. What the hell is going on with you and Alec?"

The breath was locked in my chest. My drink arrived, but I didn't touch it.

"I know you broke up," she went on softly, "but it's like the devil herself is chasing him." Her pity made my skin burn. I snapped my gaze up, fighting the tears clawing at my eyes.

"I didn't want to, Gabby. He can't keep worrying about me when he has his own job to think about. I don't want him distracted." I gave her a pointed look, and she nodded slowly. She knew my father's grip.

"I need you to tell me about-"

The bell chimed again and I froze.

Jake strolled in like he owned the place, his eyes locking instantly onto mine. Anger bolted through me, unwelcome and sharp. Gabby's gasp caught in her throat beside me, and I felt her nails dig lightly into my arm.

Gaz turned, grinning like an idiot. "Hey, Callahan. Come and sit with us."

My stomach twisted.

Oh, for fuck's sake, Gaz. My teeth ground together, and I could feel Gabby's stare like a laser burning into the side of my face. Jake pulled out a chair with infuriating calm, a ghost of a smile tugging at his lips.

"Thanks. Hope I'm not interrupting." His voice was low, dangerously velvet, his half-hooded eyes dragging over me. I wasn't fooled. Neither was Gabby.

"So, you must be Jake Callahan." She simpered, offering her hand with a smile sharp enough to cut.

"And you must be Gabrielle Statton." He didn't just shake her hand; he *kissed* it. "I've heard a lot about you."

Their eyes locked, a silent battle sparking between them.

"All good things, I hope," she purred, flashing teeth as she lifted her cocktail. We both know she was lying.

Alec would've told her everything.

The tension at the table thickened until Maddy's phone rang, making us all jump. After a quick exchange, she grabbed Gaz's arm and dragged him out, promising to be back. I barely inhaled before Jake slid into the empty space beside me, his arm brushing mine.

"I don't know if dear Alec passed on the message," he hissed at Gabby. His words were like a blade pressed to my throat. "But you need to *Back. The fuck. Off.*"

My shoulders hunched, chin nearly tucked to my chest.

"*Then leave her alone,*" Gabby growled, leaning forward, all claws now. "I'm not some pushover. I don't scare easily."

Jake didn't even blink. His eyes flicked to me, then away. "It's not just *your* life on the line." He let that hang there for a moment.

"Jossi gets hurt if you don't stop," he snarled. "If I'm ordered to kill you, she goes down with you in the middle of the night. Never to be seen again."

My stomach caved in. My breathing turned shallow. I glanced at Gabby, her golden face drained of colour.

"You expect me to simply forget?" she whispered, trembling with fury. "Forget about the bastard threatening to kidnap my friend?"

"It's bigger than this," Jake snapped, voice cracking with restrained rage. He exhaled slowly, leaning back an inch. "I've got better things for you to sink your teeth into." He dug into his pocket, then tossed a plastic zip bag on the table. I slapped a hand over my mouth to smother the scream clawing up my throat.

It was a finger. A severed finger.

Polished red nail still attached.

Gabby snatched it off the table with trembling hands, shoving it into her purse.

"And these." Jake slammed a stack of letters down, all addressed to me.

"You've been keeping my letters?" My voice cracked as I reached for them, but Gabby beat me to it.

"Trust me. You don't want to read them." Jake's voice softened, almost pitying, which somehow made it worse. "What you *do* want is to look into where Sera and Darius are. Find Fendi, and Jenna, too."

Gabby paled further, flicked a quick look at me, then back to Jake. "Why should I believe a word you say?"

He cocked his head to the side, predator-patient. "Maybe because you know who that finger belongs to. Linda ring a bell?"

I gasped, hands flying to my mouth as I whipped toward Gabby.

"She's been missing five days," Gabby whispered, clutching her bag like it was the only thing holding her together.

"The finger arrived two days ago," Jake said flatly, sliding a letter across the table. I leaned in, dread scraping through my veins.

My Dearest Jocelyn,
I have a little present for you!
She didn't want me to give it to you,
but I insisted you'd love it.
Linda sends her love, as do I, and
Darius.
Forever yours,

Sera xx

My stomach lurched. I gagged.

Gabby made a broken sound and snatched the letter, her hands shaking, tears welling.

"So," Jake leaned back, eyebrow cocked, his calm more terrifying than his fury. "We have a deal? You hunt them down and stop their little cronies from sneaking into the academy, and I'm not forced to kill you."

Bargaining lives like poker chips. How the hell did my life get here?

"Deal." Gabby's voice cracked, but her hand was steady as she extended it. Jake shook it firmly, eyes locked with hers.

"If you go back on this, I won't be able to stop my orders. I *will* come for you." His tone was light.

The promise in it was not.

"Alright." She exhaled shakily, then turned to me. "Joss, watch your back. Stay safe." She pulled me into a crushing hug, whispering fiercely in my ear, "You're protecting him. I get it. But Alec is unravelling."

I couldn't even reply. My throat was too tight. She patted my cheek, gathered her things, and was gone.

Which left me alone. With Jake.

He waved the waiter over and ordered food for both of us without even asking. And the terrifying part? I didn't care. He probably knew my order better than I did.

We sat in silence until Maddy and Gaz tumbled back in, disappointed they missed Gabby but already buzzing with talk of their prank. I barely heard them.

My mind was still on that letter. That finger.

"Hey, Joss. Are you good with a needle and thread?" Maddy asked around a mouthful of nachos, crumbs raining everywhere.

"Say it, don't spray it," Jake muttered, brushing the mess off the table.

I huffed a laugh. "Not really. Never tried."

"Well, you'd better learn." Maddy grinned, eyes sparkling with mischief. "We've got work to do."

I shook my head, bewildered, but I couldn't ignore the glitter of glee in her eyes.

After lunch, we hauled bags back to the bus. Jake helped with the heavy stuff, then dropped into the seat beside me. His shoulder brushed mine, solid and constant, his knee knocking against me with every turn of the road. I glued myself to the window, ignoring him. Trying to, anyway.

But my thoughts circled back to the letters. To *her*.

"What else was in them?" I whispered at last.

He didn't answer right away. When he did, it was low, his voice grim.

"You don't want to know, Jocelyn." His jaw clenched. "She's vile. Cruel. Petty. The kind of evil you can't unread. You're better off not knowing." His hand dragged down his face, then dropped into his lap. His eyes were shadowed, deadly serious. "She's going to make a move again, and soon."

Ice seeped through me. My arms locked around my ribs, holding myself together by force. My arm still stung at the movement, but I welcomed it. She was never going to give up.

"You're not allowed to go anywhere alone. Understand?" The order in his voice sparked a sharp flare of defiance.

"That's impossible-" I began, but his gaze cut into me, dark as midnight.

"If it's not me, then Davies. He's already agreed."

"No. You leave Gaz out of this." I whisper yelled, not wanting to draw any attention.

"He and Maddy both know what Sera is. They'd rather watch you than bury you."

"Keep them out of it!" My voice cracked with desperation. The thought of Sera's claws in them, unbearable. "Her fight is with me."

Jake leaned in, his voice dropping to a dangerous whisper.

"Sera doesn't care who she burns. She won't stop until we take her down."

My throat ached. "And how the hell *do* we do that? I'd love to stop living in constant fear. To stop flinching at shadows."

His jaw tightened. "I'm working on it. In the meantime, keep someone with you." He turned away, conversation over.

Got it.

Chapter Eighteen

Glitter was stuck in my hair, clinging to my skin in places it had *no business being*. And yet I couldn't stop grinning. Imperial Heights were going to *despise* us.

I didn't know how Maddy pulled it off, but she somehow got her hands on their uniforms for the big day. We were turning them into masterpieces of humiliation: crop tops with sequins, "*kick me*" stitched across the backs, skirts so short their asses would be on full display. But as we worked, Maddy grew quieter. Her joy slipped away, stitch by stitch.

"What's going on, Mads?" I prodded, setting down my sequins after finishing "*hot stuff*" across the back of one guy's shorts.

She didn't look up, shoulders tight. "You remember running into my mother that time we went into town?"

"Yeah?" My stomach dipped.

"Well..." She threaded her needle with a jerky tug. "She's the new dean at Imperial."

My jaw dropped.

She yanked her thread too hard, snapping it, and cursed, throwing the shirt aside.

"She wrote me a letter. Said she wanted me transferred to Imperial at the start of this year. But my dad kicked up such a stink, she wasn't allowed to."

"Oh my god." I scooted closer, grabbing her hands. "Thank the gods for your dad."

Her laugh was brittle. "Right? If she'd won, I'd have made sure I got expelled on the first day. I would never survive that hellhole."

I hesitated. "Are you sure you want to go through with this prank, then?"

Her eyes finally lifted to mine, watery but fierce. "More than ever. If she thinks she's going to scare me into submission, she's dead wrong. Imperial's going to regret the day they crossed us."

I was locking my door when Jake shut his, and I froze. There was blood, a large blotch, soaking the back of his shirt.

"Hey, Callahan," I called, and he turned slowly, one eyebrow cocked like I'd inconvenienced him.

"Yeah, Xanetto?" He drawled, crossing his massive arms.

"You've got a little something." I gestured to my shoulder. He glanced back, cursed, then unlocked his door again. In the next breath, his hand clamped around my wrist, tugging me inside.

"Hey!" I shoved at him, but his grip was iron. He slammed the door, then raked a hand through his hair. For once, he looked...frazzled. And then he stripped his shirt off.

By the gods. He was huge. Broad, scarred, muscles stacked like he was carved from stone. And damn it all, he was beautiful.

"Four assholes snuck in early this morning," he growled, trying and failing to peer over his shoulder. "Got three of them. The fourth's a knife-thrower. Slashed me before he bolted."

"For fuck's sake, sit down." My voice cracked. I pointed to his chair in the corner by his desk. He just stood there, arms crossed, watching me like he was testing whether I'd push back. "Don't make me force you, Callahan."

That got him. A slow shake of his head, a faint smirk, and then he sank into the chair, still tracking me with those infuriating eyes.

"First aid kit?" I raised both brows, hands on my hips.

He scoffed, but pointed at the bed. "Tried. Couldn't reach."

I snatched it up and knelt behind him. One look at his back and my throat closed. Scars crisscross every inch of skin, stories I'd never know carved into him like tally marks. The fresh slash on his shoulder was thin but ugly. I swallowed hard, force my shaking hands steady, and start cleaning the wound. His skin was hot under my fingertips, his muscles tensed beneath my touch.

I cleared my throat. "So...the other guy got away?"

"Unfortunately." His shoulders lifted in a small shrug. "Which means you're stuck with me until I take him out. I'm your shadow now."

I taped down the bandage with more force than necessary just to hide my shiver.

"All done." Before I could retreat, his hand snaked back, gripping mine.

"Thank you." His voice was low, and a little raw. "No one's ever...taken care of me like that before."

I looked up, and he was watching me, eyes stripped bare of all his usual armour. For once, he looked vulnerable.

My heart stuttered painfully. The moment shattered when a knock rattled the door.

"Come in," Jake called.

I ripped my hand away just as Gaz stepped inside, and froze. His gaze bounced between Jake, shirtless, and me, red-faced and guilty as hell.

"Joss is patching me up," Jake said easily, tugging on a fresh shirt.

I blurted the first thing that came to mind. "Jake's my bodyguard."

Oh gods, I wanted to *die*.

Gaz's face darkened. "What? Is this because of Sera?"

"Yeah. Everyone else thinks I'm a transfer. But I was hired to keep her safe," Jake said smoothly, already knotting his tie like he hadn't just detonated my life.

Gaz looked betrayed. "Why didn't you tell us?"

"She didn't know until she broke her arm." Jake cut in again, because apparently I didn't get a say. "Not to mention Fendi's assassins."

Gaz barked, "What?!" His anger scorched me, and I flinched.

"When I can't be with her, could you cover me?" Jake asked, grabbing his bag and slung it over his good shoulder.

"Yeah. Of course." Gaz shifted to my side, shaking his head. "You really do know how to attract trouble."

I tried to laugh, but it came out thin. "Trust me, I'd rather be invisible."

"Oh, and don't let her open mail unless I've checked it first," Jake added casually, already at the door.

Gaz frowned as he went to follow us. "Why?"

"Because the last one nearly killed her. Courtesy of Jenna."

"What the fuck?" Gaz snarled, seizing my arm. His eyes were ice, his grip too tight. "You didn't tell us?"

I stared at the floor, throat locked. He let go with a curse, dragging his hands through his hair until it stuck up in places.

"I didn't want to drag you and Maddy into my mess," I whispered. "You've got finals-"

"I'd rather flunk my last year than bury you." His voice was sharp and fierce.

Guilt gnawed me raw.

I didn't want to be the reason that they failed. They deserved better than that.

I turned the corner, and a group of third years passed, all gossiping and laughing, but a golden ponytail caught my eye. My heart near leapt into my throat as bright green eyes met mine.

I stumbled to a stop.

Sera was inside the academy. I wasn't losing my mind.

"Hey Jossi. It's *so* good to see you." She winked, and her fingers brushed mine as she kept walking. My hands shook as I turned around to watch her walk away. I mentally slapped myself and took off after them, but when I reached the corner, they'd scattered in all directions.

Did that really happen?

What the fuck is wrong with me?

A month slipped by, and things were starting to return to normal. Well, as normal as it could be here at Hellspire. I didn't see Sera again, but I swore Darius was in cooking class.

The assessor continued to walk the halls, stalking our classes with her little clipboard. Another two students disappeared. She hadn't paid me any more attention, thank goodness. But everyone was on edge, and Professor Wood more so than the others.

I'd been given a clean bill of health and could finally take the damn cast off. But they still had concerns about my memory loss after the accident. Sometimes when I woke, I'd completely forget where I was, and Maddy and Gaz would watch me with raised brows, worry pinching their mouths while I tried to remember simple things.

But I didn't have time to worry about that. Not with everything else going on.

Jake was a little distant, which suited me fine. He was constantly at my side, but he seemed too distracted to talk. I didn't miss the bags under his eyes.

I didn't sleep well either, knowing someone was out in the halls, waiting to take me out. I tossed and turned, wishing I could get a full night's sleep for the first time in months. At least now I don't take sleeping pills to get me to sleep. I'd learned that lesson the hard way.

I ran over the conversations that I'd had with my father before I returned to school, and why he was so adamant that I return. Matthew didn't agree at first, but my father had a silver tongue and was able to convince him that my staying here against all odds would work in my favour.

He had an iron conviction that I'd survive whatever was thrown at me, but I was starting to think something was going to eventually catch up with me.

Surely I'd used up my allotment of luck by now?

We were making our way back inside from another horrible escape and evasion class when a man I hadn't seen before stepped out onto the field and shook Colonel Fex's hand. He was tall, well-built and even from here, I could see a huge scar down the side of his face. His light brown hair was cropped short, military style. A shiver passed over me, making me roll my shoulders. Gaz and Maddy didn't take any notice of him, as they were bickering about who was better at escaping each other. But Jake stiffened beside me when he saw him.

"Ah, Mr Callahan. I've heard great things about you." The man approached us, and Jake came to an abrupt stop.

"Keep moving." He breathed under his breath, only loud enough for me to hear. I looked away and tightened the strap of my bag as I made my way off the field. But I looked over my shoulder to see the two having what looked like a serious conversation, and the fact that the man with the scar was staring right at me.

Unease soaked into me, anxiety flaring. I didn't know why, but I knew that man was bad news. And the fact that Jake knew who he was made me wonder if they worked together.

He'd given me a burner phone the other day, with just his number in it, in case I ever needed him when he wasn't around. Which was never. But I appreciated it, making sure to store it in my bag or pocket when I could get away with it. They were sticklers about us having our phones only on weekends.

I'd heard from Gabby and Matthew, but Alec had kept his distance. I didn't know if that was what I wanted or not. Sure, I wanted him to focus on his career, not the drama of his girlfriend. But I just wanted to talk to him, have him hold me. But I didn't deserve that. I'd pushed him away for a reason.

Chapter Nineteen

Professor Wood had us cleaning up the classroom, getting rid of any spare metal lying around. He wanted it nice and clean for when the assessor came back. She apparently made him nervous.

He made his way to my table and dumped a bucket in front of me.

"Jocelyn, do you mind taking this to the shredder? Take Sprouts with you for the muscle."

"Who?" I wrinkled my nose, having no idea who he was talking about. Wood pointed to the third year, who was happily carving something that looked like a wooden sword.

"Oh, Carl, alright then." I picked up the bucket of scraps and made my way over to his desk. "Hey, Carl, Professor Wood asked if you could help me throw this bucket of scrap into the shredder?"

"It's Mr Sprouts to you." He looked at me like I was the idiot.

"What?" I frowned, but quickly mastered my expression as he laughed.

"Nah, I'm just messing with you. I'll help." He chuckled and took one of the buckets from me.

We wandered along the dark hallway in silence, our boots scraping on stone the only sound. I'd never talked to Carl before. He preferred to keep to himself lately, but he was pretty clever in metalwork class. He could make some amazing figurines and was currently the best at making the bows and arrows. He hadn't said much since his friend Jordan exploded the other week.

I shivered every time I thought about it.

The disposal room was loud and eerie as we entered, the churning sound grating over my skin. I shivered as we made our way to the small steps, ending on a platform to the mouth of the machine.

"Is that everything?" He called over his shoulder as the shredder drowned out any other noise.

"Yeah. I've never used this thing. I didn't even know it was here." I eyed the growling beast. It was churning and grinding, constantly going. I felt the vibrations under my feet, as if the whole room were shaking.

"They call it Monkin the Muncher." He chuckled. I followed at a distance, wary of the giant shredder. "Great at disposing of...anything." He tipped the bucket of scrap in, the machine eagerly ate it up with a groan, sparks hissing. The hair on my neck prickled. I looked around, but nothing seemed out of sorts. I was about to watch Carl tip in the rest of the junk metal when I saw a shadow move out of the corner of my eye. I turned, falling back with a scream. A knife flew past my face so close that a sliced strand of hair floated down to the platform. Someone dressed in all black flew up the stairs, and if I didn't move now, I was about to die.

I ducked as another knife flew, and Carl yelled out in shock as it embedded in the stone wall behind me.

"What the fuck?" He cried, raising his fists as the attacker approached, taking the steps two at a time.

The man in black lunged, and I stumbled back as he swung for my ribs. Carl barreled into him before the blade connected, both men slamming against the railing. The machine howled, hungry and merciless, as I scrambled to my feet, my heart in my mouth.

Carl crashed backward into the railing. For a heartbeat, I thought he'd caught himself, then the man in black bent low, grabbed his legs, and *lifted*.

"Carl!" I shrieked, but it was too late.

The shredder gulped him down.

His scream was ripped away almost before it started. Blood geysered across the railing, hot against my face, coating my boots, painting the stone walls in violent red. The sound, gods, the *sound*. Bones splintering, flesh tearing, Monkin roared on like it couldn't tell the difference between man and metal.

I choked; bile burned my throat as the mist of his blood clung to me, sticky and hot.

The assassin straightened slowly, almost lazily, as he turned.

I couldn't move. My knees were jelly, my lungs locked. The shredder kept chewing, sparks and blood spitting in the air. One step. That was all he took before instinct exploded through me.

I bolted. But the floor was too slick. My boots skidded in Carl's blood, and before I could find my balance, an iron grip seized my waist. We went down hard, my scream ripping out of me, raw and desperate.

I thrashed, kicked, clawed, but he smashed his fist into my face, and white stars burst across my vision. The cry died in my throat. My ears rang as he hauled me by the ankle like I weighed nothing, dragging me toward the shredder's yawning mouth.

No. I won't go like this!

I clawed at the stone, slippery with gore, sobbing, shrieking as I writhed. He flipped me over, fist knotted in my shirt, hauling me upright. My legs kicked uselessly.

He was too fast, too strong. The ledge bit into the back of my thighs as he shoved me against it. The shredder snarled below me, as if it were hungry for more.

Then his hand clamped around my throat, and *squeezed*.

Black spots bloomed in my vision as I struggled for breath, and the world narrowed to the iron grip around my throat. My hearing fuzzed, heartbeat thundering in my skull. I clawed at his face, his chest, kicked at his legs, anything I could reach, but it was useless.

My lungs began to burn. My eyes fluttered shut.

I'm not going to go down like this.

One of my legs finally connected with the assassin's groin, with a satisfying grunt. He let go and fell to his knees, gagging. I lurched forward, blinking away the stars from my vision, taking in deep, gulping breaths. The assassin looked up, and I didn't need to think. I swung my fist back and cracked him on the side of the head, causing him to stumble to the ground. I kicked him in the chest as my anger fuelled me. My legs still felt weak, but it was him or me. And I'd prefer that it was him.

Then suddenly, I was falling.

He'd kicked my legs out from under me, and I hit the ground heavily, knocking the wind out of me.

My back hit the ground, and I swallowed my gasp. I didn't have enough air to spare.

The assassin crawled on top of me, straddling me as his hands slid around my throat.

I lashed out and poked him in the eyes as hard as I could. He swore and slapped me, but I wasn't going to stop. I was not going to die today.

I punched him in the throat, and he finally let go as he gasped for breath. I pushed him off and grabbed him by the scruff of his shirt and threw him as hard as I could.

The scream was high, broken, then cut off with a gurgle. Blood rained hot across my face, my body, soaking everything again. The sound of the machine chewing him down, grinding flesh and bone, was unbearable. I clapped my hands over my ears, fell to my knees and curled in tight, sobbing into the crook of my arm.

"Fuck sake, answer me!" Jake's voice cut through, sharp and ragged.

I blinked up at him. Panic was evident in his eyes.

"I'm… alright," I rasped, though my throat burned with every word. His curses rumbled against my ear as he hauled me up. I swayed, disoriented, before he lifted me up, but his grip was steady and solid.

I heard boots running when we reached the door, and I shut my eyes again, feeling nauseous.

A horrified gasp and a gag as they looked into the room.

"What the *fuck* happened here?" The voice sounded like Professor Wood's. I couldn't open my eyes, though. There was no way I was going to vomit on Jake.

"Please tell me she's alright?" A panicked voice sounded close, hands brushing my forehead.

"I'm taking her up to my room to make sure. I need to get this blood off." Jake's voice was sharp and dangerous, but I could hear the underlying panic.

"Let me know if I can help." Gaz had to clear his throat, but I could imagine his face was scrunched up, eyes wide as he took in the devastation of the room.

"Actually, get those two blades, then give them to me. Don't let anyone else see." Jake's voice was low, only loud enough for Gaz to hear over the roar of the shredder. It finally fell silent as Professor Wood shut it down, cursing under his breath.

"No worries. Can do."

"Thanks, Gaz." Jake started walking again as I heard Wood cursing under his breath, barking out orders to Gaz about getting the mess cleaned up. "Eyes open, Jossi." Jake barked, and I groaned. The swaying made me feel ill.

"I don't want to." I croaked, wincing when I tried to clear my throat. "I don't want to see the...blood." I gasped, and his arms tightened around me. We somehow made it to the bathroom without running into anyone, but then again, they should be in the middle of class.

Jake locked the door behind him and turned the shower on. By the time he lowered me, I could barely keep my eyes open. The sharp, metallic tang of blood clung to me, suffocating.

"Get it off," I sobbed, shuddering against the tiles. "I can't... just get it all off."

His voice was low and gentle. "Alright."

The world narrowed to his hands, careful as he peeled away blood-soaked clothes. He stripped me down with clinical efficiency, but I couldn't stop shaking. I opened my eyes once, and he was there, soaked in red, water cascading down his hair, his gaze fixed on the bruises rising on my throat. I took one look at the red water swirling and surrounding us and shut my eyes again.

"Everything. *Off.*"

His hands trembled as he unhooked my bra and lifted me slightly so he could slide my panties off.

"I need to wash your hair," he murmured, and I nodded because words wouldn't come. "Up you get." He pulled me to my feet, and I managed to stand, keeping my eyes shut as I concentrated on his hands.

The water ran hot over my scalp as his fingers worked through tangles, so gentle it made me cry harder. When he was finished, I blinked through the spray at him, shirt clinging to his body, covered in blood from carrying me.

"Get those off," I whispered. He stared at me, startled, then stripped down too, shedding red-stained clothes until there was nothing left between us but steam. He scrubbed himself clean, quick and rough, but when he faced me again, we were both bare, raw. Too damn close.

Something inside of him must have broken as he gripped my face and kissed me.

I thought that this was what I needed. I needed warmth and heat, but my stomach curdled.

He wasn't Alec.

I pushed him back, my chest heaving, lips tingling.

"I'm sorry." I gasped, attempting to gather my scattered thoughts. "I can't do this."

He pulled back, cupping my cheek with a hand that still trembled. "I'm sorry. I was too caught up in my emotions. You scared the hell out of me," he admitted, his voice low, raw. "I thought I was too late."

I didn't trust myself to answer. My throat burned, my body still shook.

Jake pressed a quick kiss to my hairline before standing back, strong arms scooping me up again. I didn't protest. I was wrung out, emptied, clinging to him because if I let go, I'd crumble.

He made a mad dash across the hall and into his room, where he lay me gently on the edge of his bed. The softness of his towel followed as he dried me with surprising care, patting my bruised throat last, his jaw tight with fury at the marks there.

Right then, I wanted nothing more than for Alec to be beside me. To wrap me up in his arms and hold me tight. But I didn't have the right to have those thoughts.

Once I was clean, Jake gave me a shirt to wear and tucked me beneath his sheets, smoothing the blankets over me like I was something fragile. My eyes stung, and for the first time since it all started, I felt safe enough to cry.

Jake sat on the edge of the mattress, brushing damp strands of hair from my face.

"Sleep, Jossi. I'll stay right here." His voice was steady now, quiet but firm, an anchor in the storm. "I'm not leaving you."

I wanted to argue, to tell him he didn't need to, that I could take care of myself, but the fight was gone out of me. I simply nodded, curling into the pillow. His weight shifted as he settled beside me, not too close, but close enough that I could feel the warmth of him, hear his steady breathing.

For the first time since being back here, I let myself believe it. That I was safe. That I was not alone.

And with Jake's quiet promise lingering in the dark, I finally let sleep take me.

Chapter Twenty

I couldn't believe I'd almost slept with my enemy.

With the man who was supposed to be my kidnapper.

What the fuck is wrong with me?

I rolled over, taking in the ridges of his scarred back as he slept, his chest rising and falling steadily and calmly.

I scrubbed my face with both hands, trying to banish the images of us naked under the spray, but they assaulted me with every blink. Better that than seeing Carl. Better that than seeing the assassin, his blood sprayed across the stone, their screams drowned by the shredder's endless hunger.

My body ached as I sat up, groaning softly. Instantly, Jake stirred, rolling toward me, those sharp green eyes snapping open, zeroing in on me like a predator. His gaze lingered on my face, then dipped to my throat. His jaw tightened, and something murderous shadowed his expression.

"I didn't know he got you in the face, too." His knuckles brushed my cheek, feather-light. He dragged a hand through his tousled hair, exhaling like he was trying to force himself to calm. "How do you feel?"

"Like shit. Everything hurts." I croaked and flopped back on the pillow, staring up at the ceiling. Anything to avoid those eyes. Anything to avoid thinking about what we almost did yesterday.

"Jocelyn." His voice sharpened, commanding. It forced me to look. With a grunt, I pushed up until I was leaning against the headboard, meeting his gaze. "I'm sorry about yesterday," he said, his tone clipped. "It shouldn't have happened."

"You can't always be there. And I'm alive."

"You nearly died, Jocelyn. They're getting too bold." He snapped, scrubbing at his face. "You probably should head out before someone sees you."

"Thanks for... taking care of me." The words tasted bitter. I threw back the covers, needing distance, making for the door. My hand landed on the handle, only to realise I didn't have my key.

I turned back, and of course, he was smirking in that infuriating way.

"I'll let you in." He winked, casual as sin.

I scowled as he rose, stretching, and moved toward me with that infuriating swagger. I followed him out into the quiet hall. He swung the door open for me with a grin, then slipped back into his own room. I stood there for a moment, forehead against the wall, forcing myself to breathe.

I almost *died* yesterday. Then I almost *slept* with my enemy. My life was so, so fucked.

The mirror didn't soften the truth. A black bruise bloomed across half my face, my lip split and swollen, my throat mottled in dark handprints. No makeup in the world would hide that. With a sigh, I stripped off Jake's shirt, tossed it onto the bed, and tugged on my own clothes. No way in hell would the Dean excuse me from class because I nearly died. He'd just be disappointed the assassin failed.

Slinging a bag over my shoulder, I locked the door behind me. Two sets of boots stopped close, and I froze before slowly turning. Maddy and Gaz. Their eyes went wide, shock twisting to horror in a single heartbeat.

"Oh, my fucking *God*." Maddy gasped, covering her mouth with a trembling hand. She gripped my shoulders before I could react and pulled me into a crushing hug. The sob tore out of me before I could stop it, raw and jagged. She shook as she cried against me, and for a moment, we just clung to each other.

When she pulled back, her eyes were red and watery. She swiped angrily at the tears. "Oh, Joss..." Her voice cracked. She inhaled, blowing out a shaky breath, trying to steel herself.

"I'll be alright." My voice wavered, my throat tight, tears threatening to spill again.

Then it was Gaz's turn. His arms were crushing, protective, like he was holding me together. But my anxiety thrummed under my skin, buzzing sharp and electric.

Everyone was going to stare. Everyone was going to ask questions.

A door clicked open down the hall.

Gaz let me go reluctantly, jaw clenching as he glared past me. I didn't have to look to feel Jake's eyes on me, raking over the bruises.

"The Dean just rang; he wants a word. About yesterday." His voice was low and hard, and it startled me. A reflex, being summoned to the Dean's office, had never ended well.

"Okay." My throat tightened. Maddy grabbed my hand, squeezing tight.

"I'll wait for you," she whispered fiercely.

I squeezed back but shook my head. "I don't know how long I'll be. Don't risk getting in trouble for me. Not while the assessor's here."

She bit her lip, then nodded, stepping back to Gaz's side.

Jake fell in at my shoulder, his voice pitched low enough for me alone. "He won't hurt you. The Dean."

"I know." My whisper came out jagged. "But my body doesn't care. It remembers." My hands trembled, my chest shuddered.

Jake stopped me with a hand on my arm. His grip was firm and unyielding. I snapped my eyes to his.

"What did Fendi do?" The growl simmered low in his throat.

"Nothing. Don't worry about it." I twisted, trying to shake him off, but his grip only tightened.

"*What did he do?*" Louder now. If he kept this up, people were going to hear.

"Nothing compared to what he did to the others. Forget it." I yanked, but he didn't let go.

"No fucking chance." His voice was steel, vibrating with fury. "Is that why he's hunting you?" He whisper yelled as my shoulders hunched up around my chin. He didn't need my answer to know. "When I find him, I'm going to drag out his pain for a very long time before I kill him." His chest heaved, his eyes burned into me like wildfire.

He let go, and I could suck in a breath, following him to the door leading up to the Dean's office. Up and up we climbed, my chest getting tighter and tighter the closer we got.

Jake knocked, and the Dean barked at us to enter. Jake held the door open for me, and I nodded my thanks. I was unable to meet the monster's eyes as I slowly sat in the chair before his desk, remembering too well what happened when I was here last time. I swallowed, my throat feeling dry.

"Someone needs to tell me what the *fuck* happened yesterday." He barked, not even bothering with a greeting. Jake's hands were white as he gripped the arms of his chair.

"An assassin attempted to take Jocelyn's life yesterday, and Carl was unfortunately caught at the wrong place, wrong time."

"And you took care of the assassin? Not leaving him alive for us to interrogate?" He growled, leaning forward on his desk, not even bothering to look at me. He pointed a finger, and I wanted to shrink in my seat.

"I should expel you, Xanetto. Two students have died because of you. You're a hazard to the school."

I felt frozen, my heart racing at the chance that he might throw me out.

What would I do if I were expelled? Father would be furious.

"Do I have to remind you who her father is? And how big of a donor he is for this school?" Jake leaned forward slightly, resting his elbows on his knees. "And not to mention the others pulling out if he does."

Orletta's eyes were narrowed on Jake, his lip almost curling over his teeth.

"She is a risk for the other students! They wouldn't be dying if not for *her*." He turned his hateful gaze to me, but I'd had enough of being treated like shit. I sat higher in my chair, shoulders back, chin up.

"It's not my fault that your niece has attempted to kill me twice in the last few months," I growled, gripping my hands together as he didn't even act surprised. He knew for sure.

"Perhaps the other students won't like to know that you're giving away our locations to third parties," I said, not hiding my anger anymore.

"Prove it." He snapped, but I didn't back down.

"It wouldn't take much convincing. You've made it well known that you favour your niece, and hate the rest of us. You haven't made your dislike for me a secret."

"Are you threatening me?" He leaned forward on his desk, and if looks could kill.

"Leave her alone, and we won't have any trouble." Jake snapped and I held my breath. This could go either way. His narrowed gaze swung between the two of us, hatred seeping from his pores, the silence stretched on.

"Get out of my office. I never want to see you in here again. Count yourself lucky, Miss Xanetto. You're on *very* thin ice."

He didn't need to tell me twice. I nodded my agreement and got the hell out of there, Jake right behind me. I tore down the stairs, taking two at a time. I needed to get out of that office. I caught my breath as soon as the door shut behind me with a thud.

"Come on, let's get something to eat. I'm starving." Jake set off to the cafeteria, and I followed with unease. Everyone was going to see my face and know what happened. They must be aware of Sera's threat to me now, but I still didn't want them staring and gossiping. I swallowed thickly as I walked through the doors, and the room fell silent in seconds. I gritted my teeth and took a tray. The ladies behind the counter sighed and handed me at least five chocolates. Bless them. I smiled, and they winked as I slipped them into my pocket. Whispers broke out as soon as I was on the move, and I sat heavily in my seat with Gaz and Maddy. But Jake sat beside me, and I turned to stare with confusion.

"What?" He mumbled around a mouthful of eggs. I shrugged and turned back to my yoghurt. My throat wasn't up for anything heavier today.

"So, anything else you need to tell us, Jossi?" Maddy asked casually as she leaned back in her chair, arms folded across her chest. I felt guilt settle like a stone as I met her hard eyes. I hated myself for lying to my friends, but I was trying to keep them safe. They didn't deserve to be dragged into my shit-storm.

I could feel Jake tense slightly beside me. I *could* tell them everything, but then I didn't think that would end well for them or me. It would probably end up with me bound and gagged in the back of Jake's car, and my friends would either be with me or dead.

I cleared my throat, but winced when it burned. Jake softly growled beside me.

"Nope. Other than Sera and Darius chasing me, and Fendi, and Jenna, and maybe Paul too."

Their eyes widened as I listed all the names of people who were currently hunting me. I looked back down at my breakfast and twirled the spoon, hating how the whole room was still staring at me.

"Then we need to buck up and make sure they know not to mess with us." Maddy cracked her knuckles, and I smiled slightly.

"I'm so damn thankful I have friends like you guys." I blinked away my tears, hating how emotional I was at the moment. She just winked at me, and Gaz grinned, waving his spoon in the air.

"We need to do something to take your mind off all this. And I know just the thing." Gaz and Maddy shared a look, and I knew it was going to be chaotic.

Chapter Twenty-One

A knocking at my door woke me around three in the morning.

I didn't answer it, and they didn't knock again, but I saw something white beneath my door. As if the person slid something under there.

I tore the envelope open with shaking hands. I chastised myself for being scared of envelopes and letters.

I've been wanting to repay you for the fart gas. And I think I know how.

You see, it's not that hard to smuggle someone into the school. My room is plenty big enough for a few extra people. The kitchen doesn't notice when I steal extra food at night.

But Sera wanted me to tell you that you're looking a little peaky. Aren't you sleeping very well?

Perhaps she could give you something to dull your pain.

I like her. I think we could be friends.

I didn't stay in my room. I ran straight to Maddy's. I didn't care that it was three in the morning. There was no way I wanted to be by myself right now.

She answered on the second knock, her lion's mane sticking up in every way. But she paled when she saw me, pulling me into her room before locking the door.

"What the hell happened?" She breathed, pulling me down beside her on the bed.

I didn't speak, only shoved the letter into her hands. Her eyes widened with each sentence.

"Joss. She's got them in the school?" Maddy looked horrified.

Her expression mirrored just how I was feeling.

"That fucking little brat." She snapped, standing up to punch at her boxing bag chained to the ceiling, leaving it swinging. "Have you seen any of them?"

My silence made her snap her head toward me, eyes narrowed. "You have, haven't you?" She took one step toward me, and I got to my feet, holding my hands out.

"Hey, I thought I was going insane!" I snapped, crossing my arms across my chest. "They would be there one minute and then gone the next." I ran my hands through my hair, feeling like a fucking mess. "You would too if you saw them standing there in their school uniform, then gone the next blink." I mashed my lips together to stop the burning in my throat. But Maddy wrapped me in a hug instead, holding tight.

"Looks like we need another fart bomb to draw the cockroaches out."

We had two weeks until we went to Imperial Heights, and the school was buzzing.

This year, we were doing an equestrian-style challenge, in which selected students had to ride through the grounds, over obstacles, and shoot targets with a bow and arrow. The most targets shot by a school won.

Professor Kiyoko and Panchette had selected the students, as not everyone knew how to ride a horse. I was one of the lucky few. I hadn't ridden in years, but we had been training the past few months, and I was actually looking forward to it. Of course, Jake was too. What couldn't that man do?

We were sneaking out tonight to set up the pranks, and I knew that Jake would come. Wherever I went, he followed.

The night air bit at my skin as we crouched in the shadow of the outer fence. Imperial Heights Academy looked more like a fortress than a school, with high walls, sleek glass buildings glowing faintly in the dark, and the occasional sweep of a flashlight from the patrolling guards. Their crest gleamed above the entrance gate, polished and perfect, daring us to even try.

"Why the fuck am I here?" Jake muttered.

"Because," Maddy whispered with glee, "you love us."

He shot her a flat look, the kind that could probably reduce lesser mortals to ash. Maddy just grinned wider, hugging the duffel bag strapped to her chest like it was treasure.

I smirked, tugging my hood lower over my face. "You can't complain now. You signed up for this the second you started babysitting me."

Jake grumbled something that sounded suspiciously like '*lunatics*', but he crouched lower anyway, scanning the grounds like he was gearing up for war. Gaz, meanwhile, was smug as hell, pointing toward the far corner of the fence where the shadows looked thick and ominous.

"Guard rotation leaves a gap every six minutes," he whispered. "They sweep, turn the corner, and we slide in right there. Easy."

Jake snorted. "You've never done an actual infiltration in your life, have you?"

Gaz's grin only widened. "Nope. But I've watched every spy movie. So basically an expert."

Maddy muffled a laugh with her hand. Even I cracked a smile, despite the hammering of my pulse. This was dangerous and stupid and reckless as hell, but it was also exhilarating.

When the flashlight beam finally swung away, we sprinted. Gravel crunched under my boots, the only noise in the still night. Jake reached the fence first, scaling it with an ease that was frankly unfair. He reached down and grabbed my wrist before I could even jump.

"Up you go, Xanetto," he muttered, practically yanking me off the ground. I scrambled for footing, but his grip was iron, hauling me up like I weighed nothing. My stomach flipped at what we were about to do.

Maddy came up next, Gaz boosting her by the ass until she was cursing him and laughing in the same breath. Then Gaz himself vaulted up, landing beside us with all the subtlety of a tank.

"See?" he whispered, grinning like a lunatic. "Easy."

"Shut the hell up," Jake growled, but a grin tugged at his lips as he went back to scanning again. We slipped across the manicured lawns like shadows, ducking low whenever a light swept past. My nerves screamed with every step, my heart pounding so hard it hurt. But somehow, impossibly, we made it to the locker room entrance without setting off alarms or being spotted.

Inside, the smell hit me first: disinfectant, sweat, and that faint chemical tang of cheap deodorant. Fluorescent lights buzzed overhead, casting everything in pale, unforgiving brightness. My stomach flipped again as we pushed inside, duffel bags slung over our shoulders.

The room was neat, orderly, rows of lockers polished and gleaming. The Imperial Heights uniforms were already laid out, pristine white and navy, crisp and folded with military precision. They looked like costumes more than clothes.

And in a few minutes, they were going to look very, *very* different.

Maddy practically skipped to the racks, her grin unholy as she pulled one of the helmets out of her bag. The fluorescent light caught the glitter instantly, making the bejewelled dick and balls sparkle like they were blessed by the gods themselves.

"Oh my god," I hissed, clapping a hand over my mouth to stifle my laugh. "Maddy-"

"Beautiful, isn't it?" she whispered reverently, turning the helmet so the sequins glared like disco lights.

Gaz doubled over, wheezing. "That's... that's a masterpiece. Michelangelo would be proud."

"God, you guys are like children," Jake muttered, but his mouth twitched like he was fighting a smirk.

One by one, we replaced the uniforms - sequined crop tops, shorts stitched with '*KICK ME*' and '*HOT STUFF*' across the asses, and the crowning glory: glitter-dicks adorning every helmet.

The air was thick with stifled laughter, my ribs aching from holding it in. Even Jake's jaw twitched as he placed one helmet back on the rack.

We were almost done when footsteps echoed in the hall.

All of us froze.

My stomach plummeted. Maddy's eyes went wide, and Gaz swore under his breath. Jake was already moving, grabbing my wrist and yanking me down behind the row of lockers. I crashed against him, his chest hard and hot under my cheek as he pulled me close.

"Quiet," he mouthed, his breath ghosting against my ear.

The footsteps drew closer, slow and casual. Hopefully, just a janitor. Keys jingled as they hummed to themselves, pushing a mop bucket into the room. I held my breath so long my lungs burned. My heart thundered against Jake's chest, and I was painfully aware of how close we were, his hand gripping my waist, my body pressed against his in the suffocating silence.

The janitor mopped for what felt like a goddamn eternity, whistling off-key, completely oblivious. My nails dug into Jake's arm, and I felt his muscles tense as though he was coiled to strike if the man came any closer.

Finally, *finally*, the janitor left, the door swinging shut behind them.

We all exhaled at once.

"Fuck me," Gaz whispered, wiping sweat off his brow. "I nearly pissed myself."

"Would've made it smell better in here," Jake muttered darkly, but his grip on me lingered a moment too long before he let go. We finished the job in record time after that, every laugh muffled, every movement quick and efficient. The last helmet went back on the rack, glittering obscenely under the lights, making sure to turn them around, so they wouldn't be discovered until it was too late.

Maddy stepped back, her eyes shining. "They're going to hate us so much."

"They already hate us," I whispered, grinning despite the terror still hammering in my chest. "This is just the cherry on top."

"More like the dick on top," Gaz snorted, and I had to clap a hand over my mouth again.

The uniforms were swapped. We could have stopped there. We *should* have stopped there. But no, because we're Hellspire, and stopping at mildly humiliating Imperial Heights would be too easy.

"Phase two," Maddy whispered, dragging the second duffel bag onto the bench with a grin that belonged to a mad scientist.

I eyed the zipper with suspicion. "Mads, please tell me you didn't-"

She unzipped it with a dramatic flourish, and I nearly choked on my own tongue.

Glitter bombs. Dozens of them. Mason jars rigged with balloons of fine powder, spray-painted tins with wire triggers, even a fucking leaf blower filled with rainbow confetti. The bag looked like a unicorn had overdosed on acid and exploded inside.

"Oh my god," Gaz breathed reverently, holding up a jar like it were a holy relic. "This is... this is art."

Jake pinched the bridge of his nose. "This is going to get us expelled."

Maddy chuckled, stuffing a jar back into the bag. "C'mon, we don't have all night. Classroom block first."

My stomach flipped, adrenaline roaring back to life as we crept out of the locker room, duffels heavy against our shoulders, our hoodies up covering our heads. The Imperial Heights buildings loomed around us, cold steel, perfect glass and pristine halls. It was the polar opposite of Hellspire's chaotic stone spires and shadowed corners. Here, everything was sterile. Controlled. Which made the thought of them choking on glitter bombs all the sweeter.

We slid through a side door that Gaz had jimmied open with a bobby pin, and I instantly felt like we were committing an actual felony. The hallways were spotless, the walls lined with smug portraits of Imperial champions past. Their eyes seemed to follow us as we padded down the corridor, ducking into the first classroom we found.

"What I wouldn't do for a permanent pen right now," Gaz murmured under his breath as he shook his head at their pompous expressions.

Maddy cracked open a desk drawer and slipped a glitter bomb inside like she was planting evidence at a crime scene. Gaz stuffed another behind the teacher's podium.

I shoved one into a supply cupboard, the jar rattling as I eased it onto a shelf of neatly stacked books.

"Imagine them opening this in front of the assessor," Maddy whispered, grinning so wide I thought her face might split. "*Pfff*. Boom. Glitter facial."

Gaz nearly cackled, but Jake clamped a hand over his mouth just as footsteps echoed outside.

We all froze.

The hallway lights flicked on, washing through the crack under the door. I pressed myself flat against the wall behind the door, heart thundering, throat so tight it ached as I held my breath. Jake's hand shifted from Gaz's mouth to my waist, steadying me, his body coiled and ready. The footsteps drew closer. A voice hummed.

Not again. Not another janitor.

The handle rattled.

Maddy clamped her hands over her mouth, eyes wide with manic glee and terror. Gaz mouthed something that looked suspiciously like '*we're fucked*'.

They poked their head inside, did a quick sweep of the room, then shut the door. The footsteps faded. The hall light clicked off. We didn't breathe until a full minute had passed.

"Bloody hell," I whispered, shoving at Jake's arm until he let go. My pulse still hammered in my throat.

We hit three more classrooms, each one faster than the last, tension ratcheting higher every time a pipe creaked or the wind rattled a window. My nerves were frayed raw, but Maddy was in her element, humming under her breath as she slipped bombs into lockers, bags, even a vent. The cafeteria was next, where we deposited most of our cache. Bring on breakfast time when their timers went off.

"Imagine the janitor turning the air-con on," she whispered gleefully. "They'll be coughing up sparkles for weeks."

Next stop: the bathrooms.

That was where things got truly insane.

The Imperial Heights boys' bathrooms were through a maze of sterile hallways, and half the bedrooms still had lights under the doors as we crept past. My pulse spiked at each creak in the floorboards, Maddy smothering giggles with her sleeve while Gaz tiptoed like he thought he was in a cartoon. Jake kept us moving with sharp hand signals, silent and deadly serious, which only made it funnier every time Gaz tripped over nothing.

We slipped into one bathroom with the door ajar, empty showers and toilet stalls. We wasted no time in hiding them in the cisterns, above the shower heads, in the cupboards.

I stuffed one into a rubbish bin, biting back laughter as I imagined some smug Imperial prick throwing rubbish in there and setting it off.

But then the hallway door slammed.

We froze.

Voices and laughter. Two guys, chatting away, completely oblivious and heading straight this way.

Not again. I don't know how much more of this I can take. Why isn't everyone in bed like they should be?

Maddy's eyes went wide. Gaz mouthed *shit, shit, shit.*

Jake didn't even hesitate. He shoved us all toward the closest shower stall, herding us inside like panicked cats, and silently closed the door. The voices came into the room. The door creaked into two toilet stalls. The guys continued talking about training, about the competition, about some poor bastard failing drills as they took a piss, one of them farting so loud it echoed through the room.

We stood pressed together in the cramped bathroom, barely daring to breathe. I was smashed between Maddy's shoulder and Jake's chest. Gaz was wedged half on top of the tiny bench, trying not to snort as he shook with laughter.

Minutes crawled like years.

One of the guys laughed at the sound. "Hey, did you hear that fart?" He chuckled; the sound of his shit hitting the water followed. I wanted to gag.

"Good one." Snorted the other. "Listen to this," I swore that I could hear him grunt as he forced his fart out, and the sound squeaked out like when you let air out of a balloon.

Both guys snorted in laughter.

Maddy's eyes blazed in the dark, and I nearly lost it, pressing my fist against my mouth to stifle the hysterical laugh bubbling up as we all began to shake.

Eventually, *finally*, the boys left, the bathroom door slamming shut again as they snuck off to the kitchen for fresh biscuits. We waited another full minute before Jake cracked the bathroom door open.

Clear.

"Out. Now," he hissed, shoving us back into the hall.

We didn't need to be told twice. Maddy had her nose pinched between two fingers as her sparkling eyes met mine. I had to bite my tongue to stop myself from blowing this whole thing.

By the time we made it to the equipment storage shed, my nerves were shredded. I wanted out. But Maddy insisted we hit it too, because what's an equestrian competition without weaponised glitter?

She shoved jars into saddlebags, Gaz lined helmets with powder packets, and I rigged a bomb inside the quiver rack, every arrow now coated in glitter, waiting to happen.

Jake didn't even help; he just stood by the door like a furious watchdog.

When the final bomb was planted, we slipped toward the back door, nerves stretched tighter than violin strings.

A dog barked as we slipped across the lawns, the sound echoing through the night. A flashlight beam cut too close, sweeping over the grass just meters away. My pulse skyrocketed, my lungs tight.

"Move," Jake hissed, "faster," pushing me forward.

We sprinted for the fence, my boots slipping on the dewy grass. Maddy scrambled up first, Gaz boosting her again, both of them laughing nervously. Jake grabbed me around the waist and all but tossed me upward. My stomach lurched, my hands scraping against the metal, but I clung and hauled myself over.

By the time we hit the ground on the other side, I was breathless, my legs shaking. We ran until the lights of Imperial Heights were nothing but a glow behind us, until the night swallowed us whole.

We collapsed in the shadows of the trees, gasping, laughing, the adrenaline still sizzling in my veins.

"Best. Mission. Ever." Gaz wheezed, flopping onto his back, a fist pump in the air.

Maddy's grin was wild and triumphant. "They won't know what hit them."

Jake leaned against a tree, his chest rising and falling, eyes sharp and bright even in the dark.

"You're all insane," he muttered, ending in a dark chuckle.

And for the first time in what felt like forever, I laughed.

Really laughed.

Chapter Twenty-Two

The assessor finally left, moving on to Imperial Heights next, and we couldn't hide the sniggers as Dean Orletta shook her hand, thanking her for her time. I just hoped she was still there for when the glitter bombs went off.

The first-year continued to wink as she passed, not caring that people were still calling her Polly Poopy Pants. She was riding on the high of knowing that Sera and Darius were doing their best to torment me. Jake obviously didn't know about them, as he never said anything. And I didn't want to share that knowledge either. I didn't want to talk to him more than necessary.

Turnbull would smile and politely greet me each time we passed in the halls, but I could feel his eyes on me, like a physical weight. All the students thought he was cool, the fun teacher. He let them play games and pranks on each other. But there was something about him that didn't feel right.

Two whole weeks passed without anyone trying to kill me, but Jake looked tired and on edge. He fitted locks to my window and extra locks on my doors. But he still had his own keys to get into my room whenever he pleased.

I couldn't let myself forget that he was my enemy. His people wanted to kidnap and use me as ransom for my father. I had no idea what they actually wanted, and Jake wouldn't tell me anything. I had no idea if Alec had caved and given them any information. I wanted to ask him, but I was scared at the same time. I missed him like crazy. Even Matthew had mentioned that Alec wasn't himself and was snappy and short-tempered. I didn't want to tell my brother that I had broken things off. I didn't need him to tell me what a stupid thing it was. I just had to live with my decision until things calmed down.

The library was one of my last sanctuaries. It was a place that hadn't seen death or torture. Plus, the others deemed it a safe place too.

I nestled down into the beanbag, a book in my lap as I studied for Disguises 101.

We were told to have something prepared at all times, so we would be confident should we need to use it. It could even be something as simple as makeup, a wig, glasses, and a hat. I had a small bag inside my backpack with those essentials. With everything happening in my life at the moment, I might need them sooner rather than later.

A scuff of a shoe sounded a couple of aisles away. I didn't react, knowing it could be any student in here for the same reason. But the hairs on the back of my neck prickled. I slid the knife from my thigh and into my palm, gripping it tight.

The worst thing about beanbags was that they were almost impossible to get out of. Especially if you were trying to be quiet. I tried to move, but it was so loud that the beans *shushed*. I stopped and racked my brain, trying to think of anything as the steps crept closer.

A whistle started quietly, but it was eerie, and I swore that I'd heard it before. I craned my neck to try to see anything, but being so low to the ground, legs and feet were the only things I could see.

A pair of steel-capped boots stopped two aisles over, but they were facing my direction.

No one that I knew of wore those kinds of shoes here. They weren't uniformly appropriate.

I slid down into the bag, gripping my blade tight as the boots started to move again, the whistling getting louder. But what I found odd was that there weren't any other noises in here. Even a library wasn't completely silent all the time. No pages being turned, no soft whispering, no sniffles or sneezes.

Shit, shit, shit.

This person wasn't trying to be quiet. They knew we were the only two in the room.

The boots stopped in the aisle right next to mine, as if they were trying to decide their next move. I was low enough to the ground that I slid off the beanbag and onto the floor with minimal sound. There was an empty shelf to my right, and if I were quiet, I could slide through it and end up behind the person.

I made sure to keep my breathing quiet, seeing as I was loud, apparently.

The boots started to move, and so did I. I slid through headfirst, glad that the shelves were metal-coated and slippery, not caring that I was collecting years of dust. I pulled myself out slowly, watching the boots almost at the end and about to turn the corner. He was still whistling, so he wouldn't hear me, anyway. I pulled the rest of my body out and crouched on the floor, gripping my knife.

The boots turned the corner, and I crept closer, keeping low so he wouldn't see me between the shelves.

"Where are you, darlin?" He cooed, and my stomach did the horrible flip-flop thing.

It was Darius.

I stood to my full height and walked around the corner. I wasn't going to hide like a coward. I'd had enough of being scared and weak. I was going to bring this asshole down.

He was rifling through my bag on the ground, unaware that I was right behind him.

I kicked him in the ass. He stumbled, landing on his hands before whipping around to snarl at me.

"I would say it's lovely to see you, Darius. But I'd be lying." I smiled as he pushed to his feet, standing to his full height.

Shit. I forgot how tall all these Hyde men are.

"Jocelyn." His thumbs hooked into his belt loops, looking a little too casual. I should have made sure we were alone. He could be here to distract me while Sera snuck up behind me.

"Don't worry, sweetheart, it's just you and me here. Sera, let me finally get my revenge." He must have seen the panic in my eyes. He took a step forward, and I took one back.

I did know how to fight, but he was a very large and very angry man.

It would take all of my skills to take him down.

"But you don't realise that I'll also be getting my revenge for what you did to my sister and mother." I snapped, gripping my blade so hard my hand ached.

"Come on then, let's play." He grinned as nerves shot through me.

I'm strong. I can do this.

He lunged, coming at me so fast for someone so tall. I ducked his swing, rolling past him as he spun. But his boot kicked out and collided with my head, sending me sprawling. Stars flashed across my vision, but I rolled away just as his foot stomped the ground beside me. I slashed out with my blade, cutting the back of his calf. He grunted, reaching down to grab the front of my school shirt. I kicked as he lifted me, hitting his shins before he slammed me into the shelves, pain cracking through my head and back.

"You can't win this," he growled, slamming me again hard enough that books fell off the shelves.

I aimed my knee and hit him in the balls, obviously not hard enough, as his fist crashed into the side of my face. Pain flared, hot and fierce as I tried my hardest to blink past it. One of his hands wrapped around my throat as he pressed his face so close to mine, his hot breath ghosted across my face.

"I will enjoy watching the light leave your eyes. Payback for killing my brother, and turning the other one against me." His hand squeezed, and dark spots dotted my vision. But I wouldn't go like this. I wasn't going to let this asshole kill me.

I moved, swift and deadly, as I hit my target. He grunted, letting go of my neck as he pushed away from me and looked down. A red stain began spreading out over his white school shirt.

"You fucking bitch." He seethed, but I didn't give him the chance to come at me again. I swung, smashing my fist into the side of his jaw, sending him crashing to the floor.

"Say hi to Damian for me." I jumped onto his chest, ripped out my dagger, and plunged it into his heart.

He coughed, blood leaking out of the corner of his mouth as he glared at me, his hatred so hot I could almost feel it.

"Fuck...you." He spat, but his eyes fluttered, and his head rolled to the side.

I sat there for a moment, trying to draw enough air into my lungs.

I'd just killed someone. But I wouldn't lose sleep over this one. He deserved to die.

I jumped off and packed up my things, ignoring the way my heart was hammering. I had to get this asshole out of here without anyone seeing me. That was going to be the biggest challenge of all.

I knew there was a window across the room; it opened out onto the grounds...the same one that Alec snuck me through to retrieve my letter last year.

It was just whether I could lift his heavy ass over my shoulder and outside.

I was willing to give it a go.

I wiped my bloody hands on my shirt and got to work. I slowly dragged him, grimacing about the trail of blood I left in my wake. I should have called someone, but right now I wanted to do this for myself. I was sick of other people stepping in and doing everything for me.

I don't know how long it took me to get him up to the windowsill and out, but eventually, he fell outside with a meaty thud. I turned back to the carnage behind me, thinking.

I dug through my bag, pulled out the burner phone, and rang Jake.

"Jocelyn." His tone was urgent, and I knew he was going to be *so* pissed. "What's wrong? Are you still in the library?" It sounded like he was moving, no doubt to come and find me.

"I'm fine...there's just a little mess I might need your help with." I bit my lip, for some insane reason, I wanted to laugh.

"Jocelyn," Jake snapped, "tell me what the *fuck* happened."

Yup, he was definitely moving now. I could hear his feet slapping on the floor.

"I've taken care of it; there's just a bit of a mess I'm sure the librarian wouldn't appreciate." As much as I didn't like the snooty bitch who ran it, she didn't deserve to have a trail of blood on her carpets.

"For fuck's sake, tell me!" he barked, and I rolled my eyes.

"So grumpy. I'll be making sure the evidence is gone. I'm sure you'll catch up with me later to tell me off." I hung up, knowing I was just baiting him, but right now, I had more pressing matters to attend to. The phone rang and rang, but I shoved it back into my pack and climbed out the window.

I looked down at the bloody mess of Darius Hyde and didn't feel one ounce of sadness or shock. I shook out my hands and started the long journey to the incinerator.

I'd never been so thankful that it was outside and away from classrooms and students.

What I didn't appreciate was that the rain thought now was a good time to bucket down, drenching me instantly and making Darius ten times heavier with his soaked clothes.

But somehow, I'd managed to drag him through the grass and into the cover of the incinerator.

Just as I was lifting him, a shadow filled the doorway. I spun, heart in my throat, thinking I was about to be caught in the act, but I puffed out a breath as Jake's furious face glared at me.

"Don't just stand there and snarl; help me get this asshole in." I snapped, my strength wavering as my arms shook. He rolled his eyes and stomped forward, taking him by the legs and helping me toss him into the giant pit of flames.

I hastily stepped back as his clothes slowly caught fire and started to burn.

Jake's hand wrapped around my arm and spun me to face him, his face red from anger.

"Don't start with me!" I pointed at his face, forcing his hand off me. "He snuck up on me in the library, and I didn't have time to stand there and call you. I took him down, and that's all that matters." I crossed my arms over my chest, aware that the rain had soaked my shirt until you could see my bra.

His jaw ticked, and he looked away for a moment before taking a deep breath, then blowing it out.

"Are you hurt?" He was trying to keep his tone calm, and it took all my remaining strength not to laugh at his pained expression.

I was seriously losing my fucking mind.

"No, he tried to strangle me, but my blade found his stomach and heart." I shrugged, knowing my face would be a kaleidoscope of colours tomorrow.

His jaw ticked, but he raised his hands to my face, his fingers gentle as he turned my head side to side, assessing me.

"Well done. But it looks like you might have a concussion. Wait here while I fetch some kerosene, to hurry things along." Jake ran off into the darkness, returning over ten minutes later with a large fuel drum, which he threw right into the mouth of the incinerator.

We ducked right as the thundering boom shook the air around us, flames spewing out of the mouth. I knew that people would have heard it and possibly come to investigate.

"Come on then, help me finish cleaning." He sighed, rubbing a hand through his hair before turning on his heel and storming away.

I threw one last glance at the incinerator and was glad to see that Darius Hyde was swiftly disappearing into ash.

Chapter Twenty-Three

We made quick work of cleaning the blood off the dark carpets, glad they weren't white or cream. We replaced the books and made it look like nothing had happened.

I was surprised when Jake left me alone to shower and head to bed just after midnight. What surprised me the most was that I slept really well.

The next morning, I wore makeup, hiding most of my bruises. I was starting to get really good at covering them. The day passed as usual, but it felt like a weight had been lifted from my shoulders.

One down, and so many more to go.

Gaz flicked his lighter at dinner, eyes darting around the room every few seconds, as if he were searching for someone. I sat down with a sigh, my body aching from last nights extra-curricular activities.

"What's up?" I leaned my arms on the table, eyes narrowed on him as he fidgeted.

"Maddy's not here. I haven't seen her since she left class." He muttered, pushing his chair back with a screech. I was about to get to my feet when a fourth-year student stopped beside me, handing me a letter. I opened my mouth to ask who it was from when they darted away, their face slightly pale. I frowned, turning it over when Gaz snatched it from my hands.

"Don't even think about it." He grumbled, using his thumb to tear the envelope open. I didn't bother with a reply, there was no convincing Gaz when he made up his mind. No wonder Jake and Gaz got along so well.

His eyes scanned over the words, his face getting whiter and whiter with every sentence. My stomach plummeted as his hands began to shake.

"Gaz?" I whispered, coming to stand beside him so I could read the letter.

JOCELYN XANETTO

I HATE YOU SO MUCH IT BURNS MY INSIDES EVERY TIME I THINK ABOUT YOU.

WHICH IS ALL THE FUCKING TIME.

<u>WHY THE FUCK WON'T YOU DIE???</u>

IF YOU WANT YOUR PRECIOUS MADELINE, COME AND GET HER.

I'M NOT GOING TO WAIT AROUND LONG. TEN MINUTES IS ALL I'M GIVING YOU.

THEN I START TAKING HER APART, PIECE BY PIECE. THEN DAVIES IS NEXT.

I'M IN THE TREES, WHERE I NEARLY HAD YOU ONCE BEFORE.

COME ALONE, OR I'LL KILL THE FERAL BITCH.

YOUR FAVOURITE DEAN.

Oh, god. This can't be happening.

I could see where the pen had gone through the paper in his rage. No wonder Gaz was shaking, deathly pale.

Fendi's got Maddy.

"I need to go. *Now.*" I snarled, walking to grab my bag to swing it over my shoulder, when Gaz stopped me with a hand on my arm.

"You're not going out there alone." He snapped in my ear, holding onto me with a death grip. "Callahan will kill me if you go out there at all."

"Fuck Jake. I'm not going to let Maddy get hurt because of me. So you can either let go, or I'm going to make you."

I growled, keeping my voice down, but I could feel eyes on us. We were making a scene.

"And you think I want her with that monster? I'm coming with you, but we're bringing Callahan." He stepped closer, and I wanted to punch him hard enough that he'd let go, but I knew that wouldn't work.

He was infuriated and scared.

Just like me.

I scrunched the note into my pocket just as Jake marched through the door. Before he could make it ten steps, we were before him, and he instantly saw the change in us.

"What's happened?" He murmured, gripping onto my other arm as Gaz let go. I went to yank away, but the possessive asshole wouldn't have a bar of it.

I reined in my growl. "We don't have time for this!" I snapped, trying to pull myself free, but Jake only stepped closer.

"You need to tell me what the fuck is going on." He pulled me outside into the hall. Gaz was vibrating beside me. His face was set in a cold mask. For the first time, he looked formidable. A little terrifying.

"Fendi has Maddy." He growled, and my stomach dropped. "He sent Joss a letter." He reached into my pocket to hand over the letter. Jake managed to unwrinkle it without letting me go.

"You're not going out there. No fucking chance."

"Yes, I am. I'm not allowing anything to happen to her. Not because of me."

"Can Joss go out there, but we sneak in from behind?" Gaz started, but the withering glare from Jake was enough to make me feel ill.

"*No.*" Was the only answer we got. "Take her and make sure you don't let her out of your sight. Let me handle it." He shoved the note in his pocket and handed me over like I was some fucking package. Gaz's fingers gripped tightly around my upper arm, but I wasn't going to give up that easily.

"I won't risk her like this. He says he'll kill her if I don't go!" I whisper yelled, my face felt flushed, no doubt from my boiling anger. "You *have* to let me save her." I ended in a sob, the emotion pouring out of me. I heard Gaz clear his throat beside me.

This couldn't be easy for him either. This was his girlfriend we were talking about.

"No, and that's final. I'll tie you up myself if I have to." Jake leaned in, baring his teeth like some animal.

"*Fuck you.*" I snarled right back.

"Get her somewhere safe." Jake glared at Gaz before stalking away, heading for the courtyard, shoulders stiff. I waited until he was out of sight before I turned back to Gaz slowly, eyes pleading.

"We need to get out there. As soon as Fendi see's Jake..." I didn't finish that sentence. I didn't want to think about what he'd do.

Fendi was clearly insane.

"You heard Callahan." Gaz's voice was forced, no doubt his throat was as tight as mine. "We need to keep you safe."

"Fuck Jake, fuck my safety. I'm going to save Maddy. She's there because of *me*."

"Don't make me tie and gag you." He whispered, but I could see the silver lining in his eyes.

"I'm so sorry, Gaz." I breathed, right before I kneed him in the balls and ran as soon as he loosened his grip. He fell to his knees with a pained grunt. "I'm sorry!" I called as I got the hell out of there.

My feet slapped on the tiles, the doors slamming open as I raced through and into the swiftly oncoming night. I wasn't going to go the main way I usually took.

There was a quicker way around the back. I headed south, pumping my legs as fast as they'd take me.

The ten minutes had to be nearly up by now.

I raced into the trees, my lungs burning, but I didn't have time to think about anything other than getting there in time.

I *had* to get to Maddy.

I saw Fendi leaning lazily against a tree, throwing a knife in the air, and catching it. Over, and over, and over as he stared at his watch.

I burst into the small clearing, gasping, white spots dancing at the edges of my vision, hands on my knees as I tried to catch my breath.

"Ah, about fucking time," Fendi grunted as he pushed off the tree. "I'm guessing you gave your little guard-dog the slip. Good." He smiled as I glared up at him. I forced myself to stand straight, putting all my anger into my words.

"Where is she?" I snapped, not wanting to take my eyes off him to search for her.

"Bring the feral bitch." He drawled, eyeing me with glee as he began to slowly circle me. "I know it won't be long until one of your dogs comes sniffing, so we'll make this quick."

I raised my chin as fear coursed through me. I swallowed it down. My fingers skimmed over my thigh in a nervous gesture as I made sure my knife was still there.

I'd slit his throat myself if I had to.

I heard muffled cursing before I saw her. Maddy's hair was falling out of her pony, a disgusting black eye was already swollen shut, and her lip was split.

I gritted my teeth so hard my jaw ached.

"You fucking monster," I growled, hands balling into fists at my sides. I spared another glance at Maddy, who shook her head slowly, a tear slipping down her battered cheek and over the gag in her mouth.

"I'll kill you for this." I snarled, hating the pain I could see in my best friend's eyes.

Fendi simply stood there and laughed.

He tipped his head back and howled with laughter. His cronies chuckled darkly, as if they thought my statement was hilarious, too.

"Oh, ignorant girl. You couldn't hurt a fly. You're too precious, too coddled to want to get your hands dirty."

But one of his goons took a not-so-subtle step toward me.

"Let her go. Right now." I kept my chin high, trying to keep my eye on three men at once. I ignored the dark shadow passing the trees behind them all. I knew it was Jake, and how he was going to kill me if I got out of this alive.

"Of course." He bowed his head, nodding to the man who held her. He shoved Maddy away from him, like she was filthy. I went to take a step to help her when Fendi yelled for me to stop.

"That's close enough. Madeline, run while you're still able to." He glared at Maddy, who would spit fire if she were able. She flipped him off and came to stand by my side, limping the whole way. She ripped her gag out and volleyed insults at the top of her lungs.

"*You fucking mother fucking asshole! I'm going to strip the flesh from your disgusting mother fucking bones and shove them up your huge mother fucking ass, you absolute waste of trash. Fucking piece of shit!*"

I had to bite the inside of my cheeks to stop myself from snorting. Now was *definitely* not the right time to laugh. But the looks on all of their faces were priceless.

"You've always had such a lovely vocabulary, Madeline Pyre. I'm guessing that you're going to die alongside your friend? So it shall be then." Fendi stopped throwing his blade in the air and took one step forward. The rest of his thugs followed suit.

Shit. I've only got one knife.

And Maddy didn't even have a weapon. But looking at her next to me, you would know that she didn't need one. She was the best in our class with Professor Kiyoko, and she was about to kick these guy's asses.

"Jake will be here any moment, and Gaz..." I winced, knowing he was going to hate me for kicking him in the balls. But I had to be here, this was my mess to clean up. "Gaz will be here as soon as he can."

I slipped my hand into Maddy's for a moment, and she squeezed back with a fierce grip. If we were together, then we could do this.

We could bring this asshole down once and for all.

Chapter Twenty-Four

I was a fair aim when throwing knives, but I didn't want to lose my only weapon. I reached under my skirt to pull my knife free, making the men snort, shaking their heads.

I must of looked ridiculous standing here with a blade that was barely bigger than my hand in my short skirt and heels. But I knew how to wield it. I knew where to shove it to reach someone's heart. Darius could vouch for that if he were still alive.

And Maddy and I had been training since we returned this year. We worked together incredibly well.

"Well, since you want to play, how about I send one man at a time, and watch while they break you, and make you bleed," Fendi smirked as he leaned back against a tree, folding one foot over the other. He nodded to one of his men, who smirked, ambling forward like a bear walking on two legs. I took a deep breath to let it settle me. I shared a brief look with Maddy, who nodded back at me.

We knew how to dance to Fendi's tune.

We let the man get close enough, who barked at us like he was a dog, hoping to scare us. But we didn't even blink. It wasn't until he swung back his arm and ran that we made our move.

Maddy ducked under his arm and rolled, jumping up behind him and kicking him in the ass. He stumbled slightly, mostly in shock. That was when I slammed my fist into his jaw, snapping his head to the side with a crack. The other men stood straighter, their hands went to the weapons on their hips. The man growled as he charged at me like a bull, but I was ready.

What the other men didn't see was that one of their own's neck got snapped by lightning-fast hands, and crumpled to the ground, then was dragged away into the shadows.

But I didn't have time to watch Jake work. I needed to focus on the asshole before me.

He was close enough for me to spin and pierce his side with my blade, slipping it right in to the hilt. He grunted, then stumbled slightly with disbelief, horror marring his face as he realised that a girl had won over him. I yanked my dagger out and kicked him in the stomach, watching him fall on his ass, hand gripping his side, blood soaking his shirt.

"Get her!" Fendi yelled, and another two men ran at us.

Jake made another kill without being seen, and my eyes locked on his. His green eyes were burning into mine, so hot that I could feel them from across the field. I swallowed.

I'd deal with his attitude later. Right now, we needed to survive this.

The two men ran straight for me, seeing as I was the one with the blade, but somehow Maddy miraculously got on one of their shoulders and had her fingers digging into his eyes, making him scream and spinning around, trying to dislodge her. I made a snap decision and threw my blade at the man coming right for me.

The dagger sank into his forehead with a sickening, dull sound. I didn't think twice as I ran toward him, just as he was falling to his knees and yanked my blade out before he hit the ground.

"*How the fuck are you doing this?*" Fendi screamed, standing straight and barking at his remaining men. "Don't just stand there, fucking take her down!" But he frowned, counting them and realised that another three men were missing. "Someone else is here. Your fucking dog." He snarled and made his way toward me. "Looks like

I'm going to have to do this myself." He snarled, gripping his dagger tightly as he came towards us. Maddy was still on the back of the other man, who was bumping into things as she slowly gouged his eyes out with her thumbs. I tried not to hear his pained screams or look at the blood running down his face.

Jake took the chance to step into the clearing and make his presence known. "Take another step, and I'm going to make you regret ever placing a hand on her." He growled low and vicious, eyes locked on Fendi as the last two remaining men came to a stop. They looked behind them and paled, realising the other men were nowhere to be seen. "I'm going to enjoy peeling you apart, asshole." Jake smiled as he took a step, but Fendi laughed quietly. It sent goosebumps over me.

"Jake Callahan. You're a slippery fiend. I'll enjoy seeing Jocelyn's reaction when I kill you. I think she's rather attached to you." He smiled, but it didn't reach his eyes.

"Enough of this!" I shouted, but it fell on deaf ears. They were too focused on each other now. I was just background noise.

So I used that to my advantage.

Maddy had somehow either knocked out the man she was piggyback riding, or he was dead. I didn't really want to know.

The first man I stabbed was whimpering on the ground, clutching his wound. I didn't need to worry about him any time soon.

I tuned out their pissing contest as they threw insults at each other. I met Maddy's eyes, and she nodded in understanding. We were going to use this moment to take him down.

Once and for all.

But just as we started to move, Fendi did something that took us all by surprise. Without breaking eye contact with Jake, he leapt to the side and smashed his fist right into the side of my face. I fell to my knees as the blistering pain ignited, a gasp tearing from my lips. I saw Jake take a step, but stopped when Fendi got a fistful of my hair and yanked me against him.

“Give up, Callahan. Let me kill the girl, and I'll be on my way.”

But Jake only laughed, and the sounds rattled me to my bones. “Sure. Go ahead.” He shrugged, placing his hands in his pockets, bluffing his ass off.

Fendi stopped just as he pulled me to my feet, his arm wrapped around my waist and spun me until I was facing him.

"How about one last kiss, sweetheart? I never did get to taste your lips. I wonder if they're as soft as your ass?" He grinned, too damn close for my liking.

I didn't hesitate as I moved as quick as lightning and buried the blade into the side of his throat, and ripped it across in one swift slice with all the strength I could muster.

He froze, eyes wide with disbelief, before his life's blood spurted out like a geyser, soaking me in seconds. His arm loosened around my waist and dropped from my hair as he slowly slid down my body, gargling as he attempted to hold his throat together with his bare hands. He fell to his knees, and without any mercy, I kicked him in the chest and sent him sprawling.

He landed on the ground with a dull thud and stayed there, unmoving.

By the time I turned around, Jake had just finished killing the last two men, and when he finally stood up straight, his eyes locked on mine.

"Fuck me, Joss. That was insanely brutal...but amazing. High five, girlfriend." Maddy stumbled over and held up her hand, narrowing her eyes when I didn't move. I raised my hand and pathetically slapped it against hers. She scoffed, but nodded with a smile tugging on her lips. "I'll take it." She muttered before sitting heavily on her ass, her head falling into her hands. "I don't feel well." She groaned.

I didn't see Jake move until he was right before me, gripping my face in his hands. "What the fuck-" he started, snarling into my face. "did you think you were doing?"

"What I had to do." I gritted out between clenched teeth. We were too close. I could feel his heaving chest brush mine with every inhale, practically toe to toe. We stood there, not saying anything as we continued to stare.

"What the *fuuuccckkk?*" Gaz wheezed as he stumbled into the clearing, eyes wide as he took in the bloody carnage. But he spotted Maddy on the ground and raced over, wrapping his arms around her as they silently sobbed.

"That was the bravest and stupidest thing you've ever done," Jake muttered under his breath. "And fuck do I want to kiss you so much right now." His words were like a slap to the face, and I sucked in a breath. But he didn't move away from me.

I couldn't stop my lip from trembling. Something in him cracked as he wound his arms around me and held me tightly to his chest, one hand stroking the back of my head.

"You did what you had to. And you were amazing." He murmured into my hair, holding me so damn tight. But I was worried how I'd crack if he let go. But he wasn't who I really wanted to be held by. "I'm coming back with you to help clean you off. Then I need to come back here to..." He didn't finish, but I knew what he was going to say.

To get rid of the bodies.

"He's actually gone." I croaked. The relief was yet to register in my brain that Fendi would no longer hurt my friends and me.

Another enemy down.

"You got him, sweetheart." For once, his ridiculous nickname didn't grate. I sobbed a little harder, unaware that Gaz had helped Maddy out of there and back to her room.

It was just Jake and I.

He pulled back slightly, a thumb grazing over my cheek, eyes narrowing at the cut that stung on my temple.

"Come on then, can you walk?"

"Yeah, I'll be right." I didn't pay attention to the whole way back inside, how we got there, or who saw us. All I noticed was him leading me into his room where he patted his bed as my mind spun. I shut my eyes briefly as he darted to the bathroom, returning with a bowl, bucket and a cloth.

Without speaking, he helped me undress and cleaned me off. I felt numb.

I just killed at least three people. It felt different from when I killed Darius.

I felt bile rise, and Jake moved the bucket under my chin as he leaned me over the side of the bed, making it just in time.

I heaved and heaved, feeling like I had absolutely nothing left by the time I was finished. Jake was there again, cleaning me up, and laying me down in his bed.

I rolled over and closed my eyes, fighting the tears.

"I'll be right back, alright?" He waited for my nod before darting out of the room.

How the hell was I going to get through this?

How the hell was I going to be able to face what I'd just done?

We got on with our lives, as if nothing had happened.

Maddy brushed off people's curious questions and stares. Gaz didn't leave her side. He slept in her room every night.

I was back to not sleeping, barely functioning, but getting there. Jake was a shadow, like always.

It took a few days, but I came to terms with Fendi being dead. That he'd no longer pose a threat.

Now I just had to remember that Sera, Jenna, and Paul were still out there.

I had more letters dropped under my door, but I didn't bother reading them. I knew there would be something taunting about how they were going to get me.

I was getting really sick of their threats.

I didn't see Sera in my classes anymore, and I didn't know if that was a good thing or not. The snooty first year - Courtney - was looking a little worse for wear.

I had other things to focus on, like passing my classes and watching around every corner, and over my shoulder.

After I accepted that, sleep came a little easier. I felt that I wanted to eat again, if only a little, and because if I didn't, Jake was going to tie me down and spoon-feed me if he had to.

Bloody alpha-asshole.

Chapter Twenty-Five

Professor Wood had apparently retired without notice and was replaced by Professor Turnbull. He smiled at students as he walked the hall, and quickly settled into metalwork class like he'd been there forever. But I didn't like the way he watched me. Jake made sure to keep well away from me whenever he was around, and I knew something wasn't right.

After class, I made sure to catch up with Jake, stopping him with a hand on his arm. He turned slowly and looked down at me with a frown. He looked around and grabbed my wrist, dragging me into a dark classroom, locking the door behind him.

"What the hell are you doing?" He hissed, glaring at me with arms crossed over his chest.

"What the hell am I doing? Who the hell is Turnbull?" I snapped back, leaning against the wall with my arms crossed too, as I glared right back.

"He's not someone you want taking notice of you."

"Well, too late for that. He's constantly watching me."

"I know." He snapped and began pacing. "We can't be seen together. He's been sent in to monitor the situation and to see what's taking me so long. He almost kicked me out about the Fendi situation, and why I didn't take you then." He stopped, and his dark green eyes snagged on me. I sucked in a breath, and my worst fears were confirmed.

"So, he's one of you then?" I breathed, and he nodded his head once. But it was enough of a confirmation that I needed. "What will he do?" I breathed, my pulse picking up another notch.

"If he thinks taking you will be more beneficial than information, he'll grab you himself."

"Oh, Gods." My knees gave out from under me, and I fell to the floor, but Jake was there, gripping onto the tops of my arms.

"I'm working on Alec to give me more information, but he's always out of contact." His voice was soft, almost worried, as he knelt in front of me. "I swear, Jossi, I'm working my hardest to not let that happen."

My breaths were burning in my chest. This was starting to feel so *real*.

"What do I do?" I pleaded, gripping onto his wrists as he continued to hold me upright.

"Stay away from him. Pretend you barely know me."

"That's not going to be so easy. Gaz loves catching up with you. It's not like you can brush them off without him getting suspicious."

"I know." He snapped, and I blinked, the anger simmering just under his skin. "Just...let me take care of it."

"I have no choice, my life is in your hands, remember?" I dropped my hands from his arms and forced myself to stand. He followed, keeping too close.

His hand slowly cupped my face, and his expression was pained as we stood there, breathing heavily in the small space between us.

"How could I ever forget?" He whispered, his thumb brushing over my cheek in a gentle stroke. I gritted my teeth and stepped away, and Jake let his hand fall to his side. I couldn't read the expression, but I sure as hell didn't want to know what he was feeling. I slipped out of the door, leaving him there in the dark as I made my way through the halls.

My heart was racing too fast.

Toxic, I reminded myself.

This was toxic behaviour.

The morning of the competition dawned clear and bright, the kind of crisp day Imperial Heights loved to brag about. Their campus was spotless, their banners flapping proudly in the wind. Hellspire's contingent looked like a bunch of pirates crashing a yacht club.

And me? I was about to climb onto a horse in front of both schools. At least the bruises on my face and throat had faded enough for me to cover with makeup. I didn't want any more eyes on me than I already had.

"Smile," Maddy hissed as she straightened my uniform. Her grin was a little too wide, her eyes sparkling with way too much anticipation. "You're about to witness glory, Joss. Sparkly, glittery glory."

Her bruises were in their greeny-yellow stage, but she wore them like armour.

I groaned, tugging at my helmet strap. The stupid thing was bejewelled with a giant, glittering crown.

Subtlety had never been Maddy's style.

We were lined up at the starting line, horses throwing their heads around, snorting when someone got too close. I hauled myself up, my body finally used to riding without me aching in areas I forgot could hurt.

Jake swung up onto his horse beside me, the animal looking like it could chew me in half. His own helmet glinted in the sun, a shimmering matching crown on his. He didn't look pleased.

"This is fucking humiliating," he muttered, gripping the reins with white-knuckled hands.

"Cheer up, Callahan," Gaz laughed from beside us, already waving a homemade banner that read *SPARKLE OR DIE*. He grabbed Maddy's hand, and they made their way up into the stands, both of them decked out in Hellspire colours of navy blue and white. "You look *magnificent*." He shouted as he sat, and I stifled my laugh.

The Imperial Heights riders lined up with us, their pristine white uniforms gleaming like they'd been ironed five minutes ago. Their helmets sparkled too, but not in the way they thought. Jewel-encrusted dicks and balls winked in the sunlight, subtle enough at first glance but horrifically obvious once you looked straight at them.

I saw the first confused faces in the crowd. Then the first laugh. Then another.

"What the hell-?" one of the Imperial riders muttered, tugging at his helmet as the jeering started. He didn't dare take it off, though, the judges were already walking the line.

Maddy was practically falling out of her seat, tears streaming down her face. "Oh gods, look at their faces!" she wheezed, clutching Gaz's arm as the Imperial assholes faced each other in horror.

Jake leaned closer to me, his jaw tight. "Stay focused. When this goes off, the chaos will be-"

A *bang* cut him off.

Every head in the stands whipped toward the far end of the arena. A cloud of shimmering pink dust exploded from the equipment shed, puffing through the open doors like a rainbow mushroom cloud. Riders and assistants nearby staggered back, coughing and waving their arms as glitter coated every inch of them.

The crowd gasped. Then the laughter started, loud, rolling and unstoppable.

"Oh, shit," I whispered, clutching my reins as my horse tossed its head. "It was supposed to start weeks ago."

Jake swore under his breath.

The announcer tried valiantly to keep control. "Ahem, just a minor... ah... equipment malfunction! Let's proceed-"

BOOM.

Another glitter bomb went off, this one in the classroom block. The windows blew outward in a shimmering rain of gold and purple dust as it cascaded across the courtyard.

The crowd lost it. People stood to see better, pointing, cheering, some booing, others clapping like they'd just witnessed a magic trick.

Maddy's mother looked like she was about to combust on the spot.

Another *boom*, and glitter poured out of windows like a goddamn volcano. Shimmering clouds erupted from vents, coating the pristine lawns in rainbow sparkles. A couple of unfortunate students burst out the doors, coughing and blinded, their uniforms now twinkling like disco suits.

It was absolute chaos.

The judge tried to call the riders forward, but no one was listening anymore. The crowd was in an uproar. The Imperial riders shifted uncomfortably, the bedazzled dicks on their helmets now glinting under the sun like shameful beacons.

Jake muttered, "This is ridiculous."

"Worth it," I whispered back, grinning like a maniac.

"*ALRIGHT!*" a voice boomed over the speakers, getting everyone's attention. "On your marks, get set, go!" He shot the starting gun into the air, and we took off.

I'd only been back riding for the past few months, but I never forgot the freedom of galloping, the wind in my hair, the complete joy of it. There were fifty targets to get, and we had to hit each one, and if we missed, we weren't allowed to go back to try again.

I saw a target hiding on my left, but an Imperial was blocking my way. I cursed her, pulled my feet out of the stirrups and knelt on the saddle.

"What the fuck are you doing?" Jake shouted from behind me, but I ignored him as we raced toward the first target.

That was when the quivers went off.

The moment the Imperial Heights riders pulled their arrows free, clouds of glitter erupted from the shafts, coating their hands and faces in fine red dust. One boy sneezed so violently that he dropped his bow. Another tried to wipe his face only to smear himself into something resembling a drag show gone wrong.

I nocked my arrow, took a deep breath and let it fly. Britney had been teaching me archery, and she was a damn good teacher. My arrow flew over the head of the Imperial, who screeched and covered her head with her arms. But my arrow hit the target. I let out a whoop as I sat back down, tucking my bow into its holder on my back. Jake was suddenly beside me, looking furious.

"What the hell, Joss?"

"I know how to ride, Callahan. So don't get your knickers in a twist." I grinned, and he growled at me, but I knew he would have also hit the target. He was deadly with any sort of weapon.

We tore through the trees and grounds, chaos puffing out all around us as glitter floated down with every arrow pulled from their quivers. Every Hellspire student cackled, and the forest was filled with laughter and angry shouts.

"You're going to fucking pay for this." A rider snarled on my left, and I ducked as he swung his bow at my head.

"Hey!" I shouted, encouraging my horse to go faster. But he hit my horse on the ass, and she screamed, rearing up onto her hind legs. I grappled with the reins, squeezing my legs for dear life. The asshole took off in front of me, and I saw Jake tearing after him.

He leaned over, grabbed the Imperial ass by the scruff of his uniform, and threw him from his horse. The man screamed as he landed in the bushes, and his horse rode off without him. I gave him the finger as I rode past his furious face as it poked out.

Asshole.

It didn't take me long to catch up, another five targets hit. I saw retaliation all around us, shouts and cries as they shoved and whacked each other.

I got lost in the moment, riding hard, shooting arrows, finding those targets, some half hidden and camouflaged.

It was a blessed break from everything that had been happening lately. And it felt like I could finally breathe.

But after an hour or so of hard riding, the finish line finally came into view. I was one of the first lot back, my horse slowing to a trot as I took in those already here. A handful from each academy.

Jake trotted in behind me not long after, his eyes glittering.

We waited until a car rumbled in behind us, picking up those who fell off or were pushed off, in some cases. We stood there together, waiting in front of our horses to hear the final results.

The Imperial Heights team was coated head to toe, sparkling like furious, *furious* fairies. The Dean's face was the colour of a tomato, veins bulging in her forehead as she barked orders to her professors.

One of the Imperial riders yanked his helmet off in frustration, only for a cascade of glitter to dump straight onto his head from a hidden balloon Maddy had rigged.

I nearly fell over laughing.

Jake pinched the bridge of his nose again.

The announcer's microphone now crackling with static and glitter dust. The crowd had turned into a carnival: kids scooping up handfuls of glitter from the grass, parents laughing until they cried, and every Imperial Heights student looking like they wanted to crawl into a hole and die.

Jake leaned toward me, his mouth close to my ear so only I could hear him. “You realise they’re going to retaliate, right? Harder than ever.”

I grinned, my cheeks aching from laughter, my stomach sore. “Let them try.”

Because in that moment, as the Imperial Heights team sat there dripping in glitter, their pride shredded and their uniforms sparkling like a drag cabaret gone nuclear, I knew Hellspire had already won.

It was about time something worked in our favour.

“It was a close count, but...” Maddy’s mother’s face soured, like she didn’t want to say the words. “Hellspire wins by five.” She grumbled, and the crowd erupted into deafening cheers. We were hugging, united as one, as we celebrated. The imperial students threw their helmets on the ground and kicked them with an angry yell.

Safe to say, we were escorted off the grounds shortly after. The bus ride home was in full celebration mode, singing, drinking, and cheering.

Maddy high-fived me as she handed me a bottle of champagne.

“Drink up, we deserve it!” She grabbed her phone and flipped through the photos and videos, chuckling like a madwoman. I watched over her shoulder and laughed with her.

Yeah, they were going to hate us for the rest of their days. Maddy posted video after video, the photos in a collage on every social media platform she was on.

We're still on a high when we reached the academy, pairs breaking off to celebrate. I felt a hand on my arm, and I turned to see a worried Jake staring down at me.

"As funny as that was, you need to be careful. I've got a bad feeling about this."

"They have no way to tie it back to me. They won't know I was involved."

"They know Jenna hates you, and that you were with Paul. They're obviously still in contact with people there. I heard a few of them mention your name today."

My stomach dropped, but I didn't let him see the worry blooming through me.

"It will be fine, Jake. Don't worry so much." I patted his arm and joined Maddy and Gaz, who would be celebrating with drinks and snacks in Maddy's room. Gaz asked Jake to join, but he claimed he had a few things he needed to do.

Good. I didn't want his broody attitude to ruin our celebration.

Chapter Twenty-Six

Much to my disgust, Professor Turnbull was now helping us under the school, organising the weapons for their drop-offs. Jake kept away, but I could feel two sets of eyes on me, his and his scarred colleague.

"Miss Xanetto." His voice raked over me as he stopped at my side, but I held in my shudder. I wasn't meant to know who he was. I paused with my hand on the lid of a crate, guns packed inside.

"Yes, professor?" I ignored my racing heart, hoping he couldn't see my pulse fluttering like a butterfly's wings.

"How are you holding up from the accident a little while ago? I heard you broke your arm?" He frowned a little, coming across as concerned. He was a damn good actor, I'd give him that.

"Much better, thank you. All healed." I tried for a smile, but it wobbled. He leaned in a little, and I desperately wanted to take a step back.

"Good to hear. You'll be right for your first delivery next week, then?"

"Yes, sir." I nodded, more than aware of Jake's gaze boring into the back of Turnbull.

"Perhaps I'll send Callahan with you, he's the one who helped you out of the truck in the accident, wasn't he?"

My stomach plummeted, and my palms began to sweat as I tried my hardest to pretend like I didn't care.

"Sure." I gritted my teeth, but he was obviously waiting for me to confirm. "Yes, he and I went on that trip."

"Alone?" He cocked his head to the side, and I tried to act like it was no big deal. His brown eyes were so dark they looked black, and his scar caught my attention more often than it should.

"Yes. They just needed us to route out the road and find a meeting place, seeing as we both know the area."

"I see." He scratched his chin, but continued to keep his eyes locked on me. "I've heard great things about you. The famous Clementine Mavis, who turned out to be Gordon Xanetto's daughter in hiding. What a crazy life you must have lived."

Oh, shit.

I swallowed, trying to give him a small smile that I hoped didn't look like a grimace.

"It sure was...different. I didn't grow up at home with my father. So we're not that close." I had to clear my throat, gripping onto the table for support. "I hardly saw him until last year when I visited for a couple of weeks. But he's a busy man, doing whatever it is that he does." I tried to convey to him that I didn't know anything, that it would be useless to take me for any information. But I knew better for him to be able to read that through my eyes.

"How fascinating." He winked, leaning in a little, "I've heard those who walked away from your father's empire end up dead."

I shrank back, eyes wide as he slowly smiled, but chuckled, leaning back.

"Have a good evening, Miss Xanetto." He sauntered off, and I was left trying to reel myself back in.

He was too dangerous, but there was nothing I could do.

The air still reeked of gun oil and smoke, clinging to my clothes. My fingertips itched, stained from handling steel that shouldn't exist on school grounds - not legally anyway. Not that legality mattered here.

Hellspire didn't just thrive on chaos; it financed it.

Jake walked a step ahead of me, his broad shoulders stiff under his jacket, a duffel bag slung casually in his grip like it wasn't stuffed with enough weapons to arm a small militia.

Usually, the weapons never left the rooms underground unless on a delivery, but Omara requested that Jake drop off a bag on his way out. And of course, when he left, so did I.

"Tell me about the syndicate," I demanded, and the way Jake's shoulders stiffened, I knew it was a subject I probably shouldn't know about.

"How the hell do you know about that?" He turned slowly and checked the halls to make sure we were alone.

"I don't know anything, but I keep hearing them pop up. I know they must be something people are scared of." I planted my feet, not going to move until he gave me some information.

He ran his tongue over his teeth before sighing in frustration.

"They're the ones who hire the students when you all graduate from here." He stalked back to me until he was a foot away from my shoes. "They will fight, tooth and claw for the ones they want, and others, they have to apply for a role. It all depends on how good your grades are."

"Is that what happened to Alec? Or did he only accept my father's offer?" Is that why the assessor came to make sure we were all up to scratch? Is that why they were concerned that we weren't good enough?

"Trust me, they all wanted *Alexander Hyde* to work for them, but he rejected each offer. Even though some of them were ridiculous." Jake shook his head, and was that a little flicker of jealousy I spotted?

"And who *are* these people? What kind of things do they do?"

Jake checked over his shoulder again. "There are arms dealers, biotech companies, private securities and soldiers, intelligence networks, black-market information brokers, and artifact smugglers. Then there's also your father." His nose scrunched, like even speaking about him left a bad taste in his mouth.

"Why do they need us? What are they planning to do?" I breathed. This was *huge*.

Is this why Father was adamant that I graduate? So I can get a good job afterwards?

"This is why the involvement in delivering these weapons, as well as M.O.D.L, is something they look for. They want the best of the best."

"But *why?*" I pushed, crossing my arms.

A noise sounded around the corner, past the east stairwell. Jake put a finger to his lips and turned around, searching.

I followed, eyes straining when movement flickered at the edge of my vision.

Instinct prickled along my skin. I grabbed Jake's arm. "Wait."

He stilled instantly, duffel bag shifting silently against his thigh as he scanned where I pointed. A figure, hood pulled low, slid across the hallway and ducked toward the kitchens. Too quiet for a Hellspire student who'd risk a midnight snack. Too deliberate.

Jake's hand went automatically to the knife clipped under his jacket. "Imperial." The word was gravel in his throat.

"Are you sure?" I whispered, heart climbing into my mouth.

He shot me a look. The one that said *have I ever been wrong about this shit?*

"Stay here." He started forward.

"Not a chance." I moved with him before he could argue, ignoring the flare of irritation that crossed his face. If we'd just finished smuggling guns out of the damn basement, I wasn't about to pretend I was some fragile porcelain doll now.

The closer we got, the louder the sounds became - muffled thuds, something crashing, the unmistakable clatter of steel hitting tile. A woman's voice shouted, sharp and angry. Then a man's yell, cut off by a metallic *clang*.

I shot Jake a startled glance, adrenaline punching through my veins.

"That's Maddy," I breathed.

We burst through the side door into the kitchens - and the scene froze me where I stood.

Flour filled the air like smoke after an explosion, dusting everything in ghostly white. Bags of sugar were split open across the counters, sticky paste coating the tiles where someone had dumped water. Pots and pans swung from hands like weapons.

In the middle of it all, Maddy was brandishing a ladle like a sword, her face flushed with rage, as Gaz swung a frying pan two-handed into the side of a masked intruder's head with a metallic *CLANG!* The Imperial crumpled sideways into a sack of potatoes, dazed but still scrambling for a knife.

Three more masked figures were circling them, one with a length of chain, another with a spray canister that hissed with some chemical stink. It was chaos - and not the funny, pranking kind Hellspire thrived on.

This was sharp, fast, and *violent*.

"Jake," I hissed, panic clawing my throat.

But he was already moving, throwing the duffel into a shadowed corner and striding straight into the fray like he'd been waiting for this.

The chaos was like a slap in the face.

I took a step, but flour stung my eyes, the air thick with dust and the sour burn of chemicals. It tasted like burnt sugar and blood in my mouth, my lungs choking on it. The kitchen's usual sterile shine, all polished steel and stacked pans, has transformed into a warzone.

Maddy was shrieking at the top of her lungs, red hair plastered to her forehead, her ladle dripping with what looked like soup as she jabbed it like a spear into the stomach of a masked intruder. He doubled over with a grunt, but she didn't stop, bringing the ladle down on his helmeted head with a wet *CLONK!* that splashed broth everywhere.

Next to her, Gaz looked like he was born for this. One hand gripped a wok the size of a shield, the other held a rolling pin like a club. He swung the pin again, the sound dull as it collided with another Imperial's jaw. The man crumpled into a pile of flour sacks, coughing and wheezing.

Jake didn't hesitate. He barreled forward, all brute force and control, moving like a storm through the haze. One Imperial raised the chain, ready to swing it at Maddy, but

Jake was there first, a flash of silver in his hand. His knife slashed low, and the chain clattered uselessly to the ground as the man screamed and clutched his forearm.

The scream jolted me into motion. My heart was a war drum in my chest, my hand darted for the closest thing I could grab - a whisk.

A fucking whisk.

Better than nothing.

"Over here, bitch!" one of them snarled, lunging for me. I jabbed the whisk into his eyes, hard enough to make him howl and stumble. I kicked his knee out for good measure, and he toppled into a mess of spilled sugar. I was suddenly hurtling toward a kitchen bench when strong arms wrapped around my waist like iron. I grunted with the impact, knocking the air out of my lungs. He grabbed a fistful of hair and tried to smash my head into the table top, but I'd managed to reach something in my desperation.

A cordless blender.

Much better.

I aimed it for his face, but he caught it, looking smug like he'd beaten me as I turned. Our eyes met, and I didn't break my gaze as I grinned and pressed the on button. Blood sprayed as he shrieked, the blades cutting into his palm. I pushed away from him, sucking in a quick breath as I took in the carnage around me.

"You alright?" Jake's voice snapped at me, rough, checking me in one glance even as he smashed his fist into another Imperial's jaw.

"Peachy!" I shouted back, adrenaline making my voice shake. The chain-wielder staggered, blood spraying down his arm, but another Imperial charged Jake from behind with a mallet. My stomach lurched.

"Behind you!" I screamed.

Jake spun, catching the attacker's wrist in one brutal twist, forcing the mallet backward until the man yelped and dropped it. Without blinking, Jake head-butted him so hard I heard the crunch from across the kitchen.

The guy collapsed like a rag doll.

All around us, it was bedlam.

Maddy tripped over a bucket of mop water, landing on her ass with a squeal, but when her attacker lunged, she hurled the bucket straight into his face. Dirty water drenched him, and before he could recover, she smashed the bottom of the bucket onto his head like a drum.

Gaz was laughing like a madman, his teeth bared as he swung his dented wok in wide arcs.

"Come on, you Imperial wankers! Who's hungry for seconds?" He bellowed, cracking the wok across another helmet with a clang that rattled the shelves. Pots crashed to the floor, clattering over the tiles.

The flour haze made it hard to see, hard to breathe. My eyes stung, my throat burned. Every movement was slippery - oil slicked the floor where a bottle smashed, and my shoes skidded as I ducked a swipe of a man with a broom. I need something bigger, my blender wasn't cutting it. My hands scrabbled on the counter, grabbing anything I could get my hands on.

A cleaver.

Better still.

The next Imperial lunged, and I slashed the cleaver across his arm, leaving a gash that sprayed the counter. He screamed, the sound muffled by his mask, but I didn't give him a second chance. I drove my knee up into his stomach, then slammed the flat side of the cleaver into his temple. He went down hard.

There were too many of them. Too fast, too coordinated. My pulse was screaming, my body buzzing with terror and fury. Then, an explosion of motion from the doorway. More boots and shadows.

"Oh, for fuck's sake," Maddy groaned. "There's more of them?"

Jake cursed, yanking me back toward him as three fresh Imperials pushed into the kitchen. His hand found my hip, steadying me, as he raised his knife like it was an extension of his body. "Stay close."

I nodded, knuckles white around the cleaver.

The new attackers didn't charge. They spread, calculated, circling us. Behind them, the kitchen doors swung wider - and for a half second, I thought the whole damn Imperial Heights had poured in.

And then the shouting started.

Hellspire shouting.

Boots thundered down the hallway. Doors slammed open. The roar of voices grew louder, swelling until it drowned even the sounds of fighting.

The school had woken.

The Imperials froze, eyes darting, realising too late what they'd walked into.

Gaz grinned wolfishly, swinging his pan up onto his shoulder. "Ohhh, boys. You're fucked now."

The kitchen door burst open again, and half of Hellspire barreled through - students wild-eyed and armed with whatever they grabbed on the way: broom handles, chair legs, even a fire extinguisher.

Chaos, complete and perfect, crashed into the kitchen like a tidal wave, but the kitchen couldn't contain it. The fight burst outward like a pot boiling over.

One moment, I was choking on flour, the next, I was being dragged with the crowd, bodies surging toward the corridors. The noise was deafening - the clang of pans, the thud of fists into flesh, shouts echoing off stone walls.

Hellspire students poured from every direction, wild-eyed and furious. I saw Britney, in her dressing gown, who swung a broom handle like she was in a medieval war. Someone else smashed a fire extinguisher into the wall, spraying foam across the floor until it turned slick. Imperial Heights fought back, black-masked and efficient, but they were outnumbered.

Chapter Twenty-Seven

Jake was a storm beside me, knife flashing as he dropped another Imperial with a brutal efficiency that made my stomach twist. He didn't stop moving, didn't stop cutting a path through them, making sure I was always just behind his shoulder.

"Stay with me!" He barked, eyes like lightning as he yanked me away from a wild swing. I nodded, but it was impossible to stay tethered in this chaos. Bodies slammed into me, someone screamed right in my ears, and then Maddy and Gaz vanished in the flood of fighters. My pulse hammered so hard I swore I could taste blood.

We spilled into the courtyard, night air slicing across my face. Torches lit up the stone walls, flickering shadows across the cobbles. And here, the real war began.

Hellspire students swarmed, howling like animals, throwing themselves at the Imperials who tried to break us. Bottles smashed, fists flew. Someone hurled a chair straight out of a window, and it exploded on the courtyard stones.

I could barely think. I could barely breathe.

Jake was caught - three Imperials closing in on him, circling like wolves. He fought back with a roar, knife flashing, fists punishing. But there were too many. He dropped one with a brutal elbow to the throat, but another slammed him into the wall, and the third lunged.

I took a step forward, and then a hand clamped down over my mouth.

I screamed, but it was smothered in a palm. One arm locked around me like iron, dragging me backward, my boots scraping across the stone. Panic detonated in my chest, raw and blinding.

"Shh, Clementine."

My blood turned to ice.

No. No, it can't be.

The voice was low, roughened, but I'd know it anywhere. I thrashed, clawing at his arms, kicking backward with everything I had, but he just chuckled in my ear.

"Stop fighting me. I'm here to save you."

Paul.

He's here.

I bucked harder, nails digging into his skin, but he only squeezed tighter, my breath choking in my throat. His hand slid up, gripping the back of my head almost tenderly, even as his other arm crushed me to his chest.

"You've been running too long, Clem," he whispered, my old name like poison. "I'm here to take you home."

Terror detonated through me. He dragged me faster, weaving through the chaos like he knew every blind spot. My muffled cries drowned in the roar of battle.

We hit the edge of the courtyard. His car waited, black and sleek, tucked in the shadows like a predator.

"No!" I tried to scream, but it was only a garbled sound against the rest of the noise out there. My heels scraped, my lungs clawed for air as he yanked the boot open with one hand, never loosening his grip on me.

"Don't worry, Clementine. I'll keep you safe. Safer than this place ever could." His breath was hot against my ear, unhinged and fervent. "You'll see. You'll love me again. I just need to break this brainwashing."

I thrashed so hard he swore, slamming me against the car until stars burst in my vision. My wrists were bound in a flash, rough rope biting my skin. He spun me, and a gag muffled my sob as he shoved me backward, the cold metal of the boot slamming into my spine.

"No, please-" My cry was cut off as he tied the gag tighter, eyes wild and shining. The last thing I saw before darkness swallowed me was Paul's face. Once boyish and familiar. Now it was twisted and mad.

The boot slammed shut with a sickening loud thud.

Dark. Airless.

My heart slammed against my ribs, tears burning down my face. Outside, the fighting raged on, muffled now by the boot's walls. I heard shouts, crashes and screams. Then a familiar roar.

Paul cursed.

The car rocked violently, as if someone had been slammed against it. I froze, hardly daring to breathe, straining to hear. Another shout. Paul's voice this time, angrier and more desperate. Then Jake's, sharp as a blade, his fury vibrating through the metal walls of my cage. I wished Alec were here, the thought of him was the only thing stopping my panic attack.

My wrists ached against the rope as I tried to get free. But I held onto one truth through the panic: Jake was here. He'd come for me, again. I shouldn't be pleased about it, but I couldn't help it.

The boot shook again. Then the hinges shrieked as it was wrenched open, light flooding in. I blinked against it, gagged sobs tearing out of me. Jake's face filled my vision - bloodied, furious, but alive.

"Got you, sweetheart." His voice was low but savage. His knife made quick work of the rope binding my wrists, and I choked as he ripped the gag free. My lungs seized on a scream.

"Behind you!" I croaked, but too late.

Paul slammed into him.

The world lurched sideways. Jake crashed into the cobbles, Paul's fists raining down. I stumbled out of the boot, choking on air, scrambling to my knees.

"*Mine!*" Paul snarled, voice unrecognisable. "She was mine before any of you! You think you can take her from me?"

Jake grunted, blocking a blow, twisting to slam Paul into the car door so hard the metal dented.

"She was never yours, you sick bastard!"

They traded punches, brutal and wild, blood splattering the ground. My heart was a runaway drum, terror a hot flood in my veins. Jake finally gained the upper hand, his fist driving into Paul's jaw with a sickening crack.

Paul stumbled and pulled a gun from the waistband of his jeans.

"Jake!" I screamed.

The shot exploded.

Jake jerked back, a crimson bloom spreading across his side. He collapsed to one knee, teeth clenched, his knife clattering away.

Paul sneered, raising the gun at Jake's head. "Now you'll see, Clementine. I'm here to protect you from men like him and Hyde." He panted, blood staining his teeth.

Something snapped in me.

I launched at him. My fists, my nails, my entire body fuelled by fury. I slammed into his arm, the gun firing wildly into the air as I smashed my fist into his face, snapping his head back. He swore, stumbling back under the sheer madness of my attack.

"You don't own me!" I screamed, voice breaking.

I drove my knee into his stomach. He doubled over with a grunt, and I seized his gun hand, slamming it against the car until the weapon dropped. He swung wildly at me, but I ducked and smashed my forehead into his nose.

Bone crunched and blood gushed. He howled into the night.

Fuck, that hurts. I groaned, my head throbbing with an instant headache.

But rage was all I knew. I grabbed the fallen gun and cracked it against his temple with everything I had. Paul's eyes rolled back as he crumpled, unconscious on the cobbles. I was left panting, shaking, my hands sticky with his blood.

"Joss!"

Maddy's voice. She and Gaz sprinted across the courtyard, eyes wide with horror as they saw Jake slumped against the car, blood seeping between his fingers.

"Oh my god, Jake-" Maddy dropped to her knees, already pulling off her hoodie to press against the wound. Jake groaned, pale but still conscious.

"Fuck-don't...don't let me black out," he muttered, trying to push himself up.

"You're not going anywhere, man," Gaz snapped, his voice raw as he crouched on Jake's other side. He hooked Jake's arm over his shoulders, grimacing at the weight. "Help me, Mads."

I staggered closer, my whole body trembling, my throat raw. "I'll-"

"No." Gaz's voice cracked like a whip. "You're covered in blood, you're shaking out of your damn skin. Let us."

I could only nod, swallowing the sob clawing up my throat as they half-carry, half-dragged Jake toward the hospital wing. His head lolled, but he gritted his teeth, muttering curses under his breath to stay conscious.

Behind us, professors stormed into the courtyard, Professor Kiyoko leading with a roar, Omara right behind her. Their voices sliced through the night like whips as they corralled the remaining Imperials. Some were already pinned to the ground, others dragged by their collars, bloodied and beaten.

Chaos finally began to crack under authority's weight, but it didn't feel over. Not yet.

I followed Maddy and Gaz, my knees weak, my ears still ringing. Every step, I glanced back at Paul's limp body sprawled on the cobbles, at the pools of blood, at Jake's pale face.

My stomach twisted.

The real war between Hellspire and Imperial Heights had only just begun.

What have we done?

Maddy and Gaz returned for Paul as soon as they'd dropped Jake off, only to find him gone.

Of course he was.

I waited in the hall out front, not sure if I wanted to go in there or not. I shouldn't be seen with him.

Turnbull couldn't know how close we'd become.

But he *knew*. He knew that Jake saved me in the accident, knowing too well he had the perfect opportunity to kidnap me. I scrubbed my hands over my face, feeling utterly exhausted.

I wasn't attracted to him. I still loved Alec, but I knew there was more to Jake and I than kidnapper and victim.

Paul was in on tonight's raid. There was no other explanation. Imperial weren't here to prank, they were out for our blood.

"Come on, you need to get some rest, clean up." Maddy tugged at my sleeve, and I turned weary eyes on her. She hadn't asked why I was out in the halls in the first place. We all knew that she and Gaz liked to sneak down to steal ice-cream, but me? What I was I doing out in the middle of the night with Jake?

I couldn't tell her, even if I wanted to. Only the ones who were invited were allowed to know.

We were walking back as loud boots sounded behind us, and I spun, heart in my throat.

"What are you three doing out of bed?" Professor Turnbull barked, quickly catching up to us.

"All hell just broke loose, if you didn't know, Professor," Gaz replied, cracking his knuckles before sticking his hands in his pockets. I heard a click of his lighter.

He was nervous.

Did he get the bad vibes off Turnbull too?

"I'm aware of that, Davies. But everyone's been sent back to bed." He stared directly at me, and I refused to shrink under his heavy gaze. "Why are you covered in blood?"

"We just dropped Callahan to the hospital, he'd been shot." Gaz gave him a cold, cutting smile. I'd never seen Gaz speak to a professor like this before.

"Callahan?" Turnbull's brows flew up, then looked over the three of us. "Are you his friends?"

"Yeah, we are. And we're dog tired, so if you don't mind, I want to clean up and get to bed."

"Of course," He smiled, bowing his head. "Off you go." Gaz went to take a step when Turnbull stood in my way. My stomach plummeted. "A quick word, Xanetto." I swallowed my nerves as my friends turned back to look at me with wide eyes. "Off you go. I wont ask again." He snapped, and Maddy paled, but Gaz gripped her hand, pulling her along. But Gaz gave me a small nod before disappearing around the corner.

Turnbull advanced on me until my back hit the cold wall behind me.

"You're covered in his blood, aren't you?" He was standing so close that I could barely breathe.

"I was attacked, then helped Jake when he was shot." I croaked, hating how nervous he made me feel. Was I getting Jake into trouble? Probably.

"Were you hurt?" He looked me over, and I shook my head. "Who attacked you?"

"I'm fine. And an ex-student from Imperial. His name is Paul Manfred."

His eyes narrowed, the scar down his face pulled tight as his jaw clenched.

"Paul Manfred..." he repeated slowly, like he was tasting the name. "And Callahan, he got himself shot protecting you?" The way he said it sent ice down my spine.

I nodded stiffly. "Yes."

Turnbull's lips twitched, almost like a smile, but it never reached his eyes. He leaned one hand on the wall beside my head, caging me in. His presence was suffocating. "Interesting. I thought Callahan knew his place better than that. He was supposed to keep a closer eye on you. But maybe he's gotten too close." He murmured, eyes raking over me.

My pulse spiked. "What's that supposed to mean?" I pretended to be dumb. I didn't want to get Jake into any more trouble.

He tilted his head, studying me like I was a puzzle piece he couldn't quite make fit. "It means," he said softly, almost kindly, "that boys like Callahan don't usually waste time playing hero unless they're after something more."

His gaze dragged down me, deliberate, and my stomach churned. "So tell me, Jocelyn, what is he after?"

I pressed my back harder against the wall, refusing to look away even as my throat tightened.

"Maybe he just didn't want me dead," I bit out, but my voice was thinner than I wanted.

Turnbull chuckled darkly, low in his throat. "Maybe. Or *maybe*," his voice dropped, intimate and cruel as he leaned in closer, "he's forgotten what his job is. He was meant to bring you to me. Instead, I hear stories about him risking everything for *you*."

I froze. The words sunk into my bones like cold water. He leaned even closer until I felt his breath on my face, the scar across his cheek stark in the dim light. "Don't look so surprised. Did you really think Callahan wandered into your life out of pure chance? He had a purpose, girl. And if he's lost sight of it-" He let the threat dangle, sharp and heavy in the air.

My chest constricted. Turnbull straightened suddenly, just enough to make me gasp for air.

"Go clean yourself up," he said briskly, like he hadn't just unravelled me with a few words. His smile was wrong, stretched too thin. "And stay out of trouble. I'll be keeping an eye on you."

He turned sharply, boots echoing down the corridor, leaving me trembling against the wall, the smell of blood still clinging to my skin.

I pressed both hands to my face, bile rising in my throat.

I didn't know what was worse: that Turnbull knew that Jake had the chance many times now, or that he was here and not afraid to take matters into his own hands.

Chapter Twenty-Eight

Since the attack, the walls felt too close. The cafeteria too loud. The silence of a night too heavy.

Maddy and Gaz constantly hovered, asking me what Turnbull wanted, as they were unable to hear him hiding around the corner. I couldn't tell them the truth, but I told them not to trust him.

Jake was still bed-bound, and he hated every minute of it. He was incredibly lucky, as the bullet gouged the side of his stomach, missing any vital organs. He demanded to be let out at least three times a day until they finally relented about four weeks later, telling him to take it easy. He ignored them, of course.

I could feel Professor Turnbull's stare burning into the back of my skull at every turn.

I can't breathe in here.

Paul had gotten away, or someone had helped him. We were no closer to finding them or figuring out how to stop them. Gabby was at a dead end, and I didn't have much left in me anymore.

I wanted to take Alec up on his offer to run away.

One overcast day, as soon as Jake slipped to the bathroom, I snuck outside. I knew I shouldn't, but I had to get some space.

The night air slapped me cold, and I drank it in like water. Stars hung low over Hellspire, and the wind carried the faint smoke of the furnace from the workshops. I wrapped my arms around myself and wandered toward the tree line, not thinking, just walking.

The darkness closed in on me, and I sucked in a long breath, holding it for a count of six before slowly letting it out. I was just so damn tired.

I pushed further, trying to ignore the fact that the last time I was out here, Fendi had kidnapped Maddy and his assassins tried to kill us, and I slit his throat.

I shivered over the horrific images now plaguing behind me eyes.

My boots crunched on gravel. Then...on something softer.

I frowned, looking down at the strip of turned-up earth at the edge of the woods. The soil was damp, darker than the rest, like it had been moved recently.

Something in me *knew* that it wasn't right.

My stomach flipped as I crouched and brushed at the dirt with my fingers. It crumbled under my nails, loose and unsettled. A sour smell leaked out, faint but enough to make bile burn the back of my throat.

I froze. There I spotted something. The edge of fabric, dirty and darkened.

No. No, no, no.

I clawed more dirt away, my breath coming in sharp, ragged bursts. And then my hand caught on cold flesh. My knees buckled, but I forced myself to scrape enough soil aside to see his face.

Professor Wood.

His eyes were clouded, half-lidded, his mouth slack in eternal silence. Dirt clung to the jagged edge of his beard, and the side of his head was caved in like rotten fruit. I stumbled back so fast I landed hard on the ground, my heart hammering against my ribs. My lungs wouldn't work, my throat closed, and I wanted to scream but no sound came out.

Dead.

He'd been murdered.

And that meant Turnbull had killed him.

I clutched my stomach as I doubled over, bile rising. The world spun, shadows lengthening like claws from the trees.

I thought of his scarred face, his eyes on me in the corridor, the way he leaned in close when no one else was around.

The ground swayed beneath me.

Jake. He'd been stretching it out, delaying whatever fate his people had laid out for me. And yet, here I was, standing over a grave that proved his people were playing this game too.

I forced myself upright, my legs trembling. I couldn't stay here. Not with him under the dirt, not with the stink of death clinging to the wind.

But the question echoed louder than the pounding of my heart: If Turnbull killed Wood...what would he do to me if he knew I'd found out? I headed back to my room, locked the door to catch my breath before heading to the bathroom.

I was scrubbing the dirt from my nails when the bathroom lock slid shut behind me and I looked up in the mirror and met Jake's eyes. They were narrowed on me, the bags under his eyes were dark, his face drawn.

"Where the hell did you just go?" He growled, and I straightened my spine, not breaking eye contact.

"The woods. I needed some air."

He closed his eyes as he scrubbed a hand down his face. He looked as exhausted as I felt.

"Why don't you sit down before you collapse." I grumbled, but he ignored me.

"Why the hell did you go outside? And alone, for fucks sake."

"I couldn't breathe!" I hissed turning so I could face him. "The walls are pressing in on me, and you know what I found out there?" I leaned in, and he crossed his arms, kicking one eyebrow up in the cocky way I hated.

"I'm sure you're going to tell me." He leaned against the wall, crossing one foot over the other.

"A fucking dead body." I hissed, and his face paled a little. "Professor Wood is in a goddamned shallow grave at the edge of the woods." I spun back around and splashed some cold water on my face, attempting to make myself feel something that wasn't horror.

"Turnbull." Jake whispered, and I nodded, drying my face on a towel.

"He told me," I breathed, and Jake flinched, taking a step toward me.

"Told you what?" He was so close I could smell his aftershave, but I couldn't meet his eyes. "Spit it out, Jocelyn."

"He told me that you've forgotten what your job is, and that you were meant to bring me to him."

"Fuck." He barked, grabbing my shoulders and spun me back around, and I had no choice but to look at him. "Him telling you the truth means they aren't going to wait much longer."

First class of the day on Monday - escape and evasion. I was beginning to hate this class.

Today, we were studying techniques that had worked in the past, but the real lesson would be tonight, around dusk. Colonel Fex had given us some reading material to analyse, before our proper lesson, where a guest would be helping us. I could almost guarantee who it was going to be.

The courtyard lights cast long shadows across the cracked flagstones, and cold air nipped at my cheeks as we gathered in a restless knot. Everyone was buzzing, half-excited, half-nervous, like kids about to play a giant game of hide-and-seek. Except this wasn't hide-and-seek. This was Hellspire, and there were no safe games here.

Colonel Fex and Professor Turnbull strode into the center of the courtyard, hands clasped behind their backs.

Turnbull's tall frame and that jagged scar cutting down his cheek catch the lamplight, making him look more executioner than teacher. He surveyed us like we were cattle lined up for slaughter.

"Tonight," Fex began, his voice sharp enough to cut steel, "you'll learn that sometimes survival isn't about fighting. It's about slipping away unseen. Escaping. Evading. If you can't do that, you'll never last in the field."

Gaz leaned down to me and muttered, "Pretty sure last time I evaded something it was cafeteria stew."

I stifled a laugh. Maddy elbowed him so hard he wheezed, and the tension lifted for a moment.

Fex paced, hands clasped behind his back, his boots echoing on stone. "You'll be working in teams. Your task is simple: evade capture while moving across the academy grounds. I will be your pursuer." He smiled, a thin curl of lips that made my stomach knot. But the look on Turnbull's face was worse. "But to raise the stakes..." His gaze dragged over us one by one,. It landed on me. "Turnbull will take a hostage that you'll need to rescue."

A ripple of laughter burst through the group. Everyone started shoving each other, jeering.

"Pick Gordon!"

"Nah, take Dylan, he's slow as shit!"

But Turnbull never looked away from me.

“Xanetto,” he said smoothly, like it was already decided.

The laughter turned into whoops and cheers. Gaz clapped me on the shoulder. “Don’t worry, Joss. We’ll rescue your damsel ass.”

Maddy’s grin dropped as she remembered my words.

Don't trust him.

But Jake... Jake didn’t laugh. He went rigid beside me, jaw grinding so tight I heard his teeth. Before I could protest, Turnbull’s hand clamped around my arm. His grip was iron, his fingers biting into my skin as he yanked me toward him. I stumbled, biting back a wince. To everyone else, it just looked like a rough prop for the game. To me, it felt like a death sentence.

“Hostage is secured and will be located in an unknown location,” he announced. His scar twisted with his smile. “Your challenge is to find her, and free her from my hold while you evade Fex.” No one saw how close he leaned, how his breath ghosted against my ear.

“Do you see how easy it would be, Jocelyn?” he whispered, low enough only I could hear. My blood ran cold. “One snap decision, and you’d already be gone.”

I wanted to vomit. Or scream. But I didn’t. I couldn’t with everyone watching.

“Everyone is to turn while I...relocate...my prisoner. Colonel Fex will tell you when your search can begin." He produced rope, real rope, not the training cuffs we'd used before, and bound my wrists too tightly. The fibers bit into my skin as he knotted them, tugging with unnecessary force. Then, with sick satisfaction, he stuffed a gag into my mouth. He forced me across the courtyard and into the trees. There were bunkers out there, and I could guarantee that was where we were heading.

He couldn't know how my heart was slamming against my ribs. But I was sure he would know how scared I was. All you had to do was look into my eyes.

I heard Fex address the class. "You have forty minutes. Rescue her, or she's gone. Begin."

Turnbull tugged me into a bunker, swinging open the wooden door and almost dragged me to a lone chair in the middle of the cold, damp room. He tied my wrists, and ankles to the chair, pulling on them and made sure they were tight.

He crouched beside me, his scarred face inches from mine, voice a razor against my ear.

"See how no one suspects a thing? How easy it would be to spirit you away while they're distracted? You should be terrified, Jocelyn. You should be begging him to finally do his job and take you. Before I do. Because if I take you, it will be so much worse."

I squeezed my eyes shut, breathing through my nose, refusing to give him the satisfaction of tears.

It *would* be so easy. But they would know it was him, but I could almost bet that Dan Turnbull wasn't his real name. We would disappear into the wind, never to be found again.

He turned and shut the door, locking me in the room with a lingering smirk. My heart was near beating out of my chest as I sat there, my wrists burning from the rope. The loud thunk of the lock still rang in the silence, and it took everything in me to remain calm.

"Enough," someone growled. His voice wasn't loud, but it cut through the silence like a blade. "What the hell are you playing at?" Jake snapped. He sounded alone.

"Relax, Callahan. I'm just following Fex's lesson. You're the one who's not playing properly. Plus, you were meant to take it easy with your wound." The smug sound of Turnbull's voice set me on edge. I hated being vulnerable, feeling out of control while these assholes dictated my future, my life.

"We both know why you picked her. This isn't a game!" Jake yelled, and I wished that I could get out of these bloody ropes. I tried to move anything, but he hadn't only tied my hands behind my back, but also my chest to the chair.

"Why are you getting so worked up?" I heard boots scuff on stone, and a grunt as if he pushed Jake in the chest. "You have feelings for her, don't you?" I hated how mocking his tone was. I could imagine him sneering. "You're ruining the mission-" He was cut off by a commotion at the door.

"Callahan? How did you find him so quick?" Gaz sounded impressed, and I heard more boots move into the small bunker.

"Get her out." Jake snapped at Gaz, but I didn't hear anyone move.

"You're going to have to get past me first." Turnbull called, and I saw a dark shadow move in front of my door, blocking the small barred window.

I heard a curse, then shouting as bangs echoed off the stones, smoke curling under my door like beckoning fingers. A bunch of students crowed in victory. My door was swung open, and I was temporarily blinded by a flash of light that someone had on their helmet.

"You alright?" Jake's voice was low, just for me. I nodded, but the truth was my throat felt tight, my chest too small for all the air I needed. My heart was still hammering, not from the ropes but from the look Turnbull gave me, like he'd already buried me in another shallow grave. Jake crouched there, eyes locked on mine, as he reached out and yanked the gag from my mouth. He made quick work of cutting my ropes, pulling me to my feet. His face was pale, sweat shining on his brow.

He shouldn't be out here, doing this physical work with his gunshot wound. But he was as stubborn as they came.

We made out way out into the bunker that was full of students in gear. Helmets, vests, goggles, and gloves. Jake kept a hand on my arm, hard enough to bruise, and the other gripping his side. I wouldn't be surprised if I saw blood through his shirt.

"Tie her up like that again," he said, leaning into Turnbull's face, voice like ice, "and it won't be the lesson I ruin."

The air went electric. Turnbull smiled, a slow and cruel thing. That scar stretched across his face, making the expression almost grotesque.

"Noted." He inclined his head as if Jake's threat was a compliment, then turned on his heel and strode back into the shadows, leaving a heavy silence in his wake.

The crowd of students slowly began to disperse, leaving us alone. Jake turned back to me, jaw tight, expression unreadable. For one awful heartbeat I thought he was going to say something about what Turnbull whispered. But he snapped his mouth shut, and pulled me along, the cold air snapping into my lungs, making me gasp.

By Jake's stiff movement, and locked jaw, it was enough for me to know this wasn't a game for him either.

I don't know what changed his mind, especially since at the start he was dead-set on his mission.

Chapter Twenty-Nine

The week didn't even seem to register as it flew past, lesson's were a blur, food didn't taste the same.

But it was Friday, only three lessons to go until the weekend.

Professor Halix stood at the front like a wiry scarecrow, fingerless gloves fraying at the seams, goggles perched on his wild hair. His hands twitched as he slammed a chipped mug of coffee onto the desk, splashing liquid across a stack of keyboards.

"If you can't break into the Dean's emails by the end of class, you fail."

Dead silence.

Gaz snorted. "You're joking."

Halix slammed his mug down so hard again that coffee sloshed onto the floor. "Does this look like a face that jokes, Davies?!"

It didn't. He looked like he hadn't slept in three years.

"Good. You have one hour. *MOVE.*"

Chairs screeched across the floor as everyone lunged for a workstation. Gaz was already typing furiously before his laptop even booted, muttering a string of curses under his breath. Maddy jabbed the keyboard with two fingers, typing *password123* in every field she could find.

"Here." Jake slid into the seat next to me, calm and collected. His fingers moved across his keyboard, smooth and deliberate. "They want us to think small, but the backdoors are hidden in the admin console. Look here."

I leaned closer, trying to follow his logic. My brain didn't move that fast. "You've... done this before."

His lips twitched. "Once or twice."

Halix stalked the aisles like a hawk, barking at random.

"TRACE DETECTED - hide under your desks!" He shouted.

Half the class screamed and dove under tables. Sparks popped from a server in the corner. Halix cackled and took a swig of his coffee.

Gaz kicked his tower. "This thing hates me."

"It's not the computer, it's you!" Maddy hissed, smacking his hand away from the keyboard.

Chaos. Absolute chaos. I almost hated this class as much as M.O.D.L. It was always ridiculous and people seemed to lose their heads.

But Jake... wasn't playing the same game as the rest of us. His eyes narrowed at the screen as he clicked through folders, deeper and deeper. I caught a glimpse of one tab he opened.

Student Records.

My stomach dropped. "Jake-"

"Shh." His voice was low and focused. He scrolled through list after list, his jaw tightening. "Something's wrong."

I leaned in. The screen flickered with names, but when he clicked on individuals - me, Jake, Maddy, Gaz, Alec, even Gabby - it was just... blank. No files. No history. Nothing.

"They're gone." Jake's whispered. "Every single one of them. Wiped clean. They were here at the start of the year."

My mouth went dry. "Why? Who would-"

"I don't know." His eyes flicked to me, something almost desperate hidden in their green depths. "But someone doesn't want us to exist."

Before I could respond, every screen in the room flashed bright red.

ALERT: TRACE DETECTED. ADMIN BREACH.

My pulse spiked.

"Congratulations!" Halix bellowed, throwing his hands in the air. "You've broken into the *real* system. Don't get caught. If the Dean calls, I was never here." And just like that, he ran out the door, cackling.

Panic ensured.

Some students yanked cords out of sockets. Others bolted for the exit. Maddy shrieked as her screen locked up, spamming error messages.

Then the door *slammed* open.

The Dean stormed in, his face thunderous, demanding to know who the hell thought it was funny to break into secured files. Students scattered like cockroaches. Someone knocked over a tower of servers, sending sparks raining across the room.

Jake locked his screen and grabbed my wrist. "Run."

We bolted through the fire exit, Gaz tumbling after us with a monitor cable still wrapped around his ankle, Maddy wheezing with laughter.

Behind us, alarms blared, students screamed, and somewhere in the distance, Halix could be heard yelling: "Lesson complete! You survived - barely! Dismissed!"

By the time we made it back to the dorm corridor, breathless and rattled, Jake hadn't said another word.

But I caught him glancing at me, his jaw tight and his fists clenched.

I knew he was thinking about the missing files.

Gone, erased like we'd never been there at all.

I made sure to sit with Maddy or Britney each cooking lesson now, so I didn't have to be paired up with Jake. It was still awkward between us since Turnbull tied me to a chair. Not to mention how pissed he was with Turnbull proving how easy it was for him to get to me.

I was distracted through the rest of the class, and in science as well. The professors were much happier now that the assessor had left, and so they let us muck around more than usual. So that meant more explosions, and some that were so big that my ears were still ringing. I was just glad it was Friday, and I could spend the weekend with my friends.

I passed Turnbull in the hall, and he winked, eyes locked on me until I turned the corner. Gaz and Maddy oblivious as they compared explosions, and whose were better and which made the most smoke.

But I couldn't forget his whispered words to me.

Miss Somali handed out our phones at dinner, and I almost didn't want to turn it on. No Alec to message, Gabby was always busy these days, and Matthew was away with work.

Everything was all tracked anyway, so it wasn't like I could ring Matthew and tell him about Jake and Turnbull, they'd probably cut the call before I could mutter their names.

Jake didn't come to the cafeteria, and I didn't see him in the halls. I rolled my neck as uneasiness crawled over me, making me constantly looking over my shoulders. It wasn't like him to not be here. My constant shadow.

"Hey, something's not right." Gaz caught up to me just as I was unlocking my door.

"What do you mean?" I frowned, looking between him and Maddy.

"Earlier, I saw Jake and Turnbull arguing, and it looked pretty heated. I couldn't hear what was said, but I could tell Jake was furious."

My stomach dropped so fast I had to hold onto the wall to stop myself from collapsing. I didn't bother with a reply as I stormed to Jakes room, yanking on the door handle. It opened, and I let it swing wide.

The room was empty.

Not a trace that anyone had been living in there for most of the year.

Oh, God. He's gone.

"What the hell?" Gaz barked over my shoulder as he looked in. Maddy was poking around the room, lifting things and opening draws.

"It's like he was never here." She breathed, and I couldn't get enough air into my lungs. I could guarantee that Turnbull got rid of him. Removed him from this mission. I stumbled back a step and leaned against the wall, trying to calm my furious heart.

"Fuck." I breathed, why did I feel so scared now that he was gone?

Because he was the only thing keeping you alive.

Because Turnbull wasn't going to wait anymore. They didn't need any more information.

"Don't trust Turnbull." I whispered again, and they whipped their heads to me. "I...I found Professor Wood in a shallow grave out in the trees."

Their shocked silence said a thousand words. Their faces paled as they looked at each other.

"Why the *hell* didn't you tell us? When did you find that out?" Maddy hissed, taking my hand in hers.

"The other day, I was too rattled to say anything. But I know he killed him, he's the one telling everyone he's retired."

"Oh, my god." Gaz breathed, pacing back and fourth in Jake's cold and empty room.

"I think he's out to get me." My pulse skyrocketed as I decided to tell my friends what his presence here meant. "He told me that-"

"What are you three doing in here?" Turnbull snapped, and I almost squeaked in shock as we spun and stared at the fake professor. "This room is out of bounds, clear out." He stepped aside, gesturing for us to leave. But he leaned in close, quiet enough only I could hear.

"Make the most of your time together, Jocelyn." His fingers grazed over my arm, and I yanked it away, cringing from him as he grinned at me. "Because your time is coming to an end."

I almost ran out of Jake's old room, hurtling into mine. Gaz and Maddy were already there waiting, eyes wide and pale.

"What the hell was that about? What did he say to you?" Gaz was there, locking my door behind him, but his hands were balled into fists.

"He told me my time here is coming to an end. He's going to kidnap me." I blurted, and their faces turned ashen. Maddy swore, grabbed her phone and dialled, sitting on my bed with a huff.

"Gabby, we need to see you tomorrow. It's urgent." She nodded her head as they talked, and I turned away, trying to get my thoughts in order.

Jake was gone.

I had become so reliant on him being there this year, without him, one of my enemies was going to kill me. How the hell did it come to this? I'd relied too much on him to always be there to protect me. I'd become weak.

"We're leaving here right now, and crashing at Gabby's place." Maddy stood, digging around my wardrobe until she yanked out a bag. "Pack for a few nights. We're not back until Sunday."

We didn't muck around as Maddy ran to her room, Gaz staying with me until I was packed, then we made a quick stop for his things on the way.

I had no idea, but Gaz had a car here tucked away in the garage. He threw our bags into the boot, then sped the hell outta there.

"Why the urgency?" I asked from the back seat, my knees up around my chin as it was better suited for tiny children, obviously.

"She didn't say, only that we needed to get our asses down there." Maddy turned and looked at me over her shoulder, eyes fierce. "What was going on between you two?"

My stomach did a funny little flop. I couldn't tell them, they would flip.

"He was my bodyguard." I met her gaze and away again, unable to breathe under her stare.

"So you've said. But you seem pretty upset to learn that he's gone. Was there more between you two?" Her eyes narrowed as she seemed to strip me to the bone by her look alone.

Should I tell her? Can I tell her?

God, she's going to be mortified.

"Something happened after...the shredder incident." My cheeks felt like they were on fire as I turned and looked out the window, but she didn't speak, letting me take my time. I took a deep breath, and blew it out my nose as I faced her.

"He's kissed me, but that's it."

"I knew there had to be something, he got under your skin too easily."

"I don't care for him like that. I love Alec, but Jake became someone I relied on, someone I think I cared for, like another brother."

"Makes sense." She leaned over and patted my knee, turning back to the front. Gaz had been whistling to himself, probably trying to drown out our conversation.

The rest of the drive was silent, except the radio crackling in and out of reception. Maddy cursed him for having an old car that couldn't connect to her phone, and not having any CD's in the car. But I couldn't pay attention to their bickering, I was too lost in my head. Where was Jake now? Was he involved at all anymore?

Would I ever see him again?

I don't care. He wanted to take you away from your friends and family.

So why did I feel so rotten about it?

Or was I just scared because I'd been using him as a security blanket?

Chapter Thirty

Gabby met us in the underground car park, ushering us inside, telling us to keep our heads down.

"As soon as we're inside, I need you to tell me *everything*." She gripped the back of my neck and hissed into my ear, making shivers break out over my skin.

She could be scary when she wanted to be.

But what I wasn't expecting was to see Alexander and Matthew waiting for us in her lounge room. My heart nearly burst at seeing him, how beautiful he was.

He instantly stood, walking our way and took my hands in his.

"Gods, Jossi. Are you alright?" His amber eyes raked over every inch of me, and I felt naked before him. My bottom lip wobbled, and he then wrapped me into a tight hug. My tears burned my throat as I cried, holding onto him so tightly I couldn't feel where I ended, and he began. "Shh, Babydoll, I got you."

He rubbed my back in soothing strokes, his other hand on the back of my head.

I didn't care that I broke things off, I just wanted somebody to hold me and tell me everything would be alright, even though we all knew things were *definitely* not alright.

Once my tears stopped, I pulled back, and his thumbs brushed them off my cheeks. I wanted to tell him everything, but I was scared.

He slipped his hand into mine and pulled me over to the couch, where he didn't let go.

"I still don't know why you two broke up," Gabby grumbled, handing us each a cup of tea. "But I get it." She shrugged when she met my eyes. "Right. I need someone to tell me what the hell has been happening at that damn school." She sat down opposite us, and placed a recorder on the table, turning it toward me.

All eyes landed on me, and I squirmed under the attention. If I were on a piano, that would be fine. But to talk? No thanks.

But they were waiting, and I guessed that it all involved me, so I took a deep breath and blew it out.

"So, I'm not sure how much you know, but the Imperial assholes snuck in and attacked us the other night."

"What?" barked Matthew, sitting forward, glaring at me, then my friends. "Like a prank?"

"Oh, no. They were after blood." Gaz leaned back, sipping his tea with his little finger in the air. I smothered my hysterical giggle. *So* not the time.

"There were heaps of them, and a fight broke out in the kitchens, before spilling outside into the courtyard where Paul kidnapped Joss, tied and gagged her, before throwing her into the boot of his car." Gaz drained his cup, and placed it down on the table with a clunk. I was too afraid to look at anyone, because I could feel it about to explode any second.

Tick. Tick. *Boom*.

"What the fuck?"

"How did it get that far?"

"Where the hell is he now?" Alec and Matthew were about to jump to their feet when Maddy whistled so loud my ears hurt.

"Enough!" she barked, and the room fell silent.

"Jake saved her, then Paul shot him. But Paul got away, someone must have helped him. The Imperials were just a distraction." Maddy barked, eyeing Matthew and Alec.

"Where is Jake? Hasn't he been attached to you like a limpet, Joss?" Gabby leaned forward, and I wanted to shake my head. And I hoped against hope that Maddy or Gaz didn't bring up that he was supposed to be my bodyguard, because Alec and Matthew would deny it.

"Jake's gone. We found his room empty this afternoon." Gaz grumbled, leaning back in his chair again.

"Why the hell is he involved in everything?" Alec snapped, and I felt my chest constrict. Had he told Matthew what happened that night in my room?

By the way he wouldn't look at him, I'd say not.

Gaz went to open his mouth when I cut him off. I needed to change the subject.

"It doesn't matter. He's gone, we need to look out for Turnbull now."

"Who's he?" Matthew leaned forward with his elbows resting on his knees.

"Dan Turnbull. He's our new metalwork teacher. But I think he killed Wood." It still made me feel sad to think about it.

Gabby and Alec sucked in a breath, looking devastated.

"Not Wood. How can you be sure?" Alec faced me, keeping my fingers in his, his thumb slowly stroked the back of my hand. How I'd missed his hands on me.

"I found him in a shallow grave, at the tree line."

"Fuck." Alec breathed, turning to Gabby. "We need someone out there to confirm."

"But that's not all, is it Joss? Didn't he threaten you just before we left?" Gaz tried to pinch a biscuit off the table without anyone seeing, but Gabby smacked his fingers without even looking. He cursed and leaned back with a huff.

I could feel the anger simmering off Alec, and Matthew had even put his phone down, giving me his full attention.

"What did he say to you, Jossi?" His voice was low and lethal, and I wasn't used to seeing my big brother like that.

"He told me that my time is coming to an end. And that he's coming for me." I barely got the words out and Matthew and Alec were on their feet, yelling about how I wasn't returning to school, or that they were coming with me.

Gabby joined in, and I blocked it out. There was no use trying to get them to listen when they were like this. Maddy reached over and grabbed my hand, and gave it a small squeeze.

"They'll sort something out."

"I know." I attempted to give her a reassuring smile, but it felt wrong, my lips wouldn't obey.

"You're not going back." Alec barked loudly to be heard over the noise.

"She's not going to pull out. Imagine how that will look on her record." Matthew got in his face, and I almost held my breath, looking between the two.

"It doesn't matter what her record is like. She's going to be working for our father."

"*No fucking way.*" Alec snapped, and the room fell silent. "I will not allow her to work with us."

"It's not up to you." Matthew pointed a finger at Alec, and I cringed back into the couch. Gabby was watching with wide eyes, taking a small step back. "She's my sister, don't forget."

"And she's everything to me!" Alec yelled, and my heart *stopped*. "She's my moon, and sun. She's the flowers in the meadows, she's the water in the ocean. I will not allow her to get involved more than she already is. She deserves better."

I was shocked. I knew he loved me, but this much?

"I didn't know you felt that way about her." Matthew took a step back, his face ashen. He turned to me and nodded. "The choice is yours."

"I don't even know what you guys do. I would like to know before I make any decisions on whether I want to work with you or not."

"We deal in elite asset recovery. Be it files, objects, or even people." Matthew tried to calm his breathing, but Alec was looking at his shoes, hands in his pockets.

Elite asset recovery. I had no idea.

"So, you steal things?"

"No. We retrieve things that were stolen before. Return things to the rightful owner."

"Or who pays us the most," Alec grumbled under his breath, and I had no idea how I felt about all of that.

"We are the people they go to when they don't want to involve the police and the media. That's why we're hardly here. We need to fly around the world to meet with clients and make sure the job gets done."

Matthew sat beside me and took my hands in his. "It's dangerous work, but we're trying to do the right thing. But it does unfortunately mean that we get our hands dirty, and make some enemies along the way."

"I think they're after something to do with father, a book or something?" I shrugged, keeping my eyes on my brother as he looked at me with sadness. But something in his eyes shifted, and he sat up straighter.

"Jossi, what does this Turnbull look like?"

"He's tall, with light brown hair, dark brown eyes, and a long scar down his cheek."

"Shit." He whispered, and his face paled so quickly that I was worried he was about to pass out. He stood and threw his hands behind his head as he paced. "And this Jake guy, what does he look like?" He turned to Gaz, who suddenly sat up a little straighter.

"He was tall, hell muscly. Black hair, green eyes. But he was solid, a good dude."

Matthew whipped around and met Alec's eyes, and they both cursed.

"Spit it out." Gabby barked, standing in the middle of the room with her arms crossed.

"It sounds like Turnbull is a man they call the Viper, his real name is Nathan Bates, and this Jake guy sounds like his right-hand man, Tyler Donovan."

Jake wasn't even his real name. I didn't know anything about him, but he knew *everything* about me.

"That's why he was always there. I should have known that night he..." Alec stops himself, and I swallowed. He was walking on very thin ice right now. We couldn't afford for the others to know.

What would Matthew do if he found out that Alec was giving our enemy insider information?

"How many times was he involved when your life was threatened? He told me he'd taken bullets for you." Alec swallowed his anger and advanced on me, and I gritted my teeth as he put on a very convincing show.

"He *has* taken bullets for me, twice. And saved me when Jenna tried to poison me." I didn't want to think about it anymore. He was always there. And now he wasn't. "I would have died if he hadn't followed me. Then when I had the truck accident and broke my arm. He had the chance to take me then, but didn't. Then again, when Imperials stormed the academy, he saved me."

"Wait. What truck accident?" Maddy leaned forward, pinning me with a hard stare. "You told us you fell down the stairs, and that he was your bodyguard." She snapped, and I felt my heart wither at the hurt on her face.

"I had to. He told me that if anyone knew, he'd take me right then and there." I pleaded, and the others cursed. "As for the truck accident, I was doing something for Wood and Omara, and needed someone with knowledge of Mangalore."

"But why lie about that, too?" Silver rimmed her eyes, and I'd never hated myself more.

"Because that's not her secret to tell," Alec butted in. "It's to do with M.O.D.L class." The lie rolled effortlessly off his tongue.

Conversation over.

“We saw them arguing just before we left, and that's when we realised that Jake was no longer here." Gaz ran a hand through his hair, shaking his head. “Why was he really there, Joss?” He turned to me, and my stomach plummeted.

I hated myself so much right now.

I didn't want to be me anymore. Life was so much simpler as Clementine Mavis.

“Jake was sent to Hellspire to gather information from me, then eventually take me to use as leverage for Father.”

There. I said it.

“But he didn't. Did he?” Maddy leaned in, and I couldn't stand to see the pity in her eyes.

“No. He-“ A noise pinged in my bag, one I hadn’t heard before.

But I had my phone in my pocket.

I pulled my bag around and start digging, and found a burner phone buried in the bottom. I shook my head, knowing Jake would have put it there.

> They’re coming. Get the hell out of there. J

Oh, shit.

“Uh, guys.” I stood, my hand starting to shake. “I think we need to leave.” I looked up at all of my friends, my loved ones were all in this room.

Now, Jocelyn!

“Like, right now.” I zipped my bag and threw it over my shoulder. Gaz and Maddy were doing the same.

“How do you know?” Alec asked, but he was also grabbing his own bag. We were making our way to the door.

“I just got a text on a burner phone I forgot I had.” I couldn’t meet his eyes. I felt too guilty.

“Joss, was it from Jake?” He gripped my wrist, forcing me to face him. I nodded, and he swore, running a hand through his hair. “Lets move out.”

We wasted no time in getting out of there. The garage was dark, but we didn’t linger. Just as I reached Gaz’s car, Alec pulled me back and kissed me hard and quick, his fingers digging into my hair. It lasted only a heartbeat, but it was everything I needed.

“Please stay safe, Jossi.” He leaned his forehead on mine, and my bottom lip trembled. “I love you.”

"I love you, too," I whispered, then he was gone. I was shoved into the car by Maddy, who was barely in her seat when Gaz was moving. We tore out of the building, Matthew, Alec and Gabby right behind us. Just as we were pulling out, three black SUVs skidded around the corner.

Shit.

"Floor it!" Maddy yelled, holding on for dear life. This car might be old, but it still had some grunt. We swerved between cars, they honked us as we shot past. We were on the bridge, the others not far behind us as we began a dangerous game of cat and mouse.

I dug my phone out of my pocket and looked at it a moment before rolling my window down and tossing it out. It sailed over the railing and down into the water. My bag was next, including the clothes I was wearing. I couldn't risk them following us because I had trackers on everything I owned. The only thing I kept was the burner phone. Maddy threw me her jumper, and I gratefully pulled it on so I wasn't completely naked. It wasn't ideal, but it might be the only thing that helped us get away.

Alec was driving the other car, and he was on our tail, between them and us, but when we got to a crossroads, we split. He turned right, and we turned left.

I just hoped that Jake didn't put a tracker on Gaz's car.

It was peak hour traffic, and they couldn't catch us without causing a serious crash. So they backed off, turned around, and probably headed back to Gabby's place.

"Lets get the hell out of here, and get you some clothes." Maddy was scrubbing her face, but I didn't miss her shaking hands.

"On it." Gaz made sure to do a few more blocks before parking in an above ground garage at the mall. Maddy wasted no time in racing into the shop for me. Gaz stayed with me in the car. I could see him looking in the mirror, then away again, as if he wanted to ask something but changed his mind every time.

"Spit it out, Gaz." I sighed, leaning back and closing my eyes.

"Did you know he was working for them?" I could hear the hurt in his voice. He liked Jake. He thought he was a decent man.

"Not until Fendi's assassins tried to take me out in the forest. Before then, I just thought he was just intense." I opened them again and met his stare. "I wanted to tell you, but I was scared. I'm sorry." I breathed, and he nodded before turning around and gripping my hand.

"Please, if anything like this ever happens, you can tell us. We know how to keep a secret."

"I know. He just *knew* everything. He's got trackers in everything, all of my clothes, bugged my phone, my room."

"Fucking asshole." He grunted, turning back around just as Maddy was coming out of the store with bags tucked under her arm. She threw one of them at me, then the rest into the boot, barking at Gaz to get the hell out of there.

He peeled us out of the carpark and we made our way back to the school, where my enemy was in plain sight.

I didn't have my phone anymore, and I didn't know anyone's numbers. So it wasn't like I could check in with them to see if they were safe. But Maddy had her phone to her ear, and rapidly chatted away, confirming they were all okay. She told them we were heading back to school before hanging up.

I felt exhausted, my adrenaline wearing off. Seeing as we had at least an hour drive ahead of us, I lay my head back and shut my eyes.

The rest of the weekend, I spent in either Maddy's or Gaz's room, going through all of my clothes and taking out the tracker chips, and flushing them down the toilet. But the truth was that we had no idea when Turnbull was going to make a move. And whether I should stay there at Hellspire, or if I should run.

That was the worst thing of all.

The week flew by, and nothing happened. No mail from Sera, no attempts on my life. Turnbull just continued to smile at me and wink, giving me a knowing grin.

I hated it. I hated *him*.

I wasn't sleeping, again too worried that they were going to take me in the night. So I slept in Maddy's bed with her. I was tired, anxious, and constantly on edge.

The second week flew by, and the end of the year was looming ever closer.

What is he waiting for?

Maddy and Gaz had their end-of-year exams, so they were locked away in the great hall until they were finished.

I did as they suggested, and spent the whole time that I wasn't in class, in the cafeteria and around people.

I was finishing up my chicken salad when a fourth-year approached me.

"Hey, I was asked to give this to you." She smiled and handed me a folded piece of paper. I was instantly on edge, not wanting to open it just in case.

"Who gave it to you?" I asked, halfway reaching for it, hesitating.

"Alec Hyde." She winked, and I let out the breath I was holding.

"Thanks," I smiled and took the note from her. He must be doing the safe thing and hiding outside, rather than breaking into my room.

I unfolded the paper, skimming over the words.

Babydoll, meet me outside in the courtyard, alone. It's urgent.

It was his handwriting, so I was confident it was really him. I grabbed my bag and hurried out of the room, taking the halls at a run. If it were urgent, he must have some information.

I came to a stop in the courtyard, the lantern on the wall providing only a small puddle of light, the rest lay in darkness.

"Alexander?" I called softly, keeping my eyes peeled for any movement, but making sure I stayed close enough to the entrance in case I had to make a run for it.

"Over here, Babydoll." He softly called from my left, and he took a small step out of the shadows. I broke into a smile and ran to him, wrapping him in my arms. But as soon as his arms embraced me, I knew I'd just made a terrible decision.

This wasn't Alexander.

I tried to pull away, but his arms were like steel bands, holding me to him. I leaned back and shoved, but his hands wrapped around my upper-arms. I could barely see his face under his dark hood, but I would know those eyes anywhere.

"Jake, let me go." I breathed, barely able to get any air into my lungs.

"You know I can't do that." His voice was low, empty of any emotion. I attempted to pull back again, but he kept a firm grip on me.

"Jake, please." I could feel tears blocking my throat, pricking the back of my eyes as I tried to see anything in his sharp gaze.

"I'm sorry, Jocelyn." He gruffly shoved me along toward the driveway, keeping one hand around my arm. A sleek, black car hid in the shadows, completely invisible unless you knew it was there. I tried to dig my heels in, but he was too strong. He pushed me against the boot, grabbed my wrists and tied the rope so tightly that it instantly burned against my skin.

I choked on a sob. He was really doing this.

"Callahan." A voice snapped from the courtyard, coming our way. My heart *sank*.

"Stay where you are." Jake barked, spinning me around so my back was to his chest.

"*Let her go*." Gaz snarled, taking another step. I felt Jake stiffen behind me, his fingers digging into my skin.

"Come any closer, and I'll have to shoot you, Gaz. I don't want to do that."

I sucked in a breath to let out in a yell or a scream, but Jake slapped a hand over my mouth.

"You don't have to do this," Gaz pleaded as he took another step, and my tears ran unchecked down my cheeks and over Jake's hand.

"I'm really sorry, man." Jake raised his hand, and I was not quick enough as Jake aimed and fired his gun.

The crack shattered the night, and I fought with everything I had as I saw Gaz crumple in on himself.

He fell to his knees, holding his stomach with both hands, and a red stain bloomed out over his white shirt.

I was kicking, thrashing, unable to comprehend what just happened.

"I'm so sorry, Jossi." Jake breathed into my ear as he turned me around and popped the boot of his car.

"Jos...si!" Gary's breathless shout was the last thing I heard before Jake hit me in the head with the butt of his gun, and everything went black.

Acknowledgements

Woah, what a ride. Even reading that last chapter as I ran over my last edits, made my throat tight. Sorry guys for the cliff hanger, but I do *so* love doing it!

Just like the first Hellspire novel, I absolutely loved writing this, from start to finish. I love living in their chaotic worlds, experiencing their highs and lows. And of course the pranks. How I wish we could get away with doing something like that.

But, that is why I write, so I can live it, and enjoy it thoroughly!

Thank you, thank you, thank you my dearest Glen. You've put up with me through another book! Yay, well done. But in all honesty – you're probably glad it's over, so I don't ask you those questions that a certain search engine would flag me straight away for being one to watch out for. But I should also thank my father Bruce for helping me with those questions too! He's always got a great idea, and how those ghastly (fun to write) things work.

Thank you to my family for always being my number one fans, and supporting me in any way possible! Thank you Laura for letting me sell my books at your Saturday market stall (Sugar Ant Ridge – for all your wonderful and delicious sourdough needs), but I'm a little worried about my Nan, Audrey reading this one...she might start to worry what's going on up in my head. And also my wonderful mother-in-law, Elisabeth – please don't tell me what you think when you read my books.

It makes me nervous.

Thank you Blake Polden (my clever fellow author) for contributing in another book, and letting me kill you in a wonderful, messy explosion. That was fun. And to Caleb for letting *Monkin the Muncher* tear you to shreds. Our Sunday's at work turn out rather fruitful when customer's aren't interrupting us.

My beta readers! Sam Sauer, Kerry Costello, Russell Montgomery and Indigo Fraser. You guys are amazing, and keep my head on straight with your reasoning and thoughts that I've completely overlooked. You've helped straighten out a chapter or even paragraph that made sense in my head, but perhaps not on paper. Thank you!

And finally, to you, the reader.

Thank you for picking up this book and stepping into this world with me. I hope you love reading it as much as I loved writing it. If it spoke to you, made you feel something, or gave you a moment of escape, I'd be so grateful if you left a review. Your support means the world to me. xx

About the Author

Alice Cornelius lives in the stunning island state of Tasmania, Australia, with her two kids and husband of fifteen years. When she's not writing, you'll find her mountain biking through the bush, camping under the stars, swimming upriver, or chasing waterfalls - always in search of her next great adventure.

Hellspire Academy – Vicious Intent is Alice's fourth full-length novel, and she can't wait to dive back into their adventures!

With many more stories brewing, this is just the beginning - so keep an eye on her socials for updates, sneak peeks, and general bookish chaos.

If you enjoyed this book, leaving a review would mean the absolute world.

Stay weird, stay wild, and thanks for reading xx

CALL FOR BETA'S

Some stories don't ask permission to stay – they sink in and haunt.
If this one did that to you, I'm inviting a few readers into the heart of what's next. It won't be clean. Or simple. There will be broken vows, stolen glances, touches that shouldn't happen, and choices that change everything. I'm looking for readers who can feel the undercurrents – who live for tension that smoulders and truths left unspoken. You'll get early access to the mess: raw chapters, tangled arcs, and maybe a few kisses that weren't in the original outline. And of course, a place in the acknowledgments – because no one survives a love story like this alone.
If you're ready to read between the heartbeats, send me a raven at: alicecornelius@outlook.com

www.ingramcontent.com/pod-product-compliance
Lightning Source LLC
Chambersburg PA
CBHW020855150726
48196CB00048B/1047

* 9 7 8 1 7 6 4 0 9 0 9 7 1 *